The Aquamarine Necklace
Janice Maidstone Mysteries - Book 1

Bonny Beswick

Print ISBNs
Amazon print 9780228634737
Ingram Spark 9780228634744
Barnes & Noble 9780228634751
BWL Print 9780228634768

BWL Publishing Inc.

Books we love to write ...
Authors around the world.

http://bwlpublishing.ca

Dedication

To the strong and compassionate women of RCMP
Troop 20 (1977)

Acknowledgements

Many things have changed since I wore a police uniform in the '70s: equipment, technology, policies, procedures, and even some legislation. On these points, I needed current insight. For advice, I went to Dick Nyenhuis, retired Calgary City Police detective, and Gus Gallucci, who retired from both the RCMP and the Calgary City Police. I appreciate their guidance, and any errors in procedure or application of law are my own.

To Rob, who took me to the gun range where I was reminded that I was never as good a marksman as I'd hoped to be, thanks for keeping me humble.

Thank you to my critique group, The Fictionists. I could never wish for a more supportive community that provided constructive feedback with an always-kind attitude.

Family and patient friends who laid eyes on the manuscript in its early stages have been a godsend. You must love me to wade through the rough parts, and for that, I love you even more.

The novel is set in the city of Calgary, Alberta, Canada. To suit the narrative of *The Aquamarine Necklace*, I have taken licence with restaurants (old and new), streets, buildings and neighbourhoods.

Table of Contents

Chapter One

My work phone chirps just as I'm about to slap bread with cheese into the frying pan. Being interrupted comes with the territory when on call, but I'd hoped to at least have lunch before facing the third callout of the weekend. I glance at the text and decide there's no time to grill the sandwich. I'll wolf it down cold on the way to pick up my partner at the station.

Scott folds himself into the car when I pull up beside his Subaru SUV in the secure parking lot at the headquarters off Westwinds Drive. I ask, "Did you manage to get a decent lunch?"

"Yah, I did, thanks. There was leftover chili in the fridge."

"Chili?" I furrow my brow.

He laughs. "Don't worry. It didn't have beans."

I turn onto McKnight Boulevard in Calgary's northeast, and head to the lower Mount Royal address we got from dispatch. A black and white is parked in the plum spot, the loading zone, right in front of the upscale condo building in the sought after residential neighbourhood south of the busy Seventeenth Avenue retail and entertainment district. The other official vehicles, the Office of Chief Medical Examiner's nondescript station wagon and the Identification Section Sprinter van, are angle-parked in the parallel spots next to it. I squeeze our unmarked Ford in the remaining space beside them. Sunday afternoon drivers slow to squeeze single file past us on the narrow side street and glare at us for the inconvenience.

Sparrows twitter in heavily pruned cotoneaster bushes along the sides of the building. Early tulips, sheltered from the winds along the south facing facade, have already started to bloom.

I squint against the grit whipped up from the street by the wind and study the new-but-made-to-look-old brick building in front of me.

Ornate iron security grills cover ground-floor windows, and heavy glass entry doors guard a locked vestibule. A uniformed cop opens the door when he sees us coming. He knows us, but still checks our badges before telling us, "Unit 1704, Top floor." On the seventeenth floor, we pull on white coveralls and protective booties from the pile in front of 1704. The fabric puddles at my feet. These garments fit very few people comfortably. At five-feet-six, I roll up the sleeves, while Scott, at six-feet-four, endures a too-tight crotch and straining shoulder seams.

We give our names and badge numbers to Viv Wilkins, another uniformed officer at the condo door. He's already filled half the page, starting with his and his partner's name and badge numbers. Then there are the paramedics, who've come and gone, the duty sergeant who came to look at the scene and initiated the call out to the Medical Examiner, the Medical Examiner herself, the Identification Section who do the crime scene analysis, and now us, the homicide unit.

My partner speaks up, "Scott Amble. 75068."

"Janice Maidstone. 74965."

The gate keeper nods. "Hey there, Bumper. How ya doin'?"

Viv was my trainer for the first six months after I left the Academy. I couldn't have asked for a better role model. He was steady and full of common sense, patient with the public, and ready with a kind word. But he constantly drummed into me the need to be alert.

"Most people are good, Bumper, but there are some looking for trouble. Whether it's to hurt someone else, or specifically a cop, ya gotta keep your eyes open. Especially the ones in the back of your head."

We were partners when I was saddled with that nickname. Bumper. In the first month or so on the job, I had a few car accidents. None of them resulted in injuries, just property damage — a fence, a light standard or two, even a rollover into a storm pond. It's not as though cops don't have accidents. It comes with the job, but unfortunately, I had them in quick succession. Our sergeant at the time dressed me down during Morning Report, announcing that if I wanted to play bumper cars, I could go to the midway at Stampede. The rest of the squad thought it was hilarious, and the nickname Bumper was born.

I give Viv a quick smile. "Doin' fine, Viv. What've we got?"

He smiles in return, then sobers when he relays the details. "Deceased is Sophia Turnbull. She's the Sophia of that restaurant. Sophia's on Seventeenth." He motions with his thumb to the north. "It's only about six blocks from here. Her fiancé found her when he came home from a stag down in Priddis over the weekend. She was on the couch. Said he didn't touch her."

He looks up from his black notebook. "His name is Maxwell Shark." He pauses. "That's Shark, like the big fish. I made the mistake of calling him Smart, like the old television show and he didn't think it was funny."

When I cock my head and furrow my brow, he adds. "Maxwell Smart? Agent 86? Get Smart?" He shakes his head. "Jeez, you're making me feel old. I guess it's before your time. Anyway, we gave him a ride to the station, and he's waiting there for you when you're ready."

He takes one more look at his notebook before shoving it in his breast pocket. "The lady across the hall popped out wondering what's going on. Her name is Stephanie Campbell. I've told her there was an incident." He finishes his briefing. "The Ident. team got here about an hour ago."

"Thanks Viv." I turn and open the door to the condo. I'm impressed by the high ceilings and large windows looking over the gentrified neighbourhood. Early afternoon sunlight shines on dove-grey walls and smoke-coloured carpets.

The place is bustling with techs in white disposable coveralls. The lead analyst, Al MacIntosh, recognizable even behind his mask, looks over from behind the coffee table. His eyes narrow and he looks ready to yell at us for disturbing the scene. I hold up both hands in surrender. He bellows anyway.

"This is my scene. Keep your hands in your pockets." He's a burly man, with a voice to match.

I tell him, "No problem, Al. Any idea how long you're going to be?"

He growls back. "As long as we need to be." He's not the ogre he makes out to be, and after a glance around, he relents. "Maybe half an hour.

"You know we're gonna hold the scene. Ya got someone working on the warrant?"

I nod. "Not yet, but we will."

Al raises his hand in acknowledgment and turns back to the coffee table. I am always pleased when he is part of the team. When not in the crime scene disposable protective gear, his wrinkled pants, wild grey hair, and drooping moustache do not inspire confidence, but Al is the most thorough, keen-eyed investigator I know.

He grunts as he lowers to his knees to scrutinize the table. He swirls a delicate brush, laden with magnetic powder, both on the surface and underside of the glass.

He and his team are taking their time. This is their only opportunity to gather evidence before the rest of us unwittingly contaminate the scene.

Beside Al, the medical examiner hunches over the body.

Dr. Monica Patel looks up from the side of the dark grey sofa. Her eyes crinkle above her mask when she flashes the barest hint of a smile. "I'm just about done. Give me a couple of minutes."

Standing inside the door, Scott and I survey the bright, sunlit suite in front of us. We shift from one foot to another, watching the techs move slowly in ever-widening circles from the sofa. One of them has a souped-up dust buster; another wields a fingerprint brush; another has a camera.

There's little chatter among them, just the rustle of their Tyvek suits, the digital clicks of a camera, and the crinkle of brown paper bags when evidence is secured inside. Neon-yellow evidence markers dot the room wherever something has been gathered.

Monica's knees crack when she gets to her feet. She strips off her gloves and tosses them into the garbage can placed at the front door with the accuracy of a pro basketball player. "I'm done, Al. Give my guys a call when you're finished, and they'll take her in. I'll let you know when I schedule the postmortem. It'll probably be tomorrow afternoon."

Al's moved into the kitchen and is sweeping his brush over the refrigerator handle. "Sure thing."

As she steps carefully around the sofa toward us, I ask, "What are you thinking? Suspicious? OD?"

"Yes, definitely suspicious. She's young. Looks healthy, other than the fact that she's dead, obviously. No signs of distress or trauma. No drug paraphernalia. I'll have more for you tomorrow."

"Can you give us a time of death?" I ask.

The examiner nods. "With the usual caution that this is an estimate, based on her body not quite ambient temp yet, I'd say she died at least twelve, but probably no more than fourteen hours ago. That would put it before midnight. Maybe around eleven. Thereabouts.

"One of you will be at the autopsy?"

I nod. "Yep. Probably me."

She replies. "I'll let you know the time."

"Thanks Monica. See you tomorrow."

I study the victim on the sofa. Long blonde hair curtains part of her face. A cashmere-like sweater and yoga pants are appropriate attire for a relaxing evening at home. Her footwear draws my attention. She's wearing a pink slipper, with an applique of kittens on top. It's well-worn, and the fake fur trim, probably cotton-candy pink at one point, is matted and faded. Earlier, I'd watched a crime scene tech retrieve its mate from under the other side of the coffee table and put it into a brown bag.

The slippers remind me of a pair of moccasins my dad gave me on my eighteenth birthday. After so many years, they've lost all colour, and the sheepskin lining is as thin as a piece of old flannel, but I can't part with them. Maybe the thought of my slippers is why hers tugs at my heart.

Our victim looks peaceful, like she's simply fallen asleep watching the evening news.

I know her by reputation. Her transformation from exotic dancer to successful restaurateur is impressive. Opened a few years before the pandemic, Sophia's on Seventeenth not only survived, but has become the go-to place for influencers, visiting celebrities, and those who want to be seen in the latest trendy eatery.

A couple of porters from the Medical Examiners' office push through the door and wait for Al's go ahead to zip Turnbull into a white body bag.

The kitchen counter-tops are uncluttered except for an Ann Cleeves paperback left face down next to a plate with a pizza crust.

I wait until Al moves away from the refrigerator, then take a peek inside. The contents are similar to what my fridge holds. Milk, some fruit and veg in the crispers, assorted condiments and a couple of pizza slices, wrapped in wax paper. A little unusual, though, is a wooden platter with an interesting assortment of items: mini-cheese wrapped in red wax, baby carrots, grape tomatoes, a mini pepperoni, a handful of goldfish crackers, and little jellybeans, sitting next to a see-through box of mini-cupcakes, some with blue, others with pink, icing. I point it out to Scott, "A weird charcuterie board, eh?"

He glances over my shoulder and shakes his head. "Who would you serve this to?"

I shake my head. "A weird uncle that shows up unannounced?"

We turn back to the living room behind us.

"This place is way above our pay grade," Scott mumbles.

The furnishings, artwork, cushions perfectly perched on the sofa, and interior-design photo books splayed on the end tables look high-end and ready for a magazine photo-shoot. Nothing looks out of place; nothing broken or tumbled onto the floor.

A mostly empty bottle of Bollinger Extra Brut champagne and two flutes sit on the coffee table in front of the couch. One glass only has a trace of liquid in it, but the other is full. Scott gives a low whistle. "Someone wanted to impress! Do you know how much a bottle of that will set you back?"

"No idea. I'm not into champagne. There's usually not anything exciting enough in my life to justify opening a bottle."

He gives me a stink eye. "Come on, Janice." He mocks playing a violin. "If you're not careful, you'll make me feel sorry for you."

I snap back, with enough lilt in my voice to let him know I'm not taking offence. "I said there wasn't anything exciting going on. I didn't say I was unhappy about it."

I wait for him to come back with some pithy remark. He doesn't. "Ok, how much would I pay for said bottle?"

"Upwards of $350."

"She owns a restaurant. Maybe she didn't buy it but brought it home with her from the inventory."

I glance at the plate on the counter. "Would you eat pizza with pricey champagne? And why are there two glasses, but only one plate?"

"Maybe she was eating the pizza and reading her book when someone came to the door. Whoever it was, had the bottle and they settled down to drink it? She left the pizza and book on the counter, figuring she'd get back to it later?"

"Could be a possibility. What do you think about that pink slipper?"

Scott glances under the coffee table where it had been. "Yah, it's a little unusual. She's on the sofa almost without a hair out of place, but that slipper's way over there. If she just slipped her foot out of it, wouldn't it be closer? And look at the glasses. Two of them, but one doesn't look like it's been touched."

As we watch, a tech places the glasses in brown paper bags and leaves neon evidence markers in their place. The pile of evidence bags by the door is accumulating while the photographer continues making a record.

We continue to look for anything out of place. In the bedroom, thick broadloom and heavy brocade fabric in colours a shade darker than the cushions in the living area create a serene and opulent sanctuary. An almost life-size photo of our victim hangs over the bed. She's wearing only a few wisps of fabric, but her demure pose and expression, as though she's about to break into a smile, make the photo more playful than sultry.

An open, leather overnight duffle sits on the bed, some contents strewn across the midnight duvet. It looks like Mr. Shark left his bag before they took him downtown to the station to await our interview.

We wander through a home office, remarkable for its organization, and both the ensuite and main bathrooms. The ensuite seems to have been her space, evidenced by organizers with cosmetics and perfume, hair ties and brushes, and a variety of over-the-counter medications. A soft flannel nightshirt hangs on the back of the door.

Mr. Shark's bathroom is decidedly more masculine with a disposable razor and Elemis Shave gel sitting beside the sink. There's a yellow evidence marker on the shelf under the vanity. I take a moment and go down into the living room to the tech who's recording evidence taken from the condo.

"There's an evidence marker in the main bathroom. What was there?"

He checks his list. "A Sharps container. You know, the bright yellow plastic jugs that hold needles?"

"Gottcha, thanks."

Al is slowly surveying the scene for a last look. He tells me, "We're done here. Once you finish your interview with the fiancé, let me know if you need us to come back and gather anything else."

I walk back to the office area where Scott's rifling through papers on the desk. "Find anything?"

He shakes his head. "Nothing that jumps out at me. I'm ready to head back and interview the fiancé."

Viv's still standing outside, ready to record the time when we leave.

"How long before your shift is over?" I ask him.

"It was over at four, but my replacement's on his way. How long are we going to hold the scene?"

I shake my head. "Don't know, at least until after the autopsy tomorrow afternoon, though."

The older cop shrugs.

An old shoulder injury objects when I squirm out of the white protective jumpsuit, reminding me to get back to the exercises the physio gave me, or else I'll lose the flexibility that was so hard to regain after the scuffle with the car-jacker a few years ago.

Scott's cursing his jumpsuit, too. The one-size-fits-all label in them is a stretch. It would be more appropriate to say one-size-fits-some. I reach over and help pull it off his shoulder. If they could take the four inches too-big-for-me, and put it on Scott's, that would suit us both.

We ball up the puddles of material and toss them into the waste bin placed at the front door. When we're done, I tell Viv, "We're going down to interview the fiancé. We'll send him back with an escort to pick up whatever he needs for a couple of days."

Viv nods. "No problem."

* * *

Before we talk to the fiancé, Scott and I stop in the office to meet with Detectives Lance Nguyen and Wayne Marshall. They've been called in to work the case with us.

I'll lead this investigation, Scott will be the Secondary, and Nguyen will take care of Search Warrants, Production Orders, and any other documentation. Marshall will manage and follow-up any tips that come in.

I sent Lance a text when we left the scene, and he's already got a sheaf of documents to hand to me.

Lance is a skinny guy who moved to Calgary and signed up with the CPS after spending fifteen years with the Vancouver Police Service. He started out on the beat, like all of us, but moved up through the ranks quickly because of his work on the coast. Not only does he have great policing experience, he also speaks a handful of languages, including Mandarin, Cantonese, and even a smattering of Russian. On the coast, he worked in the drug and gang units for years where electronic surveillance is commonplace. Lance has probably filed for more warrants, production orders, and wire taps than the rest of us combined.

He gets right to the point. "Here's the Search Warrant for the condo, and I'm just finishing one for her business. I figure you'll want that right away. What else?"

"Thanks, Lance. Yes, we need one for the business. Make sure you include office and storage spaces, not just the restaurant. We'll also need Production Orders for the CCTV cameras in the condo building, for cell and land lines for the victim, Maxwell Shark, and the restaurant. Get all of that started and we'll feed you the details on anything else when we get it."

Marshall, who's closer to fifty than forty, is leaning against Scott's desk. "You want me to handle tips? No problem. So far, I haven't seen anything on the news about her death, but as soon as the story gets out, calls will trickle in, like they always do. I suspect it'll be the regulars who see a conspiracy behind everything, but I'll tell Dispatch to put them through to me, anyway." He pauses, "If we need any more bodies to take calls, I'll let 'cha know.

"D'ya know if there's gonna be a press release?"

I shrug. "Don't know, Wayne. That's a wait-and-see. There's no COD yet."

The heavy-set detective sighs. "Wouldn't 'cha know it. I just pulled the RV around to get it ready for the season. I guess I'd better get the wife to take it back out to the storage yard, eh? The neighbours will bitch about it sitting on the street if it's there overnight."

Scott commiserates. "'Fraid so. Unless a miracle happens, you're not going to be puttering around in it for at least a couple of days."

I ignore Marshall's bitching; he's not the only one who's going to have to put in the overtime.

* * *

We open the interview room door and get our first glimpse of Maxwell Shark, laying back with his arm over his eyes, on the ugly, uncomfortable two-seater couch. Mid 30s, dressed in jeans and a skin-tight golf shirt, he shows off bulging pecs, pop-eye biceps, and a trim waist. He swings his legs to the floor, his phone pressed tightly to his ear. An expensive-looking leather jacket lies over the back of the couch.

I ask, "Mr. Shark?"

"Hey, Mom, I gotta go. I'll call ya later." He touches his phone to end the call, then runs his fingers over the hint of bristle on his head. "Yeah, I'm Max." His red eyes and blotchy face suggest he's been crying, but he lashes out. "What the hell's going on? Why am I penned up like a criminal?"

I feel sympathy for the guy. His world has been shaken, and we've carted him into an interview room, further destroying his equilibrium. "Can I get you some water? Coffee?"

He shakes his head, his chest still puffed with anger, frustration and grief.

Scott lowers himself into one chair while I take the other. "I'm Detective Janice Maidstone and this is my partner, Detective Scott Amble. I know this is incredibly difficult. You're here because we don't yet know why Sophia died. We need to ensure that your condo remains the same way it was when she died in case we need to gather more evidence. You may say that we've already looked it over, but it's possible we might need to go back for another look."

Mr. Shark shudders and seems to deflate when some of the anger leaves him.

"When can I go home? And where is she?"

I hold his eyes and explain. "She's been taken to the Medical Examiners' office. We will take you home when we're finished here so you can pick up whatever you need to stay elsewhere for a few days. And I will let you know just as soon as you can go home for good."

He hangs his head, like a hound dog after he's been scolded. "I guess that means I'll have to check into a hotel or something."

"We can help you with that," I assure him. "Now, if you feel up to it, I have a few questions for you."

Scott's sitting beside me, taking notes and observing the grieving fiancé.

I start by confirming Shark's relationship with the victim, then I ask, "You told the officer at the scene that you spent Saturday night at a house in Priddis? When did you go and what time did you get back to the condo?"

"I left about midmorning on Saturday. I had a few errands to run before meeting up with the guys, my groomsmen, down at my best man's dad's place in Priddis. I wanted to go to Vegas, but that was too expensive for a couple of them, so we decided to keep it local. At least Priddis felt like we were in the mountains someplace, instead of being stuck in the city. The house is on the golf course, you know, one of the places that looks like a country club."

I nod. I'm somewhat familiar with the exclusive properties about thirty kilometers south of Calgary in the Rocky Mountain foothills. "What time did you get to Priddis?"

"Around one. There were games on TSN, so we sat around drinking until it was time to put on some steaks."

"And you stayed the night?"

"Yah. We were all drinking, ya know, and not in any shape to drive home, even if we wanted to. None of us were moving too quick this morning and I didn't get back to the condo until a little after noon."

Tears well in his eyes. "That's when I found Soph. By the way, I told the cop that got there first that I didn't touch her, but I remember now. I did. I touched her shoulder. You know, shook it. And then touched her face."

He screws up his face to hold back a sob. "She was so cold."

He covers his face with his hands, rubbing his fingers up and down his forehead. "That's when I called 911."

"Did you touch anything else in the condo?"

"No. When I called 911, they told me not to. All I did was go into the bedroom and drop my bag on the bed. That's it. I went back into the kitchen and waited for the cops to show up."

"I noticed, Mr. Shark, there were two champagne flutes on the coffee table. Who might have been drinking with Sophia?"

He shakes his head. "No idea. Soph only drank champagne on special occasions. She didn't particularly like the stuff and complained it gave her a headache. I don't even know where the bottle would have come from. It sure wasn't in the condo when I left on Saturday morning."

"Was she expecting company? Or going out?"

He thinks about his answer, then slowly shakes his head. "I don't know. Not as far as I know, but I was looking forward to the weekend with the guys and didn't pay much attention to what we talked about on Saturday morning before I left. I know Corbin was coming over for their regular meeting, but that would have been in the morning, not the evening. And she wasn't into day drinking."

I ask, "Corbin?"

He clarifies. "Bradley Corbin's her partner at the restaurant. They got together on Saturday mornings."

After a deep, shuddering breath, he continues. "Other than that, I don't know what she was up to. I wish I'd have listened, you know." He studies his hands lying limply in his lap. "God, what am I going to do?"

I give him a brief moment. The sooner we're done here, the sooner he can begin the long process of grieving.

"Maxwell, who has access to your condo?"

"No one. Well, except we have a cleaner. And a personal assistant. He's got a key, but he's on holiday."

"Can I get their contact information?"

"Sure." He rattles off names and scrolls through his phone for their numbers.

"Do you know the name of Sophia's lawyer?"

He goes back to his contact list. "Byron Landry. Here's his number."

I shift gears. "Did Sophia have any medical issues?"

He rubs his shaved head that attempts, but fails, to disguise a well-receding hairline.

"No. Soph never got sick. She watched what she ate and worked out whenever she had the chance. In fact, we just had medicals a few months ago to update our life insurance, and she passed with flying colours."

"Had she complained of not feeling well?"

"No, like I already said, she was fine." He narrows his eyes. "Except, now that you ask, she'd been puking sometimes. I just figured it was something she ate."

He scrubs furrows from his forehead. "I don't understand what could have happened."

He looks from me to Scott. "Do you think if I had been home, it would have made any difference? Maybe if I'd been there, if she needed help, I could have done something?"

I give a one-shouldered shrug. "I don't know, Maxwell. We'll know more after the medical examiner gives us her report."

He hunches, resting his elbows on his knees.

He looks up when I ask, "Do you know of anyone angry with Sophia?"

He answers right away. "Hell no. Soph was easy going."

He gives the question more thought. "I mean, everyone liked her, but I guess every once in a while, when she had to fire someone, she might have had words with them. Especially if she found someone had been stealing from the restaurant or something. But the restaurant manager usually handled stuff like that."

"Do you know of anyone who recently got fired? Who might hold a grudge?"

Mr. Shark shakes his head. "No one comes to mind, but you'd have to ask her partner. He'd know more about that than I do."

"Did you notice anything missing from the condo? Was anything out of place?"

He looks up at me, the furrows on his brow deepening. "No, I didn't notice anything, but I didn't exactly have a chance to look around before I got dragged down here. Why are you asking? Do you think this was a robbery gone wrong?"

I shake my head. "No, not necessarily."

"Oh." He nods and runs his eyes over the interview room, as though he's mentally looking around the condo. "No, everything looked the same."

"If you notice anything missing, let us know right away."

I shift my questions back to their relationship. "You and Sophia were getting married?"

His eyes fill with more tears. "At Christmas. On the twenty-first. It's the solstice, the same day her parents got married, so it was special for her."

I ask more questions, looking as much for his reactions as I am for the answers. He seems grief-stricken, but maybe he's a good actor.

I pause. I'm not seeing any chinks I want to poke into. For now. "That's all I have for you. Do you have questions for me?"

When he shakes his head, I reach into my jacket pocket and pull out a laminated card. "Here's the contact information for our grief counselling unit. They can help with what to do next or if you just want to talk to anyone. They are really helpful, so I encourage you to call."

He stuffs the card in his pocket without bothering to look at it.

Chapter Two

We leave Shark in the hands of a uni who will take him back to the condo. Back at my desk, I check my phone, and smile.

"Something interesting, partner?" In the three years that Scott and I have been partners, I haven't dated many guys, so Scott takes advantage of my current relationship to tease me whenever he has the opportunity.

I glance up. "Mind your own business." I feign a scowl.

He laughs. "All right. Just checking. I'll let you have some private time while I go to the cafeteria. Want anything?"

"Sure. Bring me a tuna on multi-grain. And some milk."

We'll head back to the condo building to interview neighbours in a bit, but we're starving. Scott is always hungry, and the cold cheese sandwich has long since left my belly and I need fuel. When Scott leaves, I go back to the text I just received.

A couple months ago, while grabbing groceries, I ran into an old high school friend from southwest Saskatchewan. We chatted for a while, and he told me he'd just moved to Calgary. "Maybe we should get together for coffee and catch up," he said.

Terry Ellars was my high school crush, so it was easy to say yes. He was much like I remembered and over the past couple of months, I've enjoyed spending time with him. It's been a pleasant change from my relationship-scarce life since my divorce eight years ago while I was still in Patrol.

I send him a quick reply and am working by the time Scott gets back with my sandwich.

Though there are no obvious signs of foul play, I don't think Turnbull died of natural causes. Too many little things are out of place. First of all, the slipper cast under the coffee table. How would it end up under the far end of the table unless it was kicked off? If she'd just slipped out of it, wouldn't it be much closer? Secondly, the two champagne flutes and a partially empty bottle raise my spidey-sense. Why wouldn't Turnbull take the bottle and glasses to the kitchen after the company left? Or if her company was still there, why didn't they help her when she had a medical crisis? At the very least, they could have called 911. These two things are enough to make me think that whoever was there had something to do with her death.

After wolfing down our stale cafeteria sandwiches, we head back to the murder scene to canvas the neighbours. Late Sunday afternoon traffic on Deerfoot Trail is heavy so we have plenty of time to run through the preliminary details.

Scott's in agreement with me. "I keep thinking about how she looked. Maybe her company brought drugs. Maybe they spooked when she ran into trouble."

"That's a theory, but I suppose she could have taken something after they left. That would explain why no one called 911."

He mimics me. "That's a theory." He watches the traffic out the side window while I drive. "I don't know, though. We didn't find any bag or paper that the pills, or whatever, came in. The lab guys probably took whatever garbage was in the place. Maybe they came across a likely container."

"Could someone have slipped something into the champagne without her knowing?"

Scott adds. "If they did, the lab'll pick it up."

We fall silent until I say, "Let's hope the neighbours saw something."

                              * * *

A heady aroma of garlic billows into the hallway when Turnbull's neighbour opens the door. Attractive, she's a little shorter than my 5'6" and is wearing black leggings and an olive-green oversize sweater.

Her smile is generous and perfect. "Hello. I bet you're the police. I've been expecting you."

Her remark surprises me, but her candor is refreshing.

"I'm Detective Maidstone, and this is my partner, Detective Amble. We're investigating an incident across the hall. Would you have a few minutes to talk with us?"

The woman glances at me, before her eyes focus on my partner like he's catnip and she's a chocolate-point Siamese. Her eyes linger on him, and a touch of colour appears on her cheeks. I don't blame her. Scott is worth a second, even a third, glance. With his brown eyes and warm smile bracketed by dimples, he's easy to look at. He used to be a professional baseball player, and he's still got the tall, rangy build of a fielder. She smiles and steps back. "I'm Stephanie Campbell. Come on in."

It's an open concept space, similar to the layout across the hall. An extravagant bouquet of lilies sits on the massive quartz countertop in the kitchen. A bottle of wine and wine glasses, one already partly filled, sit on the dining room table set with china.

She notices me looking at the table. "I'm expecting company for dinner, but he's late. What can I help you with?"

I let Scott take the lead. He smiles, and in a deep baritone, a little deeper than normal, I notice, begins, "We won't take too much of your time, Ms. Campbell."

She motions to the low-slung slate grey sectional sofa. "Can I get you a coffee? Water?"

Scott shakes his head. "No, thank you. As Detective Maidstone said, we're investigating an incident across the hall. Have you noticed anything out of the ordinary lately?" He leaves his question vague.

She settles into a coordinating chair across from us and takes a sip from her bucket-sized wine glass. She considers her answer. "Well, it's usually quiet around here. Everyone keeps to themselves." She takes another sip, her sleek dark bob swinging against her cheek as she cocks her head, "But last night, though I didn't give it much thought at the time, I heard arguing." She motions with her head to show she means across the hall.

"Did you recognize the voices?"

"It sounded like Sophia. And I'm pretty sure the other voice was another woman."

"About what time would this have been?"

"I'd just gotten home from book club, so it was around eight. I heard them as I was coming down the hall.

"It was unusual, but I didn't think anything of it until I noticed cops showing up earlier today." She sips her wine. "Can I ask what happened? Is Sophia okay?"

Scott shakes his head. "I can't tell you much, Ms. Campbell."

She interrupts. "Oh please, call me Stephanie."

He smiles and starts again. "Stephanie, we can't discuss the situation. I'm sure you understand." He softens the refusal with another smile, the one that shows off his dimples. "Could you hear what they were arguing about?"

"No, not really. It was muffled, and I wasn't about to stand in the hallway and listen at the door. But I heard the words 'selfish bitch' when I was coming into my suite."

My partner nods, encouraging her to continue.

"I wish I could tell you more. It wouldn't have even caught my attention, but it had the sound of people arguing. You know, short sentences. The way people talk when they're angry."

"Did you hear any names?"

"No." Stephanie gives a rueful smile. "If I would have known it was important, I would have paid more attention."

"I understand," Scott soothes. "Did you notice anyone in the hallway? See anyone except Ms. Turnbull go into the condo yesterday?"

Stephanie tucks a strand of dark hair behind her ear. "Mmm, no. I don't remember seeing anyone. Like I said, it's quiet in the building, and since there are only four units on this floor, I rarely bump into anyone."

Her phone interrupts with a jazzy ringtone. She heaves a sigh. "Finally. This is probably my company buzzing to be let in. I have to get it." She answers, less enthusiastically than I might have imagined, considering the crystal, candles and beautifully arranged table-scape. "Come on up, Jack."

Scott fishes in his jacket pocket and pulls out a business card. "Well, we'll get out of your hair." He flashes his pearly whites. "If you remember anything, please call. Even something small. You never know what's important."

Her face floods with colour again when she takes his card. "I certainly will..." and studies his card, "Detective Amble."

A balding man passes us in the doorway as we leave. He gives us a curious stare and as the door closes behind us, we hear him. "Sorry I'm late. I got held up in a meeting. Who were they? There's a cop standing across the hall. What's going on?" The door closes before we hear her reply.

Scott and I take a few minutes to visit with the uniform across the hall. I ask, "Has the fiancé been back for his stuff?"

"Nope, not yet. Do you want me to let you know when he's here?"

"No. That's fine. As long as someone watches him."

"No worries."

Scott and I approach the next door down the hall and while we wait for someone to answer our knock, I say, "You made quite an impression on Ms. Campbell."

Scott feigns innocence. "You think so?"

I can't help but chuckle. Scott's got a wicked sense of humour. Being assigned as partners three years ago was one of the best things that's happened to me as a cop. He's a good cop, smart, and hardworking. Best of all, I trust him.

It doesn't take us long to canvas the two remaining condos on the floor. The owners were home, but neither heard anything unusual. They tell us they'd been glued to their televisions, watching the hockey game until almost midnight, when the Flames won after a series of overtime shoot-outs.

Since noise in condominium complexes gravitates downward, we head to the unit directly below Turnbull's. The couple in that unit have just returned from a weekend trip to the mountains and can't tell us anything.

When I ask what sort of neighbours live above them, the older woman confirms, "They are very respectful. I rarely hear much of anything, and if I do, it's just sounds of everyday life. Maybe some footsteps, or a piece of cutlery being dropped." She thinks for a moment and looks at her husband, who nods in agreement. "I don't think I've ever heard arguing or loud parties. Nothing like that."

Knocking on other doors on the sixteenth floor tells us much the same. No noise, just a regular Saturday night.

We head down to the main floor to look for security cameras. I see three. One points at the mailbox vestibule; another tilts at the door going down to the parkade level. The third covers both the front entrance and elevators.

"The neighbours were a bust. Let's hope the cameras show us something," I tell Scott.

My phone interrupts us. I turn it around to show Scott. He raises his eyebrows when he sees Shark's name.

Shark doesn't waste time. "I came back for stuff. I can't be positive, but I think some of my insulin is missing. Would your guys have taken it?"

"I doubt it," I admit to him. "We're in the building so we'll be right up."

We find Shark and his escort standing in the kitchen. The fiancé points to the fridge. "I keep the insulin in there. There should be enough for two weeks, but half of it is gone."

I pull out my phone and text Al. I know he printed the outside of the fridge but wonder if they took any of the contents.

Al texts me right back. *We didn't take anything out of the fridge. I'll send someone right over to print the inside of the fridge.*

Al's definition of 'right over' is up for interpretation, so I am surprised that we've only shuffled our feet and made meaningless conversation for about fifteen minutes before the front door opens and a tech walks in. He heads right to the fridge.

He doesn't say much. With Maxwell pointing, the tech gingerly removes, then swirls a brush over the bottom crisper drawer, and a small box from the bottom shelf. Since Maxwell has been handling both, I doubt there will be any useful prints left, but we'll give it a go.

When he's finished, the tech checks his phone. "Al wants to know if there's anything else you want while I'm here?"

I shake my head. "No."

He nods and leaves with only a "Later."

In the meantime, Shark moved to a stool at the kitchen counter. He sits, oblivious to his surroundings, staring at the couch where he last saw his fiancée. His escort finally clears his throat. "Uh, Mr. Shark, if you've got what you need, maybe we can head out?"

He slowly gets to his feet and reaches for the overnight bag at his feet. "Let's go."

I raise my eyebrows to Scott in a question. He nods. We're done here, too.

The uniformed cop standing guard at the door signs us out and sighs as he returns to his perch on the stool outside the door, watching us head to the elevator. Shark continues down to the parkade to his own ride while the rest of us get off on the ground floor.

It's about ten PM, not even twelve hours since Maxwell found Sophia's body, when we get back to the station. The rest of our four person team is sitting in a small conference room. Marshall's feet are on the table and I'm pretty sure he'd been napping. Nguyen has a stack of paper in front of him and is tapping away on his phone.

He stops what he's doing and tells us, "I'll be serving the Production Orders for phone and bank records for the key players tomorrow morning. That's for Turnbull herself, for Shark, Corbin, and the restaurant.

"I've also sent one over to the condo management company for their CCTV. Anyone else we need to paper right away?"

Scott looks at me and shakes his head. "No, good start. You're having all the results routed through you?"

Nguyen nods. "Yep. I'll let you know when anything comes in. In the meantime, I've run the victim, her fiancé, housekeeper, personal assistant, and business partner." He pulls out a sheet of paper from the middle of the stack in front of him.

"Turnbull's clean going 'way back. Not even a speeding ticket. Shark's had a couple of impaired driving convictions a few years ago. Also assault charges back in 2012 and 13. This was before entire reports were digitized, but from the summaries that got loaded to the system, it looks like he was a bartender and got in a couple of scuffles with patrons. Both sides were charged, but everything was dismissed before it went to court. I've got the names of the investigators if you want to follow up with them.

"The most interesting thing comes a couple years before that. A girlfriend claimed he stole her car." Nguyen smiles. "Shark claims he borrowed it with her permission, and the only reason she accused him of stealing it was because she found out he took some other girl out while he had the car. The girlfriend didn't like the idea that he was using her Porsche to hit up other girls. When it came down to it, she withdrew the complaint."

He pulls out another piece of paper. "The personal assistant had an illegal possession for alcohol. Long time ago. The housekeeper is pure as the driven snow."

Lance flips to another page and continues reading. "Business partner. No charges or record. He shows up as a witness on a couple of cases from years ago. I'm waiting for the files to come over from the archives and will let you know if we need to dig further."

He tidies his pile of paper and folds his hands on top. "That's it."

I tell him. "Great, thanks Lance. Here's another bunch for you to look at. The best man and the groomsmen." I hand him a sheet of paper.

He takes the paper, then teases, "Do you have a list of the bridesmaids, too?"

"Good point. I'll send along other names when they pop up."

I turn to Marshall. "Any tips yet?"

"No, it's quiet. Switchboard knows to transfer anything through to me."

I nod. "Why don't you guys head home, and we'll see you in the morning."

They don't wait for me to repeat the invitation.

I look at Scott. "Feel like interviewing the business partner now? I wouldn't mind seeing his reaction if we're the ones to break the news to him."

Scott nods. "Good idea. The sooner the better."

* * *

We get to Bradley Corbin's house on the west edge of the city close to midnight. He's in the restaurant business and probably used to late hours, but even if he's tucked in for the night, I won't lose any sleep if we wake him up.

His is an average bungalow in this affluent neighbourhood that boasts of walking trails along the ridge overlooking the Bow River, and ease of access to the TransCanada highway and the mountains. A faint blue glow flickers through a window.

I press the doorbell, wait a minute, then lay on it again to emphasize our serious intent. Finally, the porch light blinks on, and a man glares through the sidelight.

Scott and I hold up our badges.

The resident does a double take, his expression changing from anger to frustration.

He opens the door. "Can I not have a single evening without something needing my attention?"

"Mr. Corbin?" I ask, wanting to confirm the identity of the lanky, bookish-looking man. He's average height, about a half a head taller than me, and a head shorter than Scott. In spite of the late hour, his white shirt, with sleeves rolled precisely above the elbow, is tucked neatly into khakis.

In a precise, clipped British accent, he responds, "Yes. What can I do for you? What is happening at the restaurant?"

We introduce ourselves, then I tell him. "We'd like to ask you a few questions about your business partner."

"Sophia? Why? Is something wrong?"

"May we come in, Mr. Corbin?"

He stands back from the door and motions with his hand.

The smell of popcorn makes my mouth water and stomach growl. The tuna sandwich I devoured a few hours ago was not enough.

Corbin leads us to the living room, where the television is paused on a scene where Jeff Probst snuffs the flame of a discomforted survivor. The room is a combination of "modern bachelor" and "favourite aunt's chic". Corbin moves to a worn wing-back chair covered in a geometric pattern of reds and blacks while pointing us to an oxblood leather, three cushion chesterfield. Papers, a partially empty tub of popcorn, and a crystal glass with amber liquid comfortably clutter the shiny, lacquered coffee and end tables. Shelves filled with books and knickknacks sitting on antique doilies bookend the television.

"What is the issue with Sophia? We spoke just yesterday."

Providing notice of death to family and friends is a gut-wrenching part of the job. I've done it many times, but it never gets easier.

"I'm terribly sorry. Sophia has passed away."

Corbin freezes, his eyes flicking to Scott and back to me. Finally he says, "Pardon me?"

"Her fiancé found her earlier today in the condo. We believe she died sometime last night."

Corbin runs his hands through styled brown hair. He takes off his round, dark-framed glasses to rub his eyes. His fingers come away, wet with tears.

He argues, "No. That cannot be."

"Mr. Corbin, we have a few questions about the last time you saw her."

He brings a fist to his mouth and whispers around it. "Sophia? Gone?"

His breath hitches, and lips quiver. Tears threaten to spill down his cheeks. Without the owlish glasses, he looks younger than the age on his driver's license, 42.

Scott asks. "Mr. Corbin, can I get you a glass of water?"

The man stares at my partner. "Oh...no. I can get it myself."

Corbin gets to his feet and heads to the kitchen, separated from the living room by a large granite topped island. He steadies himself against the sink and fills a glass from the tap.

He takes his time, drinking an entire glass of water, then refilling it before coming back to the living room. He clears his throat and asks again. "What happened?"

"We don't know, Mr. Corbin. There were no signs of a struggle. But perhaps you can give us some insight."

He shakes his head. "What could I possibly say? She was fine on Saturday morning. I do not understand." His last words have the whine of a young boy upset at losing a favourite toy.

I tell him softly. "I understand how shocking this is. Is there anyone we can call? Would you like someone here with you?"

He shakes his head. "No, I am fine. I will call Barbara later. She is my fiancée."

"I'm going to ask you some questions. If you need to take a break, let me know."

Scott settles back with his notebook and waits for me to begin.

"Mr. Corbin, confirm with us the last time you saw Sophia."

"I saw her Saturday morning. I went over to her place for our regular weekly meeting."

"Did you usually meet at her place?"

"Yes. We preferred to meet there, instead of at the restaurant. It was quieter. No staff running about. Most of the time, Maxwell made himself scarce, so it was also private."

"Did you notice anything unusual? Did she mention feeling unwell?"

He shakes his head. "No, it was..." He pauses, "...well, she seemed pale and a bit subdued, so I asked if she was feeling unwell. A bit of a stomach upset, she said. That was so very typical of Sophia. She wanted no one to worry about her."

"Was she unwell enough to cause you concern?"

"No. I took her at her word."

"Was there anything specific on your agenda? Anything out of the ordinary?"

"No, not particularly. We are approaching our financial year-end, so we discussed that. We also talked about her plans to go on an extended honeymoon after her wedding in December." He closes his eyes briefly, then takes a breath. "Other than a day or two here and there, she had taken no respite from work for quite some time."

He shakes his head. "Gone. Impossible. The restaurant will not be the same without her."

I give him a moment, then ask, "Other than discussing her honeymoon, what else did you talk about?"

"Work issues, mostly. We reviewed seasonal menu changes, and some of the staff wanting holidays; Easter brunch and whether we need to bring in extra staff. Issues such as that."

"Did anything seem to be bothering her?"

He stares at the frozen television, rocking back and forth slightly in his chair. Just as I'm about to repeat the question, he continues. "Just the upset stomach, but otherwise, she seemed fine. Better than fine, actually. She was in good spirits and appeared relaxed. Maxwell was out for the night, so she had no demands on her time. She said she was going to do some shopping, then come home and have a quiet evening."

"How long was your meeting with her?"

"It was slightly longer than usual — perhaps three hours? We had breakfast and our meeting, then lingered over coffee. I left her place before lunchtime."

Out of curiosity, I ask, "Why was the meeting longer than usual?"

He huffs. "My fiancée and I had a tiff the night before and I was still out of sorts. It all seems so trivial now that Sophia is gone."

He pauses again, staring absently at the television.

I prompt. "Did you mention being out of sorts to Sophia?"

He nods. "I did not have to. She was incredibly perceptive and asked if anything was bothering me. But once asked, I admitted that Barbara and I had had words. Sophia had a wonderful ability to put things into perspective, to put me back on track. I thought she would have words of advice for me."

"What was the argument with your fiancée about? Did it concern the restaurant?"

"No, not directly. Our disagreement started after a meeting we had with our wedding planner on Friday evening. We met with her for a cake tasting, then went for a late dinner at Bonterra. It seemed strange going for dinner after eating cake, but there you go. We originally planned to have the cake tasting late on Saturday, but at the last minute, Barbara insisted we move the appointment to a day earlier. Friday afternoon. I forget what her reason was, but I have found it easier to accommodate her whims than to risk a scene."

He lifts his hands and lets them drop back on the arms of his chair. "Things were fine until after the cake tasting and we were on our way to dinner. I shared an anecdote involving the restaurant and Sophia. I should have known better. Barbara can sometimes be sensitive about the time I spend at work ... and with Sophia."

He sighs. "This launched Barbara into one of her jealous tirades. I have often assured her that Sophia and I were just business partners and friends, but Barbara did not like that we were so close."

I nod, encouraging him to continue.

"She and I are getting married in October, and the stress of planning has made her more sensitive. At the best of times, Barbara is high strung." He gives a small, lop-sided smile. "And has a bit of a temper. But over the years, I have learned how to manage her. When she gets into one of these states, I spend some extra time with her, and it blows over."

I interrupt him, "Would you mind giving me your fiancée's contact information in case we want to clarify anything?"

"Certainly. Barbara Stephens. And as I said, she is away temporarily, but here is her cell number." He rattles off some numbers.

"Thank you, Mr. Corbin. Now, you were telling us about the argument you had with her on Friday night?"

He sighs, lifts, and lowers his hands. "Yes. Barbara lost her temper with me, but we had a long talk and by the time I dropped her off at her condo after dinner, she seemed fine."

"And you brought this up with Sophia?"

"Yes. I admit I often burdened her with my problems. She said she would give Barbara a call and reassure her. Sophia did not want bad blood between them."

"Can you tell us more about your relationship with Sophia?" I ask.

He holds my gaze. "We were good friends. Perhaps the best of friends."

"Did you share an intimate relationship?"

He chuckles. "Oh no, Detective. Not at all. In fact, I often felt like a big brother." He pauses. "Or sometimes the tables turned, and she played the role of the big sister I never had, giving me advice."

"Did you see or speak to Sophia after leaving her place on Saturday morning?"

He shakes his head slowly and takes a deep breath, hesitating a moment. "I gave her a hug and told her I would see her next week."

He stands. "Excuse me for a moment." He heads into what I presume is his bedroom, and returns shortly, dabbing at his streaming, red eyes with tissues.

"After you left her condo that morning, what did you do the rest of the day?"

"As I said earlier, Barbara and I were to attend the cake tasting, but after she moved it to Friday, my Saturday afternoon was free. I went to the restaurant for a couple of hours to make sure everything was running smoothly. I met with Kevin, the manager of the Saturday evening shift. Then I went home."

His eyes widened briefly. "Oh, it has just come to me why Barbara changed the cake tasting. She wanted Saturday free so she could go visit her parents in Montana. But, as I was saying, back to what I did on Saturday. After leaving the restaurant, I went home and watched television until about eight thirty when Kevin called. They were having problems with the POS."

At my puzzled look, he elaborated.

"The Point-of-Sale system. Think of it as an electronic cash register. I attempted to talk him through how to re-set it, but that did not work so I had to go in."

"What time was this?"

"He called at eight thirty. It took me a few minutes, but I got to the restaurant at about nine o'clock.

"After we got the system restarted, I decided that since I was already there, I might as well get some work done. I wanted to concentrate, so I gave instructions that I was not to be interrupted."

"What time did you leave the restaurant?"

"After closing. Kevin and I walked out together. Shortly after midnight, I believe."

"Mr. Corbin, you sound British. When did you come to Canada, and how did your partnership with Sophia come about?"

A side of his mouth lifts in what could be a smile. "I was born in Canada, actually. When I was a youngster learning to talk, I had a nanny who was British. I picked up her accent. At least, that is what my mother told me."

Continuing, his hand shakes slightly when he takes a sip of water. "As to my partnership with Sophia, it is somewhat complicated. I got to know Sophia when I was working in the oil and gas sector. She had a temporary position in my department. Eventually, she went her own way and started the restaurant. She asked if I was interested in joining her as a partner and to manage the business side. It was the accounting, mostly, where she wanted my input. It seems a tremendous change, leaving oil and gas for a restaurant job, but she knew I had worked for a large restaurant group when I first gained my accounting designation."

"It must have been risky for you, leaving what I presume was a lucrative salary in the resource sector and going to a start-up restaurant?"

"Oh absolutely. Restaurants are notoriously fickle. But Sophia was charming and convincing. She was like that, you know. So warm and ...." His voice breaks. "She made me an incredible offer. She offered me equity in the restaurant in return for my commitment. Just my commitment to help her run the business. She didn't need any start-up capital because her father bankrolled the entire operation. He would have done anything for her.

"His passing a few years ago was devastating to her."

I ask, "Wouldn't it have been easier to hire a bookkeeper? Then she wouldn't have felt obliged to give up a share of the business?"

"I suppose so," he agrees. "She must have felt my business acumen warranted the sacrifice.

"It was an enormous risk going into the restaurant business, but I was ready for a change. Besides, I knew layoffs were imminent in the oil patch. I expressed to my Vice President that I had no objection to being one of those let go. The company obliged by offering me an attractive severance package which left me free to join Sophia." Tears trickle down his cheek. "It was the best decision I ever made."

I give him a minute to collect himself. "So, the restaurant has done well?"

"Oh yes. Incredibly well. After the first year, which had some start-up issues, we've had steady growth. With cost-cutting measures, we even weathered COVID and have thrived since. In fact, Sophia wanted to open another location on the southern edge of the city by the South Health Campus. Overlooking the river valley."

He pauses. "We knew it would be an enormous amount of work, but she thought it would be worth the effort. That part of the city is growing quickly and needs a great restaurant. It is a perfect fit and time to expand."

"How far along are the plans for the new place?"

"We were only at the talking stage. We had sketched designs and jotted down ideas but had not negotiated any lease or discussed this with a designer."

I nod, then return to an earlier statement he made.

"You mentioned you didn't meet at Sophia's place if Maxwell was around. Can you tell us a little about that?"

He hesitates. "Well, if he was there, he would hang around making what he thought were valuable comments, but I felt that most of the time, they were irrelevant. He acted as if he were the third partner." He licks his lips. "To be honest, he is irritating. I suspect he feels the same about me. And before you ask, I know this because Sophia told me."

"Why?"

Corbin put the almost empty glass of water down on a crystal coaster on the side table and folds his arms across his chest. "Why he finds me irritating? I do not know. But I can tell you why I feel the way I do. In addition to sticking his nose in the restaurant business, the man is vain, selfish and has an exceedingly entitled attitude. I suspect when he met Sophia, Maxwell saw dollar signs. I also believe he was stepping out on her. He has a reputation for a wandering eye."

Corbin warms to the subject. "Going back to your earlier question, Maxwell dislikes me because, in contrast to him, I valued Sophia for her hard work, not her money. She might have come from a wealthy family, and her father might have supplied the capital to purchase the restaurant, but Sophia worked extremely hard to develop the business and make a success of it. Her reputation as an exotic dancer when she was younger did her no favours, but she overcame the stigma." He almost whispers. "It is not fair. She worked so hard to make the restaurant a success."

"Was Maxwell unfaithful?"

Corbin's lips twist like he swallowed sour milk. "Most likely, but I knew of no particular woman. I have to give him credit for being discrete. I am sure if Sophia ever caught him, it would be over between them."

He pauses for a moment. "I suspect he would not take it well if the easy life, with Sophia paying the bills, ended. Under the pretty-boy exterior, he has quite the mean streak. Sophia told me that he faced assault charges for using excessive force during his time as a bartender."

"We will look into that. Have you witnessed any specific incidents of this mean streak?"

He holds up his hands as if to halt my question. "Oh, nothing specific, and I should not have brought up his past as the bartender. I may have given you an incorrect impression of the man."

"Did Sophia ever say he was unfaithful? Or that Maxwell abused her in any way?"

He shakes his head. "No, I never heard her say anything about him being verbally or physically abusive, however she was quite private with their relationship so I would not have expected her to say anything. Now that you ask, though, concerning infidelities, in the last couple of weeks, I overheard phone calls when she asked him where he was, almost as if she did not believe him. But that is just the impression I received."

I return to the subject of Corbin's relationship with the victim. "Is it possible Mr. Shark believed you had an intimate relationship with Ms. Turnbull? You told us earlier that you got along well with Sophia, and he must have seen that."

"Whatever scenarios he conjured in his own mind, you would have to ask him. My relationship with her was not romantic.

"We are, well, we were a great team. As I said, she had the people skills and understood what needed to be done to manage the kitchen. If you did not know, she learned restaurant basics from previous employment. I managed the financials, inventory management, payroll, licensing and other regulatory paperwork. We just meshed." He holds up his hands and interlocks his fingers. "Like well-oiled cogs in a wheel."

I have no more questions for the business partner, at least for now. We will need to come back to him, but I wrap things up.

"Mr. Corbin, because you were in Sophia's place on Saturday morning, we want to exclude your fingerprints from any others we find. Someone from the lab will be calling to arrange a time to meet you."

He briefly scowls, "Ah, yes, I suppose that is necessary. I prefer they come to the house instead of the restaurant."

"I'm sure they can accommodate that request. Can you give us the best number for them to contact you?"

After Scott records the number, we are done with the interview. "Thank you, Mr. Corbin, thank you for your time. Do you have any questions for us?"

He glances at us, tears filling his eyes. "No. I need time to absorb this... now that she is gone, I do not know what is going to happen."

Chapter Three

It's almost 2 AM by the time we get back to the office on Westwinds. My eyes feel like they're filled with road grit, and I'm so tired my hands are starting to shake. "Scott, I need a quick snooze. Give me forty minutes in a Quiet Room."

He nods. "I hear ya. I'll do the same with my feet up on my desk."

A couple of closet-sized rooms on our floor are designated specifically for cat naps. Their only contents are a cot, a kick-ass fan that serves both to move the stale air and to act as a white noise machine, a hanger on the back of the door, and an old analog alarm clock. I fight claustrophobia when the door closes, but the anxiety lessens when I crank up the fan and let a breeze blow over me.

Wiggling my toes when I take off my boots feels good, and I scratch my back where my shoulder holster always rubs. What with the two call outs earlier this weekend, and now Turnbull, I've been going nonstop way too long. My brain's mushy. I set the timer on my phone and momentarily consider sending a text to Terry before realizing he should be asleep. I close my eyes, imagining the breeze from the fan is wind across the prairie.

When Alan Doyle sings "I Am A Sailor" on my phone, it takes a few moments to push back the heavy, thick blanket of sleep and remember where I am. My eyes beg to close again, but I roll over and reach for my boots. Bright lights and coffee are needed to get my mind back in gear.

I make a quick detour to the locker room to brush my teeth and smooth the stubborn rooster-tail left in my hair from the pillow. My hair is nothing special, not like Stephanie Campbell's sleek bob that drew Scott's eye earlier today. Or was that yesterday?

I was a towhead when I was a kid, but my hair's darkened over the years. The colour's changing again, though, and it now has a few strands of grey catching the light. The ponytail I used to sport has been abandoned in favour of a short cut that's easier to take care of.

I'm not one to primp in front of a mirror and this morning, that's a good thing. A quick glance is all I need to confirm that I could use another seven hours of sleep. My eyes are red-rimmed, and the dark circles could look raccoon-like, if I was in an uncharitable mood and wanted to criticize myself. The short nap was better than nothing, though, and I walk less zombie-like to the canteen where I brew a couple cups of coffee and toast a couple of stale bagels. I butter the bagels, and then head to the squad room. The cavernous room is set up with four workstations. Each station has two desks butting up against each other so partners can easily share information. There's enough room for a 4 by 8 table and a large whiteboard. The open concept doesn't allow for much privacy, so a series of small offices line one wall where private phone calls and conversations frustrate would-be eavesdroppers.

Sergeant Ash, our boss, rates his own office at the end of the squad room. I've often complained to Scott that we have the shittiest location in the squad, in the boss's direct line of sight. Too often, I feel in his crosshairs, but Scott just laughs and tells me I'm paranoid.

Scott's already got a half-empty cup on his desk, but he looks happy when I hand him the bagel and coffee. "Here. Did you get much shut-eye?"

"Thanks for the bagel. I'm starving. Yah, I got half an hour or so of shut-eye. Enough for now." He looks me up and down. "You look better than you did an hour ago."

"Thanks. The nap was just what I needed. What 'cha working on?"

"Looking at backgrounds. I left the restaurant for you."

With no need for more chatter, I get to work while devouring the bagel. I wish I'd brought some peanut butter.

Half an hour later, I pull a pile of paper from the printer. "Scott, I've got the restaurant's corporate documents."

He nods but doesn't take his eyes off the screen in front of him. "Find anything?"

"Not really. It's a numbered company. Turnbull's the president. Corbin the VP. Registered shareholders, uh, just the two of them, with Sophia holding 75 per cent, and Corbin 25."

Scott nods. "Okay, Turnbull controlled the place."

"It makes sense. Given that he didn't put any money into it, she was generous to give him twenty-five."

"Can't argue with that."

"Any background on Corbin?"

He talks while he reads. "Not much more than Nguyen told us last night. No criminal record. He's in the system, though, as a complainant. He's called in on behalf of the restaurant for... a couple of break-ins. Nothing current."

"The first coffee went down fast. I'm going to get another before I start on Shark's social media. You want one?"

"Sure. Might as well. If you're doing Shark, then I'll look into Corbin's."

The two of us tap away until other guys in the squad room start trickling in and weak morning sunshine creeps across the floor.

Just after eight, my cell phone rings. Caller id: Monica Patel: OCME.

"Good morning, Monica."

Monica is in work mode and doesn't waste time on pleasantries. "I've scheduled the Turnbull postmortem for 2 PM." She pauses. "I assume you'll attend? Scott's got something better to do?"

"Thanks Monica. Yes, I'll be there." I smile.

She is well aware of Scott's aversion to autopsies. Most people think they're gruesome, but as autopsies go, this will be a breeze. It's a fresh body, no decomp or mutilations or gross stuff.

Monica's also aware of the deals Scott and I make. Heck, she's even given me ideas of things that Scott can do in return for me going to autopsies in his stead.

Usually, I think I end up with the better end of the deal, but I remember one time when I let him off too lightly. He convinced me to attend an autopsy when the body had been found floating in a slough after winter ice melted. That postmortem was God-awful. The original favour I'd extracted was that he had to write our reports for an entire month. I should have made it two.

Monica hangs up without saying goodbye, but I know her too well to take offence.

"Sorry to take so long exchanging pleasantries with Monica."

Scott appreciates my sarcasm and chuckles. "Chatty as usual, was she?"

"I couldn't get a word in edgewise."

Nguyen and Marshall arrive, looking bright eyed after their full night's sleep. The four of us huddle around a whiteboard, on which I'd marked out a preliminary timeline and put our main characters along the borders. Now we'll chart an investigative action plan.

My first note is autopsy. Beside it, I write my name. I look at Scott. "What are you going to do this afternoon while I'm busy with Monica?"

He goes to take another sip of coffee then scowls when he finds his cup empty. "I'm going to start with the housekeeper and the personal assistant, if I can track them down."

"Sounds good." I put this on the list. While I'm adding *wedding planner* on the next line, I say, "I'm curious about the last-minute change to the cake tasting. From the Saturday to Friday. Corbin says it was his fiancée's idea, but is it just a coincidence that Turnbull was murdered on Saturday? I wouldn't mind having a chat with the wedding planner."

Scott raises his eyebrows. "Any reason in particular?"

"Anything to do with Saturday night, I want to nail down. All of a sudden, from what Corbin said, his girlfriend is out of town, and he's free. Who knows, maybe the wedding planner overhead something. It's worth a chat, don't you think?"

Scott says, "Yep, makes sense. You'll set it up?"

"Sure." I look at Lance and Wayne. "How about you guys? What's on your plate?"

Nguyen pipes up. "I'll finish up with the warrants and get them served, then call the condo management company and see if they'll send over their security footage. I'd hate for them to erase anything before we have time to ask them for it."

"Turnbull got a mention on the news this morning," Marshall tells us. "It might prompt some calls. I have to stick around the office today anyway, so I'll take any calls that come in."

We're interrupted when my private cell gives a characteristic ring telling me that Mom is calling. I ignore it momentarily and ask the team, "Anything else?"

I get a round of head shakes. "Okay then. Let's debrief at the end of the day. Let me know if anything critical pops up before then."

The phone's still ringing, so I head to a small side office to take the call. "Hi Mom."

Mom never bothers me during the day, saving her rambling conversations for the evenings, so I'm worried something might be wrong with Dad. Or my brother who's running the ranch.

I'm glad I pick up. Her voice has a tremor when she says, "I know you're probably at work Janice, but I wanted to hear your voice."

Something must be bothering her more than usual. One of the roles I play in our family is to jolly Mom out of her doldrums. She's overwhelmed by the responsibility of taking care of Dad and maintaining the huge yard and garden. I do my best to cheer her up, but by the time I lift the worry from her shoulders, it often settles on mine.

When I return to my desk, Marshall and Nguyen are back at their desks across the room, and Scott's hanging up from his own call.

"How's your Mom?"

I sigh. "It's more of the same. She's overwhelmed. Dad's so forgetful. She can't let him out of her sight, or else he gets into something he shouldn't. Yesterday, when a flashlight didn't work, he got it into his mind that all the batteries in the house needed replacing. He went everywhere, even to the smoke detectors, and took out batteries. She had to go around putting them all back." I pause. "But you don't need to hear all of this. You have your own life to worry about."

He gives me half a grin. "To be honest, my life's drama-free. Let me know if I can help. And if you need to go home to handle stuff, don't worry about work. We can manage the case without you."

"Thanks, but I'll wait until the end of April. I've booked a week off to go down and try to work some magic. If things change in the meantime, I'll let you know."

Scott's parents are young and vibrant, in their late fifties, so he has yet to encounter the worries associated with their aging. He knows how lucky he is and never fails to offer help, even though there's not much he can do except lend a sympathetic ear.

He gets back to work. "While you were on the phone, I tracked down the housekeeper. I'm going to meet her this afternoon.

"Being the super-efficient guy I am," he teases, "I also got in touch with the personal assistant. I want to talk to him pronto before he meets up with Shark. Any objections if I head over there now? Then how about lunch? I can't survive on coffee and that bagel."

After meeting Scott for lunch, I head to the Chief Medical Examiners' building, only a few blocks from the river. I turn into a parking space beside one of the anonymous Identification Team's white sprinter vans.

Since Sunday morning, I've only had that forty-minute nap in the quiet room at the station. It took the edge off my need for sleep, but I crave my bed and pillow. Thank goodness for the bright sunshine that's given me a boost. Cheerful cheeps of sparrows keep me company while I walk to the blocky, single story, grey building incongruously adorned with bright red doors and trim.

I'm happy to see the familiar face behind the glass partition in the reception area. "Hi Beth. Last time I was here you were on holidays, so I haven't seen you since when? Last fall when you were selling the yearlings? How did it go?"

She returns my smile. "Better than I expected. Thanks for asking. And I've got some terrific new foals."

I notice a picture of a mare and foal on her desk. "Is this one of this year's crop? He's pretty fancy!"

"She. And absolutely! Fancy as the dickens, and just as sassy. Just like her momma." Beth displays pictures of her foals in the same way others like to show off their grandchildren.

I admire the picture, ooo-ing and aaah-ing appropriately, and then get to the business that brings me here.

"Monica's expecting me. Can you let her know I'm here?"

"Of course!" The older woman speaks briefly into the phone on her desk and nods at me. "Her assistant will be right out. Now, rather than just looking at pictures and listening to my stories, why don't you come out next weekend? I've got a couple horses that could use some exercise."

An assistant in green scrubs opens a door at the far end of the reception area and motions for me to come with him. As I do, I call over my shoulder to Beth. "Not this weekend, but soon. I promise!"

The assistant holds the locker room door open for me. I know the routine: put all my stuff in a locker for safekeeping and don protective gear. I would love to take my phone into the autopsy suite to record notes, but Monica forbids electronic devices. Some scrofulous character in another jurisdiction took unauthorized photos of an autopsy and posted them on social media. The resulting justifiable outrage at the inappropriate distribution means that a strict policy against cell phones is in place. Another example of one idiot's actions affecting the rest of us.

Monica is already getting changed. "Hi Janice." She looks over while she tucks her short hair into a cap. "Have you been home since the call out yesterday?"

"No. I'll probably go home when we're done here."

She nods. "Good. Treacle's going to be wondering what's happened."

Treacle is my old, retired cattle dog. When I can't get home, there are a couple of teenagers on my block who love to take her out for walks and fill up her food dish, but the dog misses me. "I know. I feel guilty. I don't know how people manage with kids. If my dog happens to poop in the house if I can't get home, that's not a huge deal but you can't just leave a kid on its own."

She agrees. "I'm glad I've never had to juggle kids with work. It would be bad enough if you were part of a couple, but as a single parent? How do they do it?" She knots the ties on her full-length waterproof gown and says, "Enough about dogs and kids. The body's ready for us, so I'm going to get started. Come in when you're suited up."

It takes a few minutes, then I pull on latex gloves and push through the heavy doors with their wired glass window inserts.

A whooshing of air accompanies me into the negatively pressurized autopsy suite. Through experience, I know that it's cold in here, so I wore a sweater. It takes a couple of breaths to get used to the noticeable chemical tang in the air.

I take my place off to the side where I won't be in the way and quietly introduce myself to the gowned person who's sitting on the one available stool. This is the crime scene tech from Al's office, ready to accept samples from Monica throughout the autopsy.

Sophia Turnbull's on the table under the glare of surgical lights. While Monica pulls on further protection, a face shield, and another layer of surgical gloves with an interposed layer of cut-proof synthetic mesh, the photographer takes pictures from every angle. When she's finished, she turns to the autopsy assistant. "There's something on her cheek. Do you want to collect it?"

The assistant nods and scrutinizes the area. With tweezers, he removes something and places it in a small glass vial. Then he begins to remove her clothing, starting at her feet. The single, soft pink, fuzzy slipper stands in stark contrast to the harsh and cold circumstances of this room. The other, the one cast off under the coffee table, is already at the Crime Lab.

Her scarlet painted toenails are garish in contrast to her marble-white flesh. Under the bright overhead lights, they are too vivid. Almost violent.

Sophia's underwear is a surprise. It is not what I would wear for a quiet evening at home when my fiancé was out of town. The cherry-red peek-a-boo bra and crotchless panties make me wonder if she was expecting company.

When she's naked, the photographer steps forward again. Though necessary, to be examined and photographed under the harsh lights that reveal every imperfection seems vulgar and a violation to the woman. I feel a tinge of embarrassment for her.

The flash fills the room with moments of incandescent light. I speak up, "Her fiancé who lives in the condo says he is missing some insulin."

The crime scene tech adds, "We took a Sharps container from the scene. We're looking through to see if any of the syringes have fingerprints that shouldn't be there."

Monica nods. "Do you know if she is diabetic?"

The tech and I shrug, but I reply for both of us. "Not that we know of. Her fiancé didn't mention that she was."

The photographer steps back and the autopsy assistant takes over to wash the body with a low pressure hose. Water streaming off her body drains through a filter that will catch any particulates. This material will be taken to the Crime Lab.

Monica steps forward to the table and speaks clearly into a microphone hanging from the ceiling. "This is the postmortem examination of Sophia Turnbull." She glances at the information on the small electronic screen situated on a stand at the foot of the table. "Date of Birth 16 November 1987."

I take a couple steps closer to the table.

She first examines the front of Turnbull's body. "Lividity in the buttocks and posterior aspect of the legs is consistent with the seated position of the body upon discovery. Preliminary examination of the body shows a 74 millimetre by 3 millimetre abrasion over the left sternocleidomastoid muscle. Evidence of fresh bruising on both shins, linear in nature approximately midpoint on the tibia. No other marks indicating a struggle or trauma are present. Fingernails are intact, with no visible tissue or fibre under them. Scrapings have been taken for microscopic analysis." She motions for her assistant to come forward and together, they turn the body.

After finishing the gross description, she slips on headband magnifier glasses and goes over the body again, front and back. It is painstaking. She makes occasional remarks in the microphone. At one point, she peers more intensely at a spot on Sophia's back and circles it with a black marker.

During the drawn-out process, my energy seeps away and my body cries for sleep. I stifle yawns and take deep breaths to keep alert. I try not to fidget, not wanting to distract Monica.

At last, she steps back and directs the photographer. "Take close-up photos of the area I've circled. There may be an injection site. Also, close-ups of the abrasion on the neck."

She tells us. "I'll take samples of both areas to test for residue. With any luck, something will turn up."

She walks over to me, and in a lower voice asks, "I've heard you yawning, friend. Do you want to go take a walk and come back? It will be a few minutes before I get started again."

"Thanks," I smile behind my mask, "but I think I'll get a second wind as soon as you get back to work."

Monica reaches for a blade and opens Sophia's body with a large Y shaped incision from the shoulders to mid sternum, then straight down to the pubis, continuing a quiet commentary into the overhead microphone. She removes each organ. They first squelch, protesting their removal, then make a wet slap on the table where she places them for later macro-examination. She pours the stomach contents into a container.

My mind had been wandering, but it snaps into focus when Monica asks, "Did the fiancé say anything about a pregnancy?"

"He did not."

Monica says, "From the condition of the uterus, it looks like she was about three months pregnant. She probably would have known, since I'd assume she would have taken a home pregnancy test as soon as she missed a period, let alone three of them."

"And assuming that she had regular periods," I comment.

"Well, yes, making that assumption," Monica concedes.

"I'll follow up with the fiancé. I find it hard to believe he wouldn't have mentioned this if he knew, but maybe she had her own reasons for not telling him."

Monica shrugs and continues.

A last indignity comes when Monica incises just within Turnbull's hairline and peels the scalp back. The room echoes with the whine of the bone saw so Monica can remove the top of the skull and expose the brain. To me, this is the most disturbing part of every autopsy. She severs the base of the brain stem, then with a sucking sound, the brain is lifted from its bony cradle.

When Monica is finished with the body, she turns her attention to the organs on the side table. Each one is sampled and scrutinized, then placed in a bag to be returned to the body cavity. Soon, all that's left on the table is an assortment of microscope slides and small vials containing bits for further analysis.

Finally, Monica steps back, stretching her neck from side to side, shrugging her shoulders and arching her back. The autopsy assistant steps forward and begins to close the Y incision with long looping black stitches.

Monica watches and summarizes her findings for the benefit of the recording. "There are no gross abnormalities. An early-term pregnancy is noted and after an examination of the foetus is completed, an addendum to these case notes will be made. No signs of a heart attack or stroke. Other than the abrasion previously noted on her neck, the tissue sample from the trapezius, and the parallel bruising on the shins, no other haematomas or abrasions have been observed. No obvious signs of drug abuse or smoking. Initial blood tests show no anomalies or alcohol consumption. Final lab results will be entered into the report when they become available. This concludes the post-mortem. Please show time as 4:45 PM, this date." She lists the names of all of us in the room.

After she turns off the recorder, I ask, "Is there any evidence that she'd been drinking? There was a bottle of champagne with two flutes at the scene."

Monica shakes her head. "No alcohol in her system."

"What do you make of the abrasions on her neck?"

"It could have happened by accident when she was brushing her hair, or pulling on a sweater with a sharp tag, I suppose, but I've encountered similar abrasions before when necklaces were wrenched off. Was a broken necklace found at the scene?"

I turn to the crime scene tech and raise my eyebrows.

He shakes his head. "Not that I know of. I'll double check when I get back to the lab and confirm. One way or the other, I'll let you know."

Monica continues. "The bruising on the shins — she was sitting in front of the coffee table. She could have kicked out with her legs and hit them."

"Like if she had been struggling?"

Monica nods. "That would be one explanation, although if she had been struggling, I would have expected other bruising or material under her fingernails from scratching someone."

"Why else would she kick out?"

"Well, it could be a reaction to a drug, or a seizure. If she had been injected, she could have gone into convulsions. But she didn't look disheveled and I would have expected saliva on her face, or her hair tangled, or at least her clothing messed up in some way if she had been."

I suggest, "Maybe someone arranged her body after death?"

"Maybe."

I look at the lonesome body on the table. *What happened to you, Sophia?* Monica found nothing to suggest what killed the woman, but the abrasion on her neck, and even the marks on the shins, suggests there is more to her death than natural causes. And the underwear suggests she was expecting someone. Maybe the father of the baby.

* * *

I'm not finished at the Medical Examiners' Office until close to 6 PM. I need sleep, but I send my partner a quick text to see how things went with his interviews. Inside the car it's warm and sheltered, the roaring chinook wind muffled by the insulation in the Ford. I could so easily close my eyes, just for a minute or two while I wait for his reply, but I check my personal phone for emails instead.

I curse. What now? In the short time my phone had been languishing in the locker, Terry's sent a couple of texts, and emails have flooded in from my brother and sister.

Terry wants to go for a bite to eat, but I send a sad emoji back. *Sorry, too tired. I'll probably be tied up all week. Maybe next weekend?*

He'll be disappointed and will whine about it in the next text he sends. It's a sticking point between us. He wants me to put him first. I'm not feeling that way about him yet. I'm enjoying his company, though maybe not as much as I did when we first got together. Maybe he will never be a priority.

I can't brush off the emails from my family so easily. I just spoke to Mom this morning, so what's happened since then?

My older brother Richard runs the family ranch in southwestern Saskatchewan. A few months ago, his wife dumped him for the local real estate agent, and he's had a hard time adjusting to being alone.

I don't blame him. I know how hard it is when your marriage collapses, since I went through a similar situation with my ex-husband. After a few years of questionable marital bliss, he turned out to be a philandering tomcat. I felt betrayed, sure, but my overwhelming emotion was anger. My first reaction was to take my riot baton to his ribs, but I settled for putting a dead fish under the seat in his precious car. And as soon as he was out the door, I traded him for a dog. Treacle's turned out to be a better companion than my husband ever was.

My younger sister, Emily, sent a semi-hysterical text a couple of weeks ago saying that Richard is planning to leave the ranch for Vancouver Island to, of all things, raise llamas. That's hard to fathom. Granted, llamas are less cantankerous than range cows but going from a ranch of over ten sections to a hobby farm with less than ten acres is a massive change. Does his disastrous marital situation warrant this reaction? Or is he undergoing some midlife crisis? Has the life as a rancher on the dry dusty prairie worn him down that much?

I'd phoned Richard when I first heard about his plan. We talked for over an hour and he promised not to make any irreversible decisions until we talk it over as a family when I go to the ranch at the end of April.

Before I hung up from the call, though, I couldn't help myself. "What's going to happen to the ranch if you leave, Rich? Dad can't run it anymore."

"I know he can't, but I feel trapped here. I need to get away. Get a new perspective."

He laid some guilt at my feet. "Once upon a time, you wanted to run the ranch. Now's your chance and you'd be good at it. Besides, Mom and Dad would be happy to have you at home."

When I talked to him, he sounded like the weight of the world is resting on his shoulders. I want him to be happy, but if he leaves, do I want to take his place? If I don't, who will? Do we leave Emily with the full burden of looking after Mom and Dad?

I sent a text back to my sister that night and told her to stay cool. I'd be home in a couple of months, and we could talk it out then. In the meantime, I put in all caps and used plenty of exclamation marks. DON'T TELL MOM AND DAD!!!!

What's prompted this string of emails? I look through them. At first, they are just between Emily and Rich, copied to me, but now the whole family is involved.

I scrub my face with my hands. God, I don't need this now. I know Emily means well, but it looks like she told Mom that Rich is leaving. Why didn't she just stay with the plan for another few weeks until I get home for holidays? Each email in the string gets louder. Emily's contrite. Richard is pissed. And reading between the lines, Mom's at first tearful, then ranting at Richard for deserting them when they need him most.

He's stuck in a terrible position.

I take a deep breath and re-read the emails, feeling the desperation of my sister and the anger and resentment from Richard. Even my absent younger brother, Cameron, in Toronto, finally replied with a non-answer. As I thought, the ranch is in his rear-view mirror, and he doesn't show any sign that he much cares, one way or the other.

There's nothing I can do about it right now. I'll call Emily later tonight when I get home from the gym and get her view. She and her husband, Harry, live only about ten miles from the ranch. Emily tries to drop in a few times a week. Harry's a good guy, too, and swings by for a coffee whenever he's got a job in the area. Granted, since Mom and Dad live at the end of the road, miles from their closest neighbour, that's not very often.

I'll have to call Richard, too, and once I know what's going on, I'll call Mom. I'm bone tired and not looking forward to spending my evening dealing with family issues, but from this distance, that's all I can do.

I've spent the last two decades building relationships and a life here in Calgary that fulfills me. Am I selfish in wanting to stay? Going back to the ranch would mean giving all of this up.

I rest my forehead on the steering wheel for a couple of minutes, listening to the spring wind moan through the fir trees. I hate being the peacemaker and problem solver in the family. Not for the first time, I wonder if that role helped groom me to become a police officer.

In a perfect world, I could head to the ranch now and we could work through the problem, but I don't want to leave this investigation just as it's ramping up. I want to solve the case. It's not just a matter of pride, although that's part of it. I feel a responsibility to find out what happened to the woman with pink slippers.

My phone rings, interrupting the contemplation of family issues.

"Hey Janice. How was the autopsy?" I hear the smile in Scott's voice, still pleased that he'd wheedled his way out of attending.

"We didn't find a COD, but we've got a few things to sink our teeth into. First of all, Turnbull was pregnant."

"Son of a bitch," Scott says. "Shark didn't even mention it. How far along was she? Was it too early for her to tell him?"

"Three months, so no, she would have known. Almost for sure. Strange that she wouldn't have told him, although maybe she was waiting for a special occasion."

"Or," Scott suggests, "Maybe it wasn't his."

"That's a thought. Get this, she was wearing racy lingerie. Not something I think she'd wear for just sitting around the condo by herself. To me, it looks like she was expecting company. Maybe even of the baby-daddy variety. Maybe she was waiting for Maxwell to be out of town to break the news to the father. Maybe we'll get the full scoop when we talk to the Maid of Honour."

"I agree. If not about the pregnancy, then at least maybe about a relationship with someone other than Maxwell. Find out anything else?"

"There's an abrasion on her neck. Monica thinks it could be from a necklace being ripped off. When we talk to Maxwell tomorrow, he can tell us if she usually wore a chain or something, and if it's missing.

"Her shins are bruised, too. She was sitting in front of a coffee table, so what if she kicked out and banged her shins against it? We can go over and test it out."

"Oh, I'm always up for a little scene re-enactment. D'ya want to go over now?"

"Heck no. I'm too tired. We'll find time tomorrow or the next day. But back to the autopsy. I told Monica about the syringe, right? She found a possible injection site on Turnbull's back. She took samples and sent them to the lab. And they found an interesting bit of trace on her cheek. An eyelash extension. Sophia didn't have them, so there's the question of where it came from. It was still glued to the eyelash, and we might be able to get some DNA from it. But bottom line, until we get the tox results and the reports from Al, Monica didn't see a cause of death. That's all I have."

Through a yawn, I ask, "Do you want to get together and talk about your interviews, or can things wait until tomorrow morning?"

"How about the morning? Nothing came out of them that we need to act on tonight. Besides, the first ball practice is tonight. It feels like snow, but we're going ahead anyway."

"Well, March is our big snow month. Let's hope it doesn't amount to much." I start the car. "I'm okay with meeting first thing tomorrow morning. Have a good practice!"

Hearing his cheerful "Gotcha," I hang up and send a quick text to the boss. While I'm at it, I send a quick text to Marshall and Nguyen, letting them know we'll have a briefing tomorrow at seven.

When the text whooshes away, as much as I want to go to bed, I head to the gym, my happy place. I need physical exercise, even if it's only for thirty minutes. When I work out, my focus is on the workout, and the stresses of the day, the case, and even my family worries melt away. The clanging of equipment, the good-natured banter of those around me, and the unique bouquet of sweat and endorphins always lift my spirits.

Spending time at the gym isn't just for mental health, of course. At just over five and a half feet tall, I don't have the height and bulk that the guys do, so when I first joined the police service, I spent hours in the weight room out of necessity. Though I'm strong from a youth spent throwing bales and wrangling calves, it's constant work to keep fit, and maintain the endurance necessary for my job. I'd never imagined how heavy our utility belts would be. They're loaded with a radio, gun, handcuffs, conducted energy device, extra ammo clip, and flashlight. Coupled with heavy boots and a tactical vest, carrying the extra twenty pounds around an entire shift was exhausting. I don't carry all that equipment now, but staying in shape is still a priority.

I need to work on my flexibility, too. It's always a struggle. A few years back, when tackling a recalcitrant car jacker, I tore a few muscles in my shoulder. Besides the pain and inconvenience of physio visits, I rode the desk for a month before I got medical clearance to get back on the street. The darn shoulder still needs to be babied. I shudder to think what it will be like when I get older.

I wheel the car out of the parking lot. A quick round with the weights, then I'll head for the phone calls with the family, then bed. And if I don't fall asleep first, maybe give Terry a call.

Chapter Four

The grumble of a snow blower disturbs me. I prop myself up on an elbow and peek out the window to confirm the weatherman's forecast of snow and to gauge how much extra time I have to factor into my morning routine to get to work on time. My neighbour is clearing the sidewalks up and down the block. Except for mine.

Years ago, when I was in uniform, working traffic, I gave him a ticket for running a red light. It was in a school zone, about eight-thirty, prime time for kids to be walking to school. Being in the dead of winter, it was still dark, and if he didn't notice me sitting at the intersection in a marked car, he could just as easily miss seeing a kid about to run across the street. Sure, I could have given him a warning, but his lackadaisical attitude made me think he needed more than a caution to think twice about doing this again.

The man has held a grudge ever since. He needs to get over himself.

Hearing me stir, Treacle lifts her head from the dog bed. She does her version of Downward Dog, and prowls over to give me her piercing cattle-dog stare, letting me know it's time for a morning pee and patrol of the perimeter. Though she doesn't have the physical energy she once did as a working dog at the ranch, her strength of will hasn't diminished. The intensity of her caramel-coloured eyes bends me to her wishes.

We make fresh tracks down the back alley, and I use the time to consider my family. I kept my cool last night when talking to my older brother. Growing up, he always figured he could boss me around, and now he's thinking he can simply tell me to come home, and I'll do as I'm told. He wasn't happy when I ended the call.

"For God's sake, don't do anything until I get home at the end of next month. And that includes buying any llamas!"

My call to Mom was less argumentative, but no less difficult. From the strained quality in her voice, she'd been worrying all day. So typical of her. Once she gets her mind on something, she doesn't let go. As a result, problems become so entangled, teasing out solutions is like combing curly hair without a conditioner.

She used to have a sunny disposition, but now her dogged optimism is often replaced by unproductive fretting. Maybe it's the beginning of dementia. It took about an hour last night before I could jolly her into a better mood. Thank goodness our conversation ended on a high note. I even got her to laugh at an inane anecdote about Scott and work.

After Treacle's walk, I let her roll in the snow while I take a shovel to the sidewalk and the concrete pad into my garage in the back alley.

I catch my neighbour's eye when he runs the snowblower into his garage. His response to my nod and wave is a scowl. He wants me to be pissed off that he doesn't take care of the snow on the stretch in front of my house. I don't care.

Dog walked, our breakfasts wolfed down, an enrichment toy filled with peanut butter and tiny snacks for her to nose around, and a go-cup of coffee for me, I head out the door.

The roads are better than I thought they'd be, and I make it into the squad room before Scott. I'm not surprised; he probably went for a few beers with the team last night after practice. Or more likely, their practice was cancelled when the snow started, and they spent longer than usual at the bar. I'm on my third cup of coffee when he shows up looking a little ragged. He's one of the older guys on the team and although he'd like to think he can keep up with the younger jocks, he pays for it dearly whenever he tries.

He's got a large Tim's in a death grip.

"Morning. How was practice?"

He shrugs off his coat. "Good, until it started to snow. But a couple of new guys showed up. Impressive bats. One's a pitcher, which we really need. We just might have a great team this year, if we stay healthy. Injuries killed us last year."

He sits at his desk and logs in to the various law enforcement databases. Then he sits back and takes a gulp of his coffee. "We packed it in early because the snow started and then went for pre-St. Paddy's Day beer." He shakes his head. "I'm too old for green beer."

I laugh at him. "Nursing a headache?"

"Nothing coffee won't fix." He tilts his head back and drains the cup. "And maybe a Tylenol or three. Do you have any?"

"You bet." I rifle through my desk and toss him a bottle of pills. I don't object when he needs my Tylenol 'cause he never complains when I eat his fries.

My back is turned to the door, but I recognize Nguyen's fast paced footsteps coming down the hall. I've never seen the man when he isn't vibrating with energy. Maybe that's why he's so thin. I used to think it was because he was a nervous type of guy. Since then, I've changed my mind. I've seen him at tense crime scenes. He's so cool it's spooky.

When the hands on the analog clock on the wall show seven, Marshall strolls in, wearing his signature blue flannel shirt and clenching an over-size Yeti thermal mug.

Other than the four of us, the office is still empty, so we settle around the whiteboard, instead of relocating to a conference room.

"Let's go over what we've got," I start.

"First off, autopsy results. Nothing from the lab on tox screens, that sort of thing, but the victim was pregnant. So far, no one we've interviewed has mentioned anything about that, so maybe she kept it to herself? Maybe someone knows and just hasn't seen fit to mention it. She was wearing racy lingerie, so maybe she was expecting someone to show up that evening, other than her fiancé.

"There was a small abrasion on her neck. Hard to say what caused it, although the explanation could be as innocent as a scratch from a hairbrush. Or, it could be from a necklace being yanked off her neck.

"There were also bruises on both shins. Scott and I will pop over to the scene later and check out the sofa and coffee table. See if the bruises make sense if in the process of struggling and kicking out, her legs hit the coffee table. That might explain the bruises and might also be the reason the slipper was so far away.

"Maybe the most important thing Monica found was a spot on her back that could be an injection site. Monica took a tissue sample to test for residues. Let's hope the lab comes back with something to show us cause of death."

Scott speaks up. "Remember that plate of food in the fridge, Janice? Baby carrots, little cheese, goldfish crackers? All things in miniature or baby. Now, given that she was pregnant, and that apparently no one knew, is it possible she was going to serve that plate and reveal her pregnancy that way?"

Marshall says, "Good thinking, Scott. Along with the sexy underwear, it kinda fits with entertaining a fella. And then when she tells him, he's not expecting that kind of news, and loses his temper. Killing her."

"Possibly, Wayne, except wouldn't there be signs of a struggle, and the cause of death obvious?" Scott asks.

We chew on this a moment, then I move on. "As far as interviews go, we've talked with the fiancé, the business partner, the personal assistant, and the housekeeper. Right?"

Scott nods.

"Did you get anything useful from the PA or the housekeeper?"

He hems and haws, pausing to drink the coffee he dashed down to the canteen to get. "The housekeeper dealt mostly with Sophia. Her usual day is Thursday, but last week she had an appointment and rescheduled for Saturday. She liked Sophia. Said she was kind. Not so much Maxwell. Didn't come out and say it but gave me the impression she thinks he's a snob."

I ask, "If she was there on Saturday, did she see Corbin?"

Scott shakes his head. "She didn't get to the condo until after lunch, and by that time both of them were gone. She let herself in. Nothing unusual about that. Sophia left notes if there was anything special she wanted done, and the housekeeper was almost always on her own."

My stomach rumbles. I should have had more than a bowl of cereal for breakfast. "How about the PA?"

"Well now," Scott stretches and smiles. "Jerome had more to say. He'd worked with Sophia for years, organizing both her personal and business life. Once Maxwell came into the picture, he started asking Jerome to do stuff for him. Manage his social calendar, make reservations, that sort of thing. I asked Jerome if he minded. He said he didn't. As long as he got paid, he said it didn't matter who he worked for."

"Didn't he find it awkward if Maxwell was screwing around, as Corbin hinted?"

"You'd think so, wouldn't you?" Scott agreed. "I pressed him about Maxwell having someone on the side. Jerome beat around the bush, then said he didn't know for sure, but probably, yes.

"When I asked how he could work for both Sophia and Maxwell, he said something about being professional and being able to compartmentalize."

"Do you believe him?"

"You know what? I do, actually. It didn't seem he was friends with either of them. At least, that's what he said. Just business."

Marshall scoffs. "Sounds weird, if you ask me, to work for both of them like that, and not really know what's going on. If he was keeping track of the social stuff, he'd have a pretty good idea of who was where, and when. And who with."

"You'd think so," Scott says. "But I got the impression that he did the bare minimum for Shark and didn't know him that well at all."

I ask, "Okay, if he didn't mention anyone in particular Maxwell was seeing, did he give any indication that Sophia was putting anyone else in her calendar, if you catch my drift? Anyone else who could be a candidate for the daddy-line-up?"

Scott laughs. "Good one. No, he didn't mention anyone. I specifically asked if Corbin was more than a business partner. He didn't think so. And back to Maxwell, Jerome said he thought Maxwell was more of an opportunist. He'd put the moves on most any pretty face if the opportunity presented itself."

I shake my head. "Sophia landed a real prize, didn't she? If she knew he was fooling around, do you think she'd have second thoughts about marrying him? So far, no one's mentioned anything about her getting cold feet."

"Corbin mentioned something about her seeming suspicious, but that's been it." Scott leans back and puts his hands behind his head. "If anyone knows what Sophia knew, including the aforementioned baby-daddy, it's probably the Maid of Honour. I've left a message for her to call."

Marshall asks, "Does the PA have an alibi for Saturday night?"

Scott nods. "Yep. He was at the hockey game. Showed me selfies with him and his buddies."

I turn to Nguyen. "Any problems with the warrants and orders?"

He shakes his head. "No. All are signed and have either been served electronically or will be served in person first thing this morning. We're waiting to hear from the banks with financial records for both the victim and the restaurant. I sent a Production Order to the Insurance Bureau, so we should get a list of policies where her name shows up. Let me know what else you need."

"Fantastic, thanks." I tap my marker on Corbin's name on the whiteboard. "His name came up as a witness in reference to two incidents where fatalities were involved. Anything further on his involvement?"

Nguyen shakes his head again. "Just bare bones. Death of his father and of a university classmate. The dad died from a fall in the bathtub, and the classmate died of drug overdose, apparently he went partying after he left Corbin's place. I'm still waiting for paper files from the archives for more details."

"Marshall, how about you?"

He looks at his notes. "A couple of calls last night from the regulars who always have hot tips." He shakes his head. "I'm following up on them, but don't hold your breath.

"All three of the major morning news programs mentioned her death, so calls might pick up today. I'll be in court this aft on the Waverly case, but I've got a couple civilian members ready to take any calls that come in."

"Thanks. Good luck in court." I smile, then look at Scott. "What else?"

"We have an appointment with the lawyer, Byron Landry, this afternoon. That's all I have."

We take a few minutes to brainstorm and run through ideas, then Nguyen and Marshall head back to their desks. I'm at my desk with my back to the door when I hear a voice that makes my stomach turn.

"Hello boys and girls. Top 'o the morning to ya!" A fake Irish accent oozes out of Charles Beavins. He doesn't belong in our squad room. He's the Sergeant in charge of Economic Crimes that works out of the warren of offices down the hall.

He's an imposing presence and though the guys on the other side of the squad room look up with welcoming expressions, I keep my head down and pretend to find my computer screen riveting when he angles in my direction.

I hate him and he disgusts me, but I need to get over his unwanted sexual advances. After all, it's because of him that I have my plum job in Major Crimes. If he hadn't crossed the line when he was my boss in Economic Crimes, I'd probably still be there, squinting at spreadsheets and ledgers. Or maybe back on a patrol beat because I wouldn't play his games. No, from a work perspective I'm in a better place, but career-wise, I suspect I'll be dodging the rumors he spread to the end of my service. With that in my past, it's especially important for me to be better than anyone else.

It's all I can do to mutter good morning when he saunters up behind me. He's so close I can smell his aftershave.

"How's my Bumper?" he asks.

Working for him was a nightmare. I was too shocked the first time he wagged his wiener in front of me to do anything other than sit in the passenger seat and stare out the windshield. The second time, I snarled, "Keep your fuckin' dick in your pants." He didn't get the message and continued with innuendos, too-friendly hands on my shoulder, and "innocent" brush-bys.

Maybe I should have made a complaint. Not for my sake, because I can compartmentalize the shit, but for other women he undoubtedly preys upon. I've worked with guys my entire career. I've spent countless hours cooped up in cars on surveillance, but none of the guys have made it about sex. Sure, there've been lots of jokes, off-colour comments and stuff like that, but Beavins is the only one who crossed the line. Whenever he crawls out of his hole and sniffs around, my stomach lurches.

Almost brushing against me, and too quietly for anyone else to hear, he gives an appreciative hmmm, then walks to the other side of the large room. The stench of his aftershave makes me want to vomit.

I glance up when his back is turned. When he was in his prime, he probably had a luxurious head of hair. Now, what strands remain are combed over the top of his shiny scalp. He'd look better if he shaved it all off.

I've heard he's about to get his third divorce. It's hard to imagine one woman finding him attractive enough to marry, let along three! I shudder to consider his charms and turn my focus to my notes and the screen in front of me.

Beavins' presence causes a ripple through the office. Marshall gives a hearty wave and a "Top-o-the-morning to you!" They probably worked together at some point in their service. I reel in my concerns about what stories Beavins would have told him about me.

The desk-bound guys call out greetings, then gather around the paunchy middle-aged cop. Even though he's far past his prime, he still attracts followers like the high school football star he claims he was thirty years ago. I try to ignore their bonhomie, but I've lost my train of thought and have to backspace through the last paragraph I wrote.

Scott knows the importance of playing the game and bonding with the head of the Economic Crimes Unit, so he goes over to shake hands with my nemesis.

My partner has never asked why I dislike Beavins so much. Undoubtedly he's heard whatever rumors are going around, but he hasn't fished for my side of the story. A few times, the topic of harassment has come up, mostly related to our cases or things we see in the news, and he's left empty space at the end of our conversations, almost like he's waiting for me to bring up the subject of Beavins. I appreciate that he doesn't pry. There may come a time when I'll feel like telling him, but for now, it's just nice to hope he doesn't drink the Kool-aid that Beavins is ladling out.

Scott comes back to his desk, busying himself with paper. I smile when I hear him murmur under his breath. "What a dickhead."

The prickles between my shoulder blades don't go away until the turd saunters out of the squad room. The white buzzing in my head slowly subsides and I finally concentrate on the work at hand.

I'm making notes for the upcoming interview with Turnbull's lawyer when Nguyen strikes back into the squad room. He hangs his jacket over the back of his chair before coming back to my desk with a sheaf of papers from his briefcase.

"Here," he says, laying them in front of me. "The Production Order for the Will, and for copies of any insurance policies. You're going over there this afternoon, right?"

I nod. "Thanks."

He asks, "You need anything else? If not, I got work piling up on my files."

"Sure, go ahead. If anything comes up, I'll text."

He knocks twice on my desk, and whirls away. I enjoy working with him, but if he were my full-time partner, he'd wear me out.

Scott looks up from his notebook. "I'm meeting Shark's best man tomorrow morning. Presumably his best friend, this Kristien guy should know if it was true love, or if Maxwell was just playing around."

"Sounds good. Get something we can use when we follow up with Shark."

Scott's studying an email. "The liquor distributor sent us a list of Bollinger Champagne purchasers over the last year. Two hundred bottles went to liquor stores."

He pauses, "Hello! Thirty bottles sold to Sophia's on 17th. We should be able to find out how many are still in inventory. Then maybe we can find out if any of them made their way to Turnbull's place."

I pick up on his thought. "Right and even if she doesn't like the stuff, maybe she brought it home for someone?

"Have you got a list of other purchasers?"

"Yep. I'll follow up with the liquor stores who received some of the stock. If they've sold any, I can't see anyone peeling off three C notes for a bottle of champagne. Most or all of the transactions will be with a credit card and we can track them. The numbered companies on the list are probably restaurants and bars."

I make more notes on the whiteboard then move to the next item. "Do we have Sophia's cell phone records yet?"

Scott checks, "Nope, and before you ask, we don't have the security camera file yet, either."

He stretches, grimacing when he lifts his arms over his head. "Want to head over to the scene and check out the sofa, then go for lunch?"

"Sounds like a plan," I say, and grab for my coat.

Chapter Five

Only two days since Sophia Turnbull's death, and without anyone moving about the condo feels hollow. The only sounds are the hum of the refrigerator and the whisper of traffic speeding away from the lights a couple blocks away at 17th and Fifth.

Keeping with the plans Scott and I made, I pull my worn slippers from the shopping bag I brought from home this morning. I slip them on and take a seat on the sofa where we'd found Sophia. Comfortable though the expensive furniture may be, I am uneasy sitting here.

"It doesn't feel right sitting here. In Sophia's spot," I tell Scott.

He tries to lighten the mood by referring to his favourite old sitcom, "Like you're sitting in Sheldon's spot?"

"Yah, maybe. Let's get this over with."

"So, tell me again what Monica found?"

"Sophia's shins were bruised about halfway up her leg." I extend my legs until they contact the heavy coffee table in front of me. "Yep, I'm about her height and I'd get bruises in about the same place."

I reach forward and shove on the furniture. "Ugh, this is heavy. No way it would have moved just by her kicking it."

Scott hefts one end. "I agree. And the carpet underneath has a distinct imprint of the table leg, so we'd have noticed if it was out of place."

He gets down on his hands and knees to peer at the under-surface. "And I can see where the crime scene techs brushed for prints under here, just in case someone'd moved it and didn't wipe off their fingerprints.

"So now what?"

"There were bruises on Turnbull's shins, but no petechial haemorrhaging to show strangulation, so it doesn't seem there was a struggle. Monica didn't find brain lesions, so if Sophia had a seizure, it could have been caused by drugs."

"Well, in either case, you'd think her clothes would have been messed up. They weren't, except for the slipper. So, what if she did struggle, and someone moved her into the sitting position where we found her, and straightened her clothes after she lost consciousness?"

"Crime scene guys didn't find any sign of that. No drag marks on the carpet, and since the housekeeper vacuumed it earlier in the day, those would have been obvious. All we found were a few footprints."

Scott came over to stand in front of me. "What would happen if the killer held her down to prevent her from falling off the couch? If she was kicking, she'd still get the bruises on her shin and lose the slipper. Let's test it. Pretend you're having a convulsion, and I'll hold you down." He reaches forward and places his hands on my shoulders.

I buck and thrash, kicking out my feet and hit the coffee table harder than I'd planned.

"Damn it, ouch."

Scott lets up the pressure on my shoulders. "Sorry."

I reach down and rub my shins. "No, it wasn't you. It was me kicking the table. That could explain the bruises on her legs."

"But you'd think," Scott says, "if someone applied enough pressure on her shoulders to hold her still, there would be bruises there, too."

"Don't forget there was a stray eyelash on her cheek. That could have been transferred."

"Oh, right." Scott glances at the end of the sofa. "There were pillows here on the day we found her, right? They're not here now. They must have been taken to the lab. But, what if one of those was used to hold her down?"

When we try to imagine the scenario, I suggest, "Can we mimic a pillow if you fold up your jacket? And try this again?"

"Sure. Let's give it a try."

Scott shrugs out of his jacket and once he folds it in a ragged rectangular shape, he asks, "Ready?"

"Do you mind if we move the coffee table first? I don't need more bruises."

We move the table out of the way, then when I mimic a convulsion, moving from side to side, back and forth, Scott takes the jacket and leans his body weight against it and my chest. Neither of us wear fragrance at work because it can interfere with our ability to smell other, often less pleasant, things at crime scenes, but I catch a whiff of something woodsy from his shirt. For an instant, my mind goes places it shouldn't with a platonic partnership. When I start to fight back, those thoughts disappear.

At first, I move tentatively, and am unable to move, triggering my claustrophobia. This prompts me to struggle in earnest, grunting with the effort to throw myself off the couch. Near enough that I hear his breath in my ear, Scott presses harder. As my feet flail, one of my slippers flies across the room.

"Okay, that's enough." I puff.

Unruffled, Scott shakes out his jacket and puts it back on. "It didn't take that much to hold you in place because I could lean over you and use my body weight as an advantage. This didn't take strength, so it could have been a woman. Maybe the person that the neighbour heard arguing with Turnbull? That could explain the eyelash thing on her cheek, too."

I nod. "As long as Turnbull was having a seizure, not actively fighting and scratching the killer, this scenario could work. Maybe we'll get lucky and there will be some transfer of hair or saliva on the cushion or to Turnbull's clothes. Something to compare when we get a suspect."

Rubbing my shins, I'm satisfied with our explanation. "Right then. Let's head out and talk to the lawyer."

Byron Landry's office is in a converted warehouse in one of the city's original neighbourhoods, close to the confluence of the Elbow and Bow Rivers. On the sandstone facade, a modest bronze plaque advertises the law firm. Once inside, along an exposed brick wall in the reception area, signage announces *Our Partners and Associates*. Rows of framed portraits trail across the wall. I assume the larger frames showcase the partners, while the modest photos are the associates.

The middle-aged woman behind a rich walnut reception desk greets us with a smile. While tidy, it has a short stack of files on the corner, and an open document on the desk protector in front of her. Her tone is professional when she greets us. "Welcome to Marshall, Bennett and Landry. How can I help you?"

We introduce ourselves and say we have an appointment with Byron Landry.

"I'll tell him you're here. Can I get you a coffee or water?"

She closes the file on her desk, then trundles down the hall, moving with a hitch in her gait, and reappears in a few minutes. "Byron is on the phone, but he will be out in just a minute."

Surprising us, it really is just a minute before a rotund gentleman comes down the hall. He resembles his photo on the wall, except now he has less hair, another chin, and has ditched the business suit for a casual sweater and khakis. No tie. He leads us to a conference room, where six Aeron chairs surround a teak table. A coordinating credenza lines one wall, facing a wall of windows looking over the eclectic Inglewood neighbourhood main street.

Even before Landry sits down, he shakes his head. "Sophia's death is shocking! I suppose if you're here, there must be something irregular about it."

Scott pulls out his notebook while I address the lawyer. "Just to confirm, you are Sophia Turnbull's lawyer?"

He nods, his double chin quivering slightly, and sniffs. "Yes, I represent both her personal and business affairs. That includes her restaurant, Sophia's on Seventeenth."

"How long has she been a client?"

"Let's see." Landry sniffs again and opens one of the many files on the conference table. "Oh, it's been years. Perhaps twenty. Ah, yes, the first correspondence I had with her is dated 2003. This was well before she opened the restaurant, of course."

He looks up, his brown eyes peering from behind thick glasses, and dabs at his nose. "One of the senior partners represented her father, and when it came time for her to need representation of her own, I was recommended. It started simply with drafting her will, and I have been her legal counsel ever since."

He pulls another tissue from his pocket and apologizes. "This time of year, I have terrible allergies." He sneezes, then asks, "Can you provide me any details of what happened? I spoke briefly with Maxwell, but he didn't say how she died."

"The cause of death has not yet been determined, Mr. Landry, but as you can imagine, we have concerns that a healthy, young woman would pass away so suddenly..."

He interrupts. "So, you don't know what happened?"

I shake my head and continue. "We would like to ask you a few questions, if you don't mind."

"No, please go right ahead. But first," he motions to the thick folder beside him. "Here is a copy of her will. I suspect you're going to want to see it. I asked Mr. Shark, the executor, if I could provide you with a copy and he had no issue with it. Do you want me to review the major beneficiaries?"

"Ah, I would appreciate that," I stammer, surprised by his proactive gesture of giving us the document. I lay the Production Order on the table in front of him. "Here is the paperwork for your files."

He glances at it briefly, then places it aside.

The lawyer runs his finger down the will in front of him. "Well, let's see. Sophia directed Maxwell to receive her personal assets — cash, her investment portfolio, and the condo. Her company, the bulk of which is the restaurant, comprises the rest of her estate. I would estimate her net worth at approximately ten million dollars. Subject to probate, of course." Landry looks at me, waiting for my next question.

"Any life insurance policies?" I ask him.

"As far as I am aware, there is one policy on her life, plus the standard policy on the business." He runs his finger down a list. "Ah, yes, there is a term policy with a payout of five million dollars to Maxwell." He rifles through the papers at his side, and nods. "And... a copy of that policy is in here for you."

"And the disposition of the restaurant?" I ask.

"The company holding the assets of the restaurant was owned jointly by Bradley Corbin and Sophia. Sophia directed her share, seventy-five per cent, be transferred to Mr. Corbin in the event of her death. In addition, although you haven't asked, the insurance for the business contains a clause for key man insurance, payable to the surviving partner, in the amount of one million dollars. Key man insurance is a standard provision in most business policies."

Scott's wide-eyed surprise probably mirrors my own. "Sophia left him the restaurant?"

Landry shrugs. "She told me Corbin took a substantial risk in leaving a lucrative position in the oil patch to help her build the business and deserved to be thusly rewarded. She said that Mr. Shark wouldn't need it and, in fact, wasn't suited to be a restaurateur."

"Did she have more than a business relationship with Corbin?"

He taps his lips with a pen but is circumspect. "Given the generosity in the disposition of her assets, one might think so. They were friends, certainly, and had been for many years, but I saw no evidence they were more than business partners. As to leaving him the business, though it is not my place to tell a client how to distribute their estate, I discussed it with her. She said there was no one else she felt deserved it."

"Did you know she was pregnant?"

Landy's left eyebrow arches. "Goodness, no. I did not."

"Does that surprise you?"

"Indeed, it does. I do not recall her ever expressing a desire for children. Not that I would have expected her to talk to me about it, of course. In any case, she probably wouldn't have felt the need to discuss something of that nature with me until it was time to make accommodations in her will."

"And those accommodations would mean less of her estate going to either Shark or Corbin?" I ask.

"That would have been the case, likely, yes."

I have a few more questions about the business and her relationship with Corbin before switching to the fiancé. "Is Mr. Shark a client of yours?"

"No, he is not." The lawyer folds his hands on top of the files in front of him.

He takes a deep breath and holds it; a sure sign he's got something he wants to say. So, I wait.

He taps the pen, end over end, on the desk. "I have little use for Mr. Shark. As he is not my client, I may share my thoughts without breeching privilege. Please keep in mind that most of what I know about him has come from well-placed sources. His parents died when he was quite young and left him with a reasonable inheritance. Apparently, he rapidly ran through it and has since had a propensity to attach himself to wealthy women who've paid his way in return for his company. Apparently, when he found Sophia, he pledged her his fidelity, and she believed him. However, as undoubtedly you know from the many characters you encounter in your line of work, leopards do not change their spots. In my opinion, he is still a womanizer.

"Honestly, I believe his attraction to Sophia, at least at the beginning, was due to her wealth. Whether over time it grew into true love, if one believes in those sorts of things, I cannot say."

"Was Sophia aware of Maxwell's past? Or of any infidelity?"

Landry purses his lips for a moment. "She knew of his reputation but thought he had changed. At least, that's what she told me a few years ago. Since then, it never came up in our conversations, but recently I sensed she had suspicions. At our last meeting, for example, she asked several questions about the rights of a common law spouse. Did Maxwell have the same rights now in their common law relationship, as he would when they married. Things like that."

I asked, "Did he?"

Byron answered succinctly. "Yes."

"Would you say he's better off with her dead, or if she was still alive?"

Byron gives us a wry grin. "Dead. If she found out he was catting around on her, he would have found himself unceremoniously out on his rump."

* * *

Tiffany Meldrum, Sophia's Maid of Honour, is waiting for us at the entrance to the elementary school where she teaches Phys Ed. It's four o'clock so most of the kids have scattered like feral cats. I see a few teachers still at their desks while we walk down the hall. We pass bulletin boards covered with green shamrocks and Happy St Patrick's Day posters on the brisk walk to her office beside the gymnasium.

Her desk is cluttered with paper. Sports jerseys, a few trophies, and an opened box of t-shirts, still in their plastic wrap spill onto the windowsill and side tables.

The teacher takes a sip from her neon-pink water bottle. Her eyes are red; her face is splotchy.

"Our condolences, Ms. Meldrum," I begin. "This is a difficult time."

She nods. "I can't believe it." Fat tears stream down her cheeks. "She wasn't sick or anything, and I know she would have told me if she was." Meldrum looks at me. "Do you know what happened?"

I shake my head. "The Medical Examiner hasn't determined the cause of death."

The gym teacher slumps into the chair behind her desk.

"I was Sophia's oldest friend," she tells us. "Even when she was an exotic dancer, when others turned their nose up at her career choice, she and I kept in touch."

I wonder what was it that bonded these two women. In appearance, at least, they are opposites. Sophia, looking at her social media photos and closet, was stylish, fashionable, and perfectly manicured and coiffed. Tiffany, in contrast, would most generously be called pleasant looking. Her hair style looks courtesy of MagiCuts in the mall, and her clothing is more Costco than Holt Renfrew. Career-wise, Tiffany holds a steady, traditional job, while Sophia took a meandering and somewhat provocative path.

"When was the last time you saw or spoke to Sophia?" I ask.

Tiffany closes her eyes and takes a deep breath. She contains her tears. "Soph worked crazy hours at the restaurant, and I'd been getting my girls' volleyball team ready for a tournament, so although we talked on the phone, we hadn't actually seen each other for a couple of weeks."

Her words come freely. "When we talked, it was almost always about the wedding. Mostly, it was just about the problems she was having."

I ask the obvious question, "What sort of problems."

"Well, about who was going to be on the guest list, her dress, lining up accommodation for friends from out of town. And then, she called late last week about her reception. The hotel called and asked if Sophia would consider changing her venue. Weird, eh?"

She looks at us. "That's bonkers. Like, can you imagine changing the venue at this late date? The wedding is in only nine months."

I'm not particularly interested in wedding plans, but I ask anyway. "Why would the hotel ask her to change the venue? Are they doing renovations or something?"

Tiffany shakes her head. "No, but the hotel was vague. Sophia thought maybe someone with deeper pockets wanted it, or maybe some celebrity is coming to the city. But she wasn't sure."

She takes a sip from the water bottle. "I get it. The Crystal Ballroom at the Pallisades is beautiful and prestigious. The food is amazing, too. I'm not surprised there are lots of requests to have an event on the same day, especially since Sophia and Maxwell were getting married on December 21, the solstice, but I can't imagine anyone asking, or expecting, a bride to change their plans like that." She pauses, "I mean, unless I misunderstood what Soph was talking about."

Tiffany slowly shakes her head. "And then, after all that, she texted me last Friday and said she had something to tell me. I figured it was just another wedding thing, and I begged off. I told her I was too busy, but we could get together sometime this week. To be honest, I was tired and needed a break."

"Too much wedding talk, eh?" I prompt.

Tiffany laughs, but there's no levity in it. "Nothing but. Always problems. Aren't there always?" She fiddles with the flip-top lid on the water bottle and looks at me. Am I supposed to agree with her? The planning of my ill-fated wedding started with a drunken *Hey, why don't we get married*, then fifteen minutes in front of a marriage commissioner, before ending less than five years later with *Oh my god, how stupid could I have been!* But I pretend I know what she's talking about and smile.

"Anyway, Sophia wanted to have her reception in the Crystal Ballroom on the winter solstice. It's the date her parents got married, and it turns out that it's one of the most popular wedding dates in the year. Venues and caterers are booked years in advance."

She gets side-tracked. "When I get married, if I ever get married, I'll pick a day in the off season, when prices are lower." She shrugs. "But money wasn't an issue for Soph."

"She didn't have trouble booking the ballroom?"

"No," Tiffany confirms. "She booked it ages ago. But then, like I said, she thought someone else wanted the space. Soph was upset about it, but I don't know why. She had it booked and paid the deposit so she should have just ignored it."

Tiffany's eyes fill with tears again. "That was the last conversation I had with her. It was about stupid wedding stuff, and I didn't even pay attention. What's worse. I never told her how much I loved her."

The conflict over the wedding venue adds an interesting twist to the investigation and I make a mental note to follow up on it later, to see where it goes.

The Maid of Honour sniffs. "I wish we would have talked about something that made her happy, but she seemed to want to unload her problems on me. At least, that's the way it seemed. She was good at not letting other people see when things were bothering her, but I wasn't so lucky. I got to see and hear it all."

I encourage her to continue. "What else was she upset about?"

Tiffany sighs. "Maxwell."

"Oh?" I encourage. "Anything in particular?"

"Well, he isn't always easy to get along with." Tiffany shakes her head. "He's a child sometimes, you know?"

"Really?"

"Yes, well, she was always having to remind him about his blood sugar. Reminding him about errands he was supposed to do. Things for the wedding. I mean, after all...." She shakes her head. "Sophia worked crazy long hours at the restaurant, and what does he do? He goes to the gym and goes out with the guys. He makes a big deal about how he's a writer and how creative he is, but he doesn't know a preposition from a participle. And so Soph had to do everything. On top of running the restaurant!" Tiffany snaps at us. "I think he was using her, and I don't know why she didn't see it."

"Had anything in their relationship changed? Were they getting along?"

The gym teacher grits her teeth. "Sophia was head-over-heels about him. But lately I think there might have been something else."

"What could it have been? Do you think he was fooling around on her?"

"I don't know, but I wouldn't put it past him. He always had a wandering eye, you know?" She glares at Scott when she says this, as if he's the one who cheated on Sophia. When she looks back at me, I sense Scott giving me a Who Me? glance.

I ignore him and continue to question Tiffany. "But you don't know for sure?"

Tiffany shakes her head. "No." She thinks for a moment. "But if he was and she ever found out, she'd turf him so fast he wouldn't have time to change his boxers. Sophia might have been forgiving about a lot of things, but being unfaithful was not one of them.”

“Were you and Sophia really close?”

“Absolutely. Since high school. Then, even after we graduated, we stayed close.”

“She was an exotic dancer, wasn’t she?”

“Yes, but that came a little later. She was a waitress for a while and hooked up with a chef. That’s where she got interested in the restaurant business.

“I’m not sure what made her decide to be a dancer, though. She’d always been athletic and was a cheerleader in high school. Somewhere along the way she took some dance classes and suddenly, she stopped waitressing and started dancing in the strip club. I know the money was good, but she didn’t really need it. Her dad took care of her bills. She’d always been a daddy’s girl, so maybe she wanted to try being a bad girl for a while.

“Then out of the blue, again, she quit dancing and got a job in the oil patch. Soph said the club had been fun, but it was time to get a job where people didn’t automatically assume she was a hooker.” Meldrum quickly glances at Scott, then back at me. “She wasn’t, you know, a hooker. Well, she may have dated a fellow she met at the club, but it wasn’t like a prostitute situation. I never met him, and she didn’t talk about him. And of course, that’s also where she first met Maxwell. He was a bartender.”

She pauses, like she’s lost her train of thought, so I prompt, “Her job in the oil patch?”

“Oh, yah. It was just a temp job. A change more than anything else, I think. Her boss at the company was Bradley Corbin, and they got along really well. I don’t think she was challenged by the job, though, and decided she wanted another change. When her dad sprung the money to open the restaurant, Soph convinced Corbin to come on board.”

“So, she was close to Corbin?”

"Absolutely. They were best buds." She shrugs. "I think he's a posh nerd, maybe that's partly because of his British accent, but they clicked."

"Anything more than just friends?" I probe.

She thinks for a moment. "I wondered about that, but I don't think so. She'd started seeing Maxwell while she was still a dancer, and I don't think she went out with anyone else. Even if she and Bradley had been dating before Maxwell came into the picture, I'm pretty sure that stopped. And now, Bradley's engaged, you know, and seems committed to his girlfriend. And she's loaded, so he has plenty of motivation to keep her happy. I don't think he'd be doing anything to risk her kicking him to the curb."

"Do you know of anyone with a grudge against Sophia? Any past boyfriends who were unhappy with the way things ended?"

"I don't think so." She pauses a moment and studies the ceiling. "No, I can't think of anyone she didn't get along with. The last two guys she went out with, before Maxwell, were really nice guys. And that's going back a few years. Neither of them was serious and they parted on friendly terms. Both of them are married now. One moved to Toronto to work in head office for some bank. The other guy is away climbing in South America. A real mountain goat."

"You said she was dating someone while she was dancing. How about him?"

"I never knew his name. I don't know why, but Sophia was close-mouthed about him. When I asked her, she'd just shrug. Just some guy to spend time with, she'd say, but I wondered if was married, something like that."

Scott shifts in his chair, distracting Tiffany. She smiles at him, maybe making amends for glaring at him earlier, before continuing. "Even if you were mad at Sophia, you couldn't stay mad at her for long. She had this wonderful smile and a way that made you feel special...." Tiffany's voice fades away and tears well in her hazel eyes.

"Do you by any chance have the contact information for the other guys she dated? The fellow in Toronto? And South America?"

"Yes, I do. They are on the list for wedding announcements. I don't have the list here, but I can check it when I get home and send it to you."

She widens her eyes. "Oh no. Do you think I have to let everyone know the wedding is off?"

"You probably should talk to Maxwell about that," I say. "Now, Tiffany, can you remember if she wore any particular jewelry?"

Tiffany didn't hesitate. "Yes. She wore her engagement ring, of course, but she also always wore a necklace. It was an aquamarine pendant on a gold chain. She never took it off."

"Do you remember seeing it the last time you saw her?"

She shrugs. "No, not specifically. I might have noticed if she wasn't wearing it, but I don't recall. Sorry."

I've waited to bring up the pregnancy, in case Tiffany brought it up on her own. I suspect it might be a surprise to her.

"Sophia didn't mention why she wanted to meet with you last weekend?"

Tiffany shakes her head. "No. I just assumed it was wedding stuff."

"Did you know Sophia was pregnant?"

The mouthful of water the gym teacher just took goes down the wrong way and she has a fit of coughing before managing, "What? Did you say pregnant?"

I nod.

"No, no way. She couldn't be. She told me Maxwell had an accident when he was a kid, or something like that. Or, no, maybe he had a vasectomy because he never wanted kids. To be honest, I kind of forget because she told me a long time ago. But she definitely told me he couldn't have kids."

She shakes her head. "So, no, she couldn't have been pregnant."

"Well, the medical examiner determined she was pregnant. About three months along."

Tiffany's firm. "Nope. I don't believe it."

"If Maxwell was sterile, then Sophia must have been having sex with someone else."

"No. Sophia was loyal to Maxwell. I know they had issues, but what couple doesn't? And I can't see her having an affair. It just wouldn't be like her. Maxwell must have lied about being shooting blanks."

"But she didn't talk about anyone else? Even mention another name in passing?"

"No."

"You said earlier that she and her business partner were friends. Any chance they could have hooked up?"

Tiffany looks down at her desk for a few seconds, then shakes her head. "No... but I guess it's possible. Sophia never said anything about him to make me think anything went on. And I can't believe she'd cheat on Maxwell. But... I guess ... Maybe?"

I give her some room to think. After a moment, she continues.

"No. I can't see her and Bradley fooling around. He's not her type, you know. He's got a pencil up his butt, and like I said, he's engaged and he just doesn't seem the type to screw around.

"Anyway, I don't know where she would have found the time to see anyone. She was always busy with the restaurant or Maxwell. When she wasn't working, she liked being at home, so she wasn't out partying or anything, either."

I ask, "Tell me a little about Corbin's fiancée. How well did she and Sophia get along?"

Tiffany shakes her head. "Barbara Stephens? They didn't. Not really. I mean, they were, I guess you'd say, cordial. Sophia didn't have a problem with Barbara, but Barbara definitely had no use for Sophia.

"Barbara's family is old money, and she comes across as old-fashioned herself. I think she is, or I guess, was always suspicious of Sophia wanting to take Bradley away from her."

"But there was nothing to those suspicions?"

"No, I don't think so. But that's from my point of view. She might say something different."

I turn to Scott, who's been taking notes throughout the interview. "Scott, do you have any questions?"

He shakes his head. "No. I think you've covered everything."

"Tiffany, thank you for talking to us this afternoon. I know it's not been easy. Do you have anything else you think we should know?"

She shakes her head, sniffing and dabbing at her eyes with a sodden tissue. "No, I'm shocked about the pregnancy. I wonder, do you think that's what she wanted to talk about when I blew her off last week? I feel even worse now that I didn't take the time to listen to my friend. What if she needed me to help her decide what to do about it?"

"That's something we will never know, Tiffany."

She continues, almost as if I never spoke, "But I suppose I should make some calls and cancel her wedding dress. That sort of thing." She looks up at me. "Or will Maxwell be taking care of it?"

I shrug. "I don't know. Maybe if you make a list of the things you think need to be done, you can call him and ask what he plans to do."

I pull out a business card and get to my feet. "And if anything comes to mind about arguments she had, things she might have said that seemed off, please call me."

She nods. Scott and I leave Tiffany making notes on a piece of foolscap, wiping tears from her face.

Even on a Tuesday afternoon, Sophia's on Seventeenth has a line-up of patrons, mostly dressed like office workers, looking for Happy Hour cocktails. Scott and I push our way to the front, ignoring glares from those who think we're cutting the line. A hostess greets us at the podium, but even heavy make-up can't hide her puffy eyes and red nose. When we identify ourselves and ask to speak with Bradley Corbin, she allows her smile to fade and shoulders to sag. "He's in his office. Down there." She points down a hallway, past the arrows to the restrooms.

A small plastic sign tells us which of the multiple doors down the hall is the office. I knock, and a voice within calls, "Come in."

The office is small and cluttered. It would feel claustrophobic except for a second door which is propped open, letting in a cool breeze from the back alley. Papers, a few coffee cups, mostly still half full, and an open laptop clutter his desk.

A straight back chair beside the desk holds a large cardboard box with Libby's Ketchup markings. In it are a few pictures, a couple of mugs, and some files. A jacket and sweater are neatly folded across the back of the chair. I raise my eyebrows in a question to Corbin.

"I am gathering Sophia's things to return to her fiancé. She and I shared this office and ..." he takes a deep breath, "...I believe Maxwell would want these."

He raises his hands to cover his face. When he lowers his hands, tears trickle down his cheeks.

I give him a few moments, then begin. "Mr. Corbin, after having some time to absorb your partner's death, has anything come to mind that you think we should know? Arguments? People who might be angry with her?"

He slowly shakes his head, his brow furrowed in thought. "No, I do not think she was having trouble with anyone. Perhaps a few minor disagreements with our head chef when she thought he was being more obstinate than necessary, or arguments with Maxwell. Nothing else significant comes to mind."

"Can you elaborate..."

We are interrupted when the door bursts open. A young man with a white chef's jacket hurries in. He's holding his hand, wrapped in a white kitchen towel, high in the air. "Mr. Corbin, I cut my hand. I need to go for stitches. Chef told me to come and let you know we're going to be shorthanded for lunch service."

It must be quite some cut because blood is already seeping through the towel. Corbin reacts. "Oh, for God's sake. Chef can figure it out. Get out of my office!"

The cook scuttles out, and Corbin scrubs his face with his hands. When he looks at us, his face has gone as white as the young man's uniform. "Sorry about that. Staff know better than to come to me with injuries. I cannot abide the sight of blood."

He picks up the phone on his desk and dials. "Bring me a Perrier. With lime." He returns his attention to us. "Sorry about the interruption. You were asking?"

"I was asking, can you elaborate on the sort of arguments you overhead between Sophia and Maxwell?"

"Oh, trivial things, really, such as when he did not show up when he said he was going to, or he spent too much money on another new watch. That sort of thing. Sophia was always reminding him to watch his blood sugar and became frustrated when he failed to pay attention to it. If you are not aware, he is a diabetic."

I nod and wait a few moments. "Anything else?"

He runs his fingers through his hair, then rests his head on his hands for a moment, before looking at both of us. "No. But may I ask a question?"

"Of course. Go ahead."

"The questions you are asking lead me to believe you think someone harmed her. Do you?"

"At this time, there's no specific reason for us to believe that foul play is involved, but in case we find something that changes that view, it's important we ask questions now, while memories are fresh."

"Hmm." He thinks for a moment. "I cannot believe anyone would want to hurt her. But if someone did, I hope you find them. She was a beautiful, kind woman and I will miss her very much." His voice cracks and he reaches for a tissue.

He looks at the photo on the wall. It is of him and Sophia toasting each other with champagne. He sees me looking at it. "That photo was taken when Sophia and I were celebrating the restaurant's first anniversary."

He seems lost in his memories, then turns back to me. "What else do you want to know?"

"What did Sophia plan to do on Saturday after you left?"

He snaps. "Did you forget? You already asked me that question on Sunday night, and I answered it. She told me it was going to be a quiet day. Maybe shopping and an evening at home."

I ignore his peevish tone. "Thank you. You said Barbara was jealous of Sophia?"

He reaches out to touch a framed photo sitting on the corner of his desk. "Did I say that? I misspoke. It was more an issue of insecurity, rather than jealousy.

"People assumed Sophia was a party girl and a flirt, but her heart was kind. She wanted people, including Barbara, to like her, and I believe they were comfortable with each other. However, Barbara fixated on how pretty and popular Sophia was, and this triggered her insecurities. I suppose she knew I adored Sophia, and it occasionally caused problems."

"Yes, it would be awkward if the two of them were at odds," I sympathize. "We may want to follow-up with your fiancée. Can you give us her contact information? And for your wedding planner, too?"

He writes on a yellow sticky note and passes it to Scott. "Barbara is visiting her parents in Montana."

"I'm not sure why you want to speak to our wedding planner, but her name is Vi Lance." He pulls out his phone. "I have her number, but Barbara is the one who deals with Vi." He gives a wry smile. "I just show up where and when I am instructed and sit back and listen to the two of them magpie back and forth."

I smile to be polite. "Mr. Corbin, you said you were at home on Saturday night, but you came down here to the restaurant and met with the manager. We will need to confirm your whereabouts, so can you give me his contact info?"

He jots a number and hands it to me. "Kevin was off yesterday and today but will be back on shift at 4 tomorrow. Though I am not sure why you feel it is necessary to confirm my whereabouts, I am sure he will confirm that my vehicle was in its regular parking spot the entire evening."

"Thank you."

I glance quickly at Scott, signaling with a minuscule nod to pay extra attention to Corbin's reaction to my next question.

"Mr. Corbin, were you aware that Sophia was pregnant?"

His eyes widen and his mouth drops open, working like a fish out of water. "Pregnant? No, I was not."

He pauses a moment, then continues with more poise. "That makes it doubly tragic that Sophia is no longer with us. Two lives have been lost, not just one."

He shifts his gaze back to me. "Did Maxwell know?"

I shake my head. "That she was pregnant? Apparently not."

Corbin lifts a well arched brow.

I ask, "Does that surprise you?"

He shrugs. "That she did not tell him? Not particularly, if I am honest. As I recall, she told me that

Maxwell had no interest in children, and perhaps Sophia wished to deal with the situation on her own."

"What do you mean, deal with it on her own?"

"Terminate it, of course."

"Without discussing it with Maxwell?"

"Who is to say? Can one ever truly know what goes on with another couple?"

"Can you elaborate?" I press.

He sighs. "What I mean," he enunciates clearly, "Is that Maxwell may have known about the pregnancy, but does not want you to know. He may have given Sophia an ultimatum. Him or the child. Perhaps he feels guilty."

"Did Maxwell often issue ultimatums to Sophia?"

Corbin shrugs. "I have no idea. My comment was simply a suggestion."

"And there is no chance the child was yours?"

Points of red appear on Corbin's cheeks. "I told you that we did not have a romantic relationship. How many times must I repeat myself?"

I let a small smile cross my lips. "As many times as I ask."

"Were you and Sophia *ever* intimate?"

Corbin sits back in his chair. "That is an entirely inappropriate question."

Since he hadn't answered my question, I repeat it. "I am not meaning disrespect to her, but I would like to know. Were the two of you ever intimate?"

He tosses his hands. "We were close friends for years but never strayed into the physical. And it is certainly none of your business, even if we had."

"Thank you. That wraps up my questions for now. I'm sure we will need to speak to you again, but in the meantime, if something comes to mind, no matter how trivial you think it might be, here's my number."

I leave my card on the desk, then Scott and I head out.

* * *

The spring sunshine's made quick work of last night's snow, and the streets are mostly dry when we leave the restaurant. Scott glances at me. "Let's hash over the interview while we have supper. I'm starved."

"Me, too. How about there?" I point up the street to a fried chicken joint. "But let's get take-away. I'd like to go home and let Treacle out."

When I first brought the black and white cattle dog home from the ranch a few years ago, she could hold it an entire day. There's a pee pad in the back entryway, just in case, but she gives it wide berth and will cross her legs until her eyes float rather than make a mess in the house. I usually ask a couple of dog-crazy, neighbourhood kids to take her out if I'm going to be late, but this week they're off on spring break.

My mouth waters and fingers twitch toward the bag of food on the short drive to my house. Scott reads my mind, and without taking his eyes off the road, growls. "Don't even think about opening that bag."

I cross my arms and give him a death glare. I'm hungry.

When we get to my house, Scott takes Treacle's leash from the hook beside the door. "I'll take her around the block while you set out the food. Do not start without me." Treacle's fond of my partner, and dances around him, tail wagging furiously. She nudges him with her nose when he takes too long.

My dog takes full measure of strangers before accepting them into her family. She embraced Scott quickly, but that's not always the case.

With Terry, even though he's been in my life for a few months, Treacle is still wary. The feeling's mutual. He says he doesn't like or trust dogs because he was bitten as a little boy. Okay, I understand his reasoning, but that doesn't explain Treacle's reaction. She glares at him when he comes over.

Not long after we started going out, he stayed over. In the morning, I came into the kitchen after a shower and found her growling at him from the doorway to my office."

"Treacle!" I scolded. "What's wrong with you?"

She gave me an apologetic tail wag, and him a whale eye, before going to her dog bed.

I asked Terry, "Why is she acting this way?"

He shrugged. "No idea. She must be PMSing.

His response was crass, but our relationship was in its infancy, so I obligingly laughed. "She's not a PMSing type of dog." I let the matter drop, but later when I went into my office, I saw my laptop had been moved. Had Terry been poking around?

I wish I had asked him, but it's too late now.

Waiting for my partner and dog to come back, I have enough time to put kibble in Treacle's bowl, pour milk for Scott and me, and throw a load of laundry in the machine.

Scott has an insatiable appetite. I constantly battle extra pounds while he eats whatever and whenever he wants. It isn't fair. He ordered the fried chicken dinner, complete with fries, biscuits, gravy, and a tub of creamy coleslaw. It taunts me while I plunge my fork into a tossed salad with a grilled chicken breast splayed on top. The chicken is juicy and tender, but I feel deprived. Thank goodness Scott doesn't object when I take a few of his fries.

I ask, "Do you think Corbin's the father of Turnbull's baby?"

Scott strips the meat off a drumstick and talks while he's chewing. "Well, he seems genuinely broken up about Turnbull, and shocked when we told him about the pregnancy." He pauses. "But he could be a better actor than I give him credit for. As for being just friends? I don't believe it. Even if they moved past it, I'd put money on them screwing in the past."

Scott watches while I dip a French fry in the gravy. "Did you notice how defensive he was about it?"

"I sure did. We should be getting a DNA sample from him to do a paternity test."

My partner pauses in forking coleslaw into his mouth. "Yah, but we don't have to shake that tree just yet. I mean, we don't even have a COD. And we may be jumping the gun. Maybe Maxwell knew about it all along."

Chewing on the last bit of romaine, I renew my train of thought. "But getting back to Corbin. The last-minute change of the cake tasting and his fiancée heading out-of-town bugs me. All of a sudden, it frees up one, or both of them. Let's follow that up. You're interviewing the restaurant manager about Friday night? See if he can give us insight into Corbin and the arguments he had with his fiancée."

Scott nods, gnawing the meat off a chicken wing."

I let him chew. "And something else. We've got the wedding planner's contact info. Let's find out what her take is. Maybe Stephens bitched to her about Sophia. Or about Corbin spending too much time with Sophia. How jealous was she? She was supposed to be in the States on Saturday night, but could she be involved? We need to make sure she was there."

Scott points at me with a bone. "No problem. I'll call. It's the least I can do since you went to the autopsy. And we've got the building CCTV to review. Hopefully one of these characters shows up, Corbin, Shark, or the fiancée, and we may have our killer."

He talks around a bite of biscuit, slathered with gravy. "Do you think Corbin was afraid he was going to get pushed out of the business once Maxwell and Sophia got married? Is Maxwell interested in the restaurant?"

I ignore his glare when I take another French fry. "By the way, don't think you're off the hook yet for the autopsy. I just haven't come up with something suitable. But you asked a good question about Corbin's motivation. From what we've heard, Maxwell doesn't seem to be the type to put his nose to the grindstone for the hours it takes to run a successful restaurant."

We think about that for a few bites, then I present a different idea. "How about this for Shark's motivation? Maybe Sophia found out he was screwing around, and she was going to kick him to the curb? He'd lose access to her money."

"Well, maybe, but if he was at a party in Priddis, and if she was at home, apparently arguing with some woman, how did he do it? It's at least forty minutes from Priddis to the condo. There and back, with a few minutes to kill her, that's over an hour and a half. If Maxwell left the party to kill her before midnight, someone would have noticed him gone."

"I know, I don't have all the answers, but it's possible. Right? Anyway, I'm just floating the idea. And we need to find who she was arguing with."

Scott nods. My partner's nothing if not agreeable, especially when his belly is full.

* * *

Back at the station, we wrap up our progress with Nguyen and Marshall. "Only a handful of tips, just the usual wackos saying followers of Charles Manson killed her. When we release a COD, I expect more," Wayne reports. "Anything yet from Dr. Patel?"

I shake my head. "Not yet. And before you ask, nothing back from Al's group, either."

I look at my team. "Tomorrow, Scott and I are going to go back to the fiancé. We'll look at his alibi. Ditto for the business partner. We need to track down the woman who was arguing with Turnbull on Saturday night. What's happening with the security cameras, Lance?"

Nguyen shakes his head, "Nothing yet from the condo manager." The furrows on his forehead tell me he's got something to say. "If the fiancé has an alibi, and if we suspect he might have a dolly on the side, could he have conspired with said dolly? Maybe she was the one arguing with Turnbull on Saturday night, killing her while Shark was in Priddis."

Scott pipes up. "If that's the case, you'd think the sidepiece would be more than casual. So far though, all we've heard is Maxwell's propensity to fool around, but we haven't actually found a girlfriend. We need those CCTV pictures."

"In the meantime," I look around at the team, "Anything else? If not, let's call it a day."

* * *

Treacle greets me at the door, her stub tail wiggling her whole body. Scott's quick-around-the-block with her earlier wasn't enough, and she's eager for more. I clip on the leash and off we go. When we get back, she looks with longing eyes, first at me, then at the cupboard where I stash her kibble. Even though she had her supper at the same time Scott and I had our chicken, just like me, she wants a snack. I don't want to spoil her, so I run her through a few tricks to justify the few crunchy nuggets I toss her way. Once she's taken care of, I open a bag of crunchy nuggets for myself, Cheezies, and check the mail while I rub her belly with my foot.

The mail carrier delivered nothing but junk. I toss the flyers and crap in the recycling bin, throw the laundry into the dryer, then head to the gym for a late workout. Even after nine, there are a few die-hards pushing iron and using the cardio equipment.

The Police Service has a fabulous gym. It's equipped with every piece of equipment a person could want, but it's not my style.

I go to a neighbourhood place. It's not equipped nearly as well, and there's often a line up for machines, but there's no cop-talk. I'm just Janice. Not "Janice from Major Crimes". Most people don't even know I'm a cop, and I like it that way. We focus on our routines, and if there is any chatter, it's more likely to be about nutrition, sports, or television shows. Not work.

Terry's in pretty good shape and says he works out. I've thought about asking him to come with me to my gym, but I prefer working out on my own, without distractions.

Some cops rely on booze and drugs to unwind; I choose the mind-clearing exhaustion of iron and sweat to chase away thoughts of bad guys and office politics. Today, though, worrying about family fills my mind.

I checked my voice mail before I left the house. My heart sank; Mom left another message. I know Richard promised to put off making any plans to leave until I come home, but Mom's fretting. She sees her lifetime spent on the ranch, working in the wind and dust, snow and cold, all for naught. I heard her voice tremble. *Janice, your dad and I built this place for you kids. It will break my heart if we have to sell.*

I want to tell her it will break mine, too.

The place will sell quickly if a 'for sale' sign goes up. It's a huge parcel of land, fenced, with good water and access. The main house where Mom and Dad live has four bedrooms. It's well maintained and a couple of years ago they renovated the bathrooms and kitchen. Three mobile homes are just down the road for ranch hands and their families. Granted, the farmstead is about ten miles from the nearest neighbour, but the gravel road is in good shape.

Our cultivated fields and pastures with native grass and natural water sources are mostly perfect for raising fat and happy cows. The exception is a swath of land that butts up against the US border. It's desolate, rocky, and deserted, with exposed sandstone bluffs, cactus, scorpion and rattlesnakes.

Growing up, everyone assumed my older brother Richard would take over the ranch. If Richard didn't, they figured my younger brother Cameron would step up. It turns out Cam was far more interested in music and artsy stuff, and his reaction to becoming a rancher wasn't just no. It was HELL NO!

I don't think Dad and Mom ever considered that a girl, either me or my sister Emily, could take over, even though we did the same chores as Richard and Cam. With ranching off the table, I decided to go into law enforcement. I remember breaking the news to Mom and Dad.

It was the Victoria Day long weekend, and we were in the kitchen having breakfast. Dad was drinking coffee and Mom was fussing over something on the stove. I said, "Mom, Dad, you probably should know I've applied to the Calgary City Police."

Dad stopped mid sip, and behind me, Mom's spoon went still. Dad slowly put down his cup, so softly it didn't even tink on the saucer. "Did you now?"

I nodded. "They're actively hiring, and the pay and benefits are pretty good."

Mom wiped her hands on her apron and sat at her place at the other end of the table. "Jan, are you sure? You'll be dealing with the worst of the worst, you know. And it's dangerous."

"More dangerous than Richard being out in the middle of a whiteout looking for calves? Riding a rank horse? Working with machinery? You know farming and ranching have the highest incidence of accidents of almost any job?"

Her lips tightened, knowing I spoke the truth.

"You're going to have to work with men who don't think you belong, Jan. They won't make it easy for you."

I got up from the table, took the percolator from the stove and topped up our coffee cups. "You may be right, Mom, but I can handle it. Besides, times are changing. Those guys will come around, eventually."

And now, here I am looking over my shoulder, wondering if after all I've done to make a life here, I'll go back to the dust, wind, and worry about drought, fire, sick cows, and hail. I'll go back and face the dangers that I reminded Mom about so many years ago.

Going back wouldn't be all bad, of course. There are plenty of wonderful things about the ranch. It would be a life with wide open spaces, the smell of rain soaking into prairie soil, the sound of a meadowlark on a fence post, and the night canopy of stars in an infinitely dark sky.

My mind struggles with the choices I face, but by the time I complete my gym routine, I am physically drained and mentally at ease. I hold on to the feel-good hormones until I walk into the house and see the reminder note I left on the counter. Phone home.

It's late, but I know Mom still likes to stay up and watch The National News, so I might as well get this over with. Of course, I want to talk to them but wish their underlying tension didn't waft onto me. They forget, or maybe they don't even realize, how they overlooked me twenty years ago when I could have made a life there. Now they think I'm their saviour. Now they think I wouldn't want to be anywhere else.

I'm surprised when Dad answers the phone.

"Hi Dad! It's good to hear you!"

There's a slight pause on the line. I picture him trying to place my voice; brow furrowed and eyes searching the room. "Hello Janice." His gravelly voice, now with a slight tremor, brings back memories of our long talks while we rode behind the cows and calves, moving them from winter to summer pasture. He's normally a quiet man, but something about the solitude of those long cattle drives brought out his sense of humour and penchant for storytelling. God, I miss those times.

We chat now, mostly about inconsequential tidbits. Gossip about neighbours, the weather, and the latest antics of new puppies. I'm not sure if he's remembering things, or if his failing mind is fabricating. Regardless, I love to hear him ramble on. Eventually, I hear Mom in the background.

"Is that Janice? I want to talk to her. Here, give me the phone."

Dad mumbles something I can't quite make out, and suddenly, Mom's on the line.

"Hello Janice. Sorry I didn't answer the phone."

I laugh. "That's okay. It was nice to say hi to Dad. He's sounding pretty good, I think."

We chat for the next twenty minutes or so, mostly about a new litter of puppies. My contribution to the conversation consists of an occasional *Really?* Or *That sounds amazing, Mom.* Finally, she winds down and predictably laments, "Oh Janice, this call is costing you a fortune. I should let you go. Next time, call collect."

I laugh, as I always do. "Don't worry Mom. It doesn't cost much. Besides, it's worth it just to talk to you." Could I even call collect anymore, or is that a thing of the last century?

"Well dear, I always say if you watch your pennies, the dollars take care of themselves."

"You're right Mom. Those are wise words." I want to end the call on a bright note, so she goes to bed happy. "Keep your eye on the mailbox. I sent you a new garden catalog earlier this week. I found it at the bookstore and thought you might like to go through it and decide what to plant when I'm down to help you at the end of next month. It's full of great ideas."

"Well, thank you, dear. I'll pay you for it when you come down."

Chuckling, "No need. It's a present."

I smile when I hang up the phone. Hearing her laugh makes me happy.

Chapter Six

Scott motions to the coffee cup sitting on my desk when I get to the office on Wednesday morning. "It should still be hot.

"I just confirmed Meldrum's alibi. Her principal confirmed they were at a volleyball tournament all Saturday afternoon, then at a staff function afterwards that didn't wind up until close to midnight."

I take a sip of my coffee. "Thanks for this." I throw my jacket over the back of my chair and strategize with Scott about our upcoming interview with Shark. "His reaction to the pregnancy will be interesting. And then to the girlfriend thing. Let's see if he thought Sophia was on to him. Do we have his bank statements?"

"Not yet. Do you think he'd be dumb enough to pay for a hit out of his bank account?"

I shake my head. "People never cease to amaze me. Greed makes them, I don't know... Stupid? Blind? He benefits with her out of the way with payouts from both the life insurance and her will. Maybe not as much as if they'd gotten married, 'cause he'd be able to ride that gravy train as long as he kept his nose clean and pants zipped, or as long as she didn't find out about his screwing around. But if he thought she was going to dump him, he might not want to take a chance on that 'happily ever after' scenario."

Scott doodles on the edge of a notepad. I see the beginnings of what seems to be an octopus, but I could be wrong. "You know, even if he knew about the pregnancy, why would that be a motive to kill her? He may not have been happy about it, but I can't see that being reason enough. Can you?" Scott frowns.

"Not really, no, but motives don't have to be logical."

We ponder and I'm draining my first cup of coffee when a new email pops up. "Hey, something from Monica."

Scott comes around to my side of the desk and looks over my shoulder.

Monica wrote: *Lab results and toxicology back. No illegal drugs in Turnbull's system. Waiting on tissue sample results. Stomach contents are consistent with pizza. COD still undetermined. Fetus age estimated eleven weeks.*

"Well," I sigh. "Damn. I was hoping we'd have the COD. I'll bug Al. Maybe he'll have something."

Scott points at another item in my inbox. "Looks like we have the building camera footage. Forward it to me and I'll get started on it while you call Al."

"Sure," I click the message Scott's way, then reach for my phone.

"Al. This is Janice over in Major Crimes. Anything yet on the Turnbull suspicious death?"

Scott, eyes glued to his monitor reviewing the camera footage, smiles when he hears Al's booming voice over the phone. "Bumper, who do you think I am? A miracle worker? Don't have anything else to do?"

I let the familiar gruff manner roll off my back.

"Anything you've got would be appreciated, Al."

The seasoned crime scene investigator gives a heavy sigh. "All right. Let me grab the file." I hear rustling, then the groan of his office chair when he settles back. "We got the clothing and trace from the Medical Examiner's Office late yesterday afternoon."

I hear papers shuffling, then he comes back, "...No fingerprints on the glasses on the table, or on the table itself. Wiped clean, but there's a partial print on the bottle. The syringes in the Sharps container? There were plenty of prints on all but one of them. The prints were smudged, but a few had enough points that they look like they belong to Shark. What's strange is the one syringe that's clean as a baby's heart. Kind of interesting, don't 'cha think? We're looking at the residue in that one to see if it differs from what's in the rest.

"We've got some hairs and dander from the throw pillows. Give me someone who shouldn't have been there and we'll see if there's a match."

More paper rustling. "That's about it. We're backed up here like Deerfoot after the first snowstorm. Did Monica find a cause of death?"

I shake my head, picturing the major traffic route filled bumper to bumper with impatient drivers. "Nope."

"All righty, then," Al acknowledges. "Talk soon." Before he hangs up the phone, I hear his gruff voice yelling to someone in his office.

I look over at Scott. His chin's cradled in his hands, eyes staring at his monitor. "You heard all that?"

He nods without taking his eyes from the screen. "Yep." He blinks hard and sits back.

"These video files are crap. For such an upscale building, you'd think they'd have high-res cameras. The only useful thing I could pull out of them is that no one used the back entrance, from the alley, into the building. Whoever killed her used the front entrance." He pauses, "Or it was someone already in the building."

"What about the parkade?" I ask.

Scott points to a sheet of paper in front of him. "Yah, I looked. I've got the license plates of the vehicles using the parkade door from 8 AM until midnight. We will need to check the registered owners, but that won't take long. Not that many of them. I can do it this afternoon."

He stands and pulls on his jacket. "C'mon, time to talk to Maxwell."

On the way down the elevator, he asks. "Do you want me to take the lead with Shark?"

"Yep, sure. Do you need me to remind you what to ask?" I tease.

"Thanks, but I've got it covered." He ticks off on his fingers, "Pregnancy. Girlfriends on the side. How he benefits from her death. What he thinks about Corbin being left the restaurant."

"That should do it. I bet we get an earful when you ask him about Sophia leaving Corbin the restaurant."

I wait until we're in the car to give Maxwell a call, asking him where he is.

* * *

Tenth Avenue, paralleling the tracks across from the downtown core, used to be lined with warehouses, storing goods for the Canadian Pacific Railway. Through the decades, warehouses gave way to ugly, gravel parking lots for downtown office workers. The few buildings that remain are being renovated for offices, condos, and designer furniture stores.

A moving truck is double parked in front of one of these buildings. There's no elevator, so we dodge sweaty men carrying furniture while we jog up the stairs. On the third floor, one of the doors has a highly polished stainless-steel plaque advertising Shark Enterprises. We don't bother knocking.

Inside, rough, reddish brick contrasts with creamy white walls and huge triple pane windows. Industrial, but fashionable pendant lights hang from ceilings that must be ten feet high. Plush carpet, matching three-cushion sofas facing each other, and a gigantic television mounted on the wall make the space look more like a luxury living room than an office. A pillow and folded blanket sit on one end of the sofa.

On the other side of the room, there is a glass-topped pedestal desk, behind which Maxwell Shark presides. He's tapping away at the computer, artsy glasses perched on his nose.

He's dressed similarly to the last time we saw him — a golf shirt, at least one size too small, and blue jeans.

Not bothering with pleasantries, he demands. "Have you found out why she died?"

"Good morning, Mr. Shark, no," Scott replies, taking the lead, as we had agreed. "We expect results from tests in a week or so."

The fiancé scowls. "People keep asking me what happened, and I have nothing to tell them." His voice rises with his frustration. "How long are you going to keep her? I'm trying to plan a memorial service."

"Sorry, I don't know. The Medical Examiner is the one who makes the decision." Scott's voice is gentle. "I can only imagine how difficult this is for you."

"Damn right it's difficult," Maxwell sputters. "Everything's just hanging in the air." He takes a deep breath. "I suppose you know I'm the executor to her will?"

He doesn't wait for Scott to respond.

"I want to get her estate settled as quickly as I can."

He brusquely points to the sofas. "You might as well sit down. I'm going to make a coffee. Would you like one? Espresso? Latte?"

"Thank you," Scott smiles. "I'd love a plain coffee. Black, please."

I pipe up. "That would be nice, thank you, Mr. Shark."

"Call me Maxwell." The tone is begrudging, and the accompanying fleeting smile doesn't reach his eyes. For a moment, he reminds me of his last name.

He turns to what I assumed was a closet. It's a mini-kitchen, complete with an impressive line-up of liquor bottles and glassware, a full-size stainless-steel fridge, and a commercial grade espresso machine.

Once we're settled with coffee in front of us, Scott wastes no time in getting to the point. "Have you given more thought as to anyone who might have wanted to harm Sophia?"

Maxwell slowly shakes his head. "No, as far as I know, she got along with everyone."

Scott doesn't wait any longer to ask the pivotal question. "Maxwell, did you know that Sophia was pregnant?"

Maxwell barks a laugh. "Hah. Good one. No, she wasn't."

Scott waits.

Maxwell looks at me, then back at Scott. "That's a shitty thing to say, man. Of course she wasn't pregnant. Why would you say that?"

"The medical examiner found she was eleven weeks pregnant. Did you not know?"

"No. I had a bad bike accident when I was little and damaged my nuts. She couldn't have been pregnant."

He pauses, the colour draining from his face. "Wait. Are you serious?"

Scott nods.

From the silence of the office, we hear the rumble of a locomotive pulling a long line of cars down the tracks outside.

Maxwell runs a hand over his shaved head. "Well, shit, maybe I've got swimmers after all. After all these years...unless..." His brow furrows. "Are you telling me that Sophia was screwing around on me?"

Scott shakes his head. "That's not what I'm saying. All I'm saying is that she was pregnant when she died. Is it possible she was seeing someone?"

Maxwell flushes. "Absolutely not. Sophia was faithful. I would have known if she wasn't."

"Could there be another explanation?"

The man shrugs. "I don't know. I can't explain it. I mean, I'm pretty sure it couldn't have been me. Should I give you a DNA sample or something?"

Muscles in his face twitch while he considers the possibilities. He looks close to tears when he finally speaks. "Pregnant? Wow. I could have been a dad?"

"If it isn't yours, can you think of anyone it might have been? Or someone she might have confided in?"

"The only person she spent much time with was Corbin. But it wouldn't have been him. And if she confided in anyone, it would have been Tiffany. That's her Maid of Honour. They were best friends, or as close as she was with anyone other than me."

Scott nods, "Thanks, Maxwell. We've already spoken to Tiffany and she told us that Sophia wore a necklace. Can you tell us about it? Did she always wear it?"

The fiancé tilts his head to the side and half closes his eyes. "Yah, it is a blue stone with a gold chain. She never took off. I asked her about it once and she said she'd gotten it as a gift. I assumed it was from her dad."

He looks quickly from Scott to me. "Wasn't she wearing it when...?"

Scott shakes his head. "When you get back to your condo, I'd like you to take a look and see if you can find it. In the meantime, though, do you have a picture of it?"

Maxwell shakes his head. "It wasn't particularly valuable or else she would have listed it on our insurance rider. I don't have a photo of it specifically except..." He looks across the room at photos on the wall.... "You could see it in any picture of her. It might have to be enlarged to get the detail, but I'm sure you have fancy equipment that could do that."

He points across the room at a large photo of him and Sophia. "You can take that if you like, as long as you promise I'll get it back."

"Thanks Maxwell. I'll get this back to you as soon as I can."

Scott clears his throat. "I'd like to talk a bit more about your relationship with Sophia and Bradley Corbin."

Maxwell narrows his eyes. "Sure. I'm not sure what my relationship with Corbin has to do with this, but yeah, go ahead."

"How did you meet Sophia?"

Taking a deep breath, Maxwell begins. "It was years ago, when she was still dancing. I worked the bar at the club, and she used to come over between sets. We'd talk and pass the time.

"She was real classy, you know. Yeah, she was a peeler, but her show was tasteful. And boy, could she move! Later, once I got to know her better, she told me she used to be a cheerleader in high school and took dance for a while. You could really see that." He looks into the distance as if picturing her. Then he glares at us. "She just danced, you know. People assumed she was a hooker, but she never left with any of the customers. She didn't take drugs; she didn't do tricks.'

I wonder if that's true, or if it's just wishful thinking on his part.

I catch up to him in mid-sentence "...hook up until later, though, after she stopped working at the club," he says. "She'd already been working in the oil patch, with Cenovus or Gulf, I forget which. I asked her out, on a real date, you know, and once we started dating, things moved pretty fast. Things felt right, you know, and I moved in with her after just a few weeks. About a year later, we decided to get married. That was a couple of years ago."

"What do you do for a living, Maxwell? Do you still tend bar?"

He shakes his head. "No. No more late-night bar tending for me."

Scott abruptly changes the subject. "Do you have a temper?"

Shark furrows his forehead. "What do you mean?"

"I mean, do you often lose your temper?"

He shakes his head. "No. Not really. No more than anyone else, I suppose. Why do you ask?"

Scott observes him. "You were twice charged with assault. Tell me about those charges."

Shark flips his hand, dismissing the question. "God, that's ages ago. Not much to tell. It happened when I was tending bar. Both times, a customer got rowdy, and I helped the bouncer. I don't even know why I got charged."

"Bartenders don't usually get involved with removing people, do they?"

"Well, not usually, I guess. But the jerks had been lippy with me, so I wanted them to know I wasn't going to put up with that shit."

"What do you mean?"

Shark looks down at his hands. "I roughed them up a bit, just enough to let them know not to mess with me. And the charges got dropped, so, you know, it really wasn't serious." He makes it a point to emphasize that fact.

Scott pushes. "But I guess you could say you lost your temper?"

"Maybe. A little. But like I say, no one got hurt and nothing came of it."

"Either time?"

"No. Neither time." Shark's voice is sharp. "Now, if you don't mind, what other questions do you have?"

"Can you tell me about the car theft charge?"

His cheeks colour. "Fuck. That was crap. An old girlfriend told me I could borrow her car and then got pissy when I did. When the cops realized she overreacted, they withdrew the charge."

"That must have made you angry. Did you think about retaliating?"

"Well, ya, I was furious. Wouldn't you be?" Shark admits, "I hired a lawyer to send her a nasty letter, but I stayed out of it. The last thing I wanted her to do was say I'd bullied her. Nah, it wasn't worth it. I don't think I even talked to that girl again. I mean, I was planning on breaking up with her, anyway." He scowls at Scott. "And why are you bringing up this old shit, anyway? You should be looking for who killed Sophia."

Scott ignores Shark's questions. "Maxwell, if you're not bar tending anymore, what do you do?"

"I'm an author," Maxwell smiles proudly, puffing out his over-developed chest even more. "That's why

Sophia leased this office. I couldn't concentrate at the condo, so we thought I'd get more work done here."

"Oh," Scott returns the smile, building back rapport after pressing Shark on his background. "Have you written anything I might have read?"

"Oh, I haven't published yet. I'm working on my first novel. Still doing research."

Scott leans forward, putting his elbows on his knees. "That's interesting. What's the book about?"

Maxwell seems to have forgotten his irritation about being questioned about the assault charges and warms to the new subject. "Well, it's a mystery. It's about a bartender who's really into weightlifting. Leaving the bar one night, he sees something he shouldn't, and then he's framed by the mob. He teams up with a cop to prove that he's innocent.

"Like I say, I'm still doing research, so maybe I could pick your brain about some investigative techniques, the mind of a cop, that sort of thing."

I'm sure it takes all Scott can manage not to roll his eyes. "The plot sounds really interesting, and of course we can talk about techniques, but maybe some other time, after this case."

Maxwell's smile fades a bit. "Oh, ah, sure. Some other time."

"So you write full time?"

Shark shakes his head. "Well, it's not a full time job. I take care of myself and spend a few hours a day at the gym."

He smooths the fabric over his chest and looks down at his arms. He's proud of his pop-eye biceps and swollen pecs, but to me, even though I'm a bit of a gym rat, I find the excessive musculature distasteful. I always wonder if the obsession with big muscles is compensating for a small penis. I haven't shared that opinion with anyone except Monica. She laughs at me but doesn't disagree. She's probably seen more penises than I have. You know, on account of her being a doctor and all.

Scott probes, "Sophia must have worked long hours at the restaurant. How did that affect your relationship?"

Maxwell heaves a sigh. Is this an exaggerated response to impress us, or to make us feel sorry for him? "Yeah, she worked long hours. It was real hard on me."

He cocks his head and looks down at his lap, blowing out another long breath. "It was lonely, ya know? But she loved the restaurant and the excitement of being around all the people. I wanted to support her passion, so I never told her how lonely it was."

"Did working long hours with her business partner ever worry you?"

Shark scoffs. "Corbin? He's too busy keeping an eye on the books. I never saw him ogle Sophia, and believe me, I watched him like a hawk. To tell you the truth, I don't think he has the balls to make a move. He knows I'da punched his lights out if he ever crossed the line."

"So, you're confident he wasn't the father of the baby?"

Maxwell scoffs. "As sure as I can be."

"Did you spend much time with him? Get to know him?"

Shark shakes his head. "I didn't spend any more time with him than I had to. Sophia was always dragging me to things where we had to sit with him and his fiancée, though. She even invited them over for dinner a couple of times."

He rolls his eyes. "Those evenings were endless. Having to make conversation with Corbin, with his hoity-toity attitude. And what's-her-name? Barbara. Have you met her? I'm pretty sure the only reason Corbon's with her is because her daddy's loaded and she's going to inherit a fortune. It can't be for her personality and it sure as hell isn't for her looks.

"She follows Bradley around like a love-sick puppy, but don't let the meek act fool you. At the drop of a hat,

BAM! she can turn into a raving bitch." Shark snorts. "Maybe she has a personality disorder or something. Anyway, I tried to get out of hanging around with them whenever I could."

"So, you don't get along?"

"Well, I wouldn't quite say that." Maxwell backpedals. "I mean, I don't want to spend time with him, but if I have to, I can have a conversation with him. And I guess when it comes down to it, all that really mattered was that he was good for the business and he and Soph got along.

"But his usefulness was coming to an end, ya know? I figured once we got married, I'd join Soph in the business and we'd send him packing. Buy him out and I could take over his share."

"That'd be taking on quite a job. How would that affect your work as an author?" Scott quizzes, managing to keep the sarcasm out of his voice.

"Yeah, well, no problemo. And you know, lots of authors do their writing in just a couple hours a day. If they can do it, there's no reason I can't."

"Did you talk to Sophia about these plans to move Corbin out of the business?"

"Yah, well, I mentioned it in passing, but I thought I'd wait until after we were married to really get into it. I didn't want to rock the boat beforehand, you know. Keep things calm."

He takes a sip of his flat white. "But I guess I wondered what she'd say. When I first brought it up and told her I could replace Corbin, she wasn't as keen about it as I thought she would be."

"You think maybe she wouldn't have agreed to it?"

"I'm sure I could've talked her into it." He gives a sly smile. "I can be pretty persuasive when I want to be."

"What's going to happen to the business now that she's gone?" Scott probes.

Shark's pretty boy face morphs into a scowl. "You know, she left the business to Corbin. Why'd she do that?" He throws up his hands. "It makes no sense at all, and I'm going to check into whether she could do that. It should've come to me."

"So, it was a shock when you found out?"

He sneers. "Yeah, well, the whole week has been quite a shock, don't 'cha think?"

Scott changes lanes. "You said earlier that it was lonely with Sophia working such long hours. Did you look for company to help get you through that loneliness?"

Shark lifts his eyebrows, then furrows his brow, as if he can't decide whether to look angry or innocent at the insinuation. He settles on incensed. "Just exactly what are you inferring?"

Scott gentles his voice. "Hey, I'm just wondering, Maxwell. Sophia was working a lot; you were lonely. Hell, I can understand if you spent time with someone else. It wouldn't mean you didn't love Sophia. Just that you needed some company."

As Scott hopes, Shark thinks he has a sympathetic ear. He nods, putting on a woe-is-me face with sad eyes. "She was always working. Day and night. She didn't come until after midnight and was too tired for sex, but she expected me to be all warm and waiting to rub her feet. Not fair, is it?"

Scott warms to his role as sympathizer. "Absolutely not. Not fair to you, for sure. Who could blame you if there was someone else, you know? Just short term while she was working such long hours."

Max takes the bait. "Yah, right? You get me. So, yah, I might have hooked up once or twice."

Scott smiles, just another guy who understands. "I totally get you, Max. I understand. But just once or twice?"

Maxwell rewards him with a sly, crooked smile. "Well, maybe." Shark remembers I'm in the room and glances over to make sure I'm not giving him the evil eye.

Scott draws Shark's attention away from me. "Anyone in particular?"

Shark shakes his head. "No, absolutely not. Never anyone more than once or twice. I didn't want no girl to get the wrong idea and think it was a long-term thing. I kept it real casual."

"Did Sophia know about this?"

"Oh, hell no. Soph was too busy working." Then he pauses. "Well, at least I don't think she knew. Anyway, it's not as though I would'a broke things off with her over any of these girls. She was a good egg. One of a kind."

He pauses, then admits. "But you know, a few weeks ago she asked if there was anything I wanted to tell her. If everything was okay. I told her she was imagining things."

"What do you think she would have done if she found out?"

"God, she'd have my nuts!" Maxwell confirms what the lawyer, business partner and Maid of Honour had already claimed.

He sits in quiet repose for a moment, draining the last dregs of his coffee. "You know, I was crazy to take a chance with any of those women. It wasn't worth the risk."

* * *

The moving van is gone when Scott and I leave the building. Scott starts the car and blasts the heater to take the chill off the air. We're not getting the heat of the sun yet because it's hiding behind Bankers Tower. I fasten my seatbelt and turn to Scott. "I have a hard time seeing what would attract Sophia to a guy like Shark."

Scott pulls a stick of gum out of his pocket and pops it in his mouth. "I know what you're saying, but maybe he's an acquired taste. And like my grannie used to say, there's a lid for every pot."

I shrug. "I suppose. At least Sophia didn't leave him the restaurant."

Scott shakes his head. "No, but why leave it to Corbin?"

"Who else?"

"I don't know, but it makes me think there was more to their relationship than he's letting on," Scott says.

"Might have been. Back to Shark, though. I have a hard time believing he didn't know what was in the will before she died. Wouldn't she have talked things over with him if he was her executor? Don't people usually do that?"

"Maybe he wasn't listening," Scott says. "I get the impression it wouldn't have been the first time."

I nod, then bounce back to Corbin. "If he knew Sophia planned on leaving him the business, plus the key man insurance, that would be about eight million dollars worth of incentive to get her out of the way."

"He seemed broken up about her death, but they could have been crocodile tears. For that much money, even I could muster authentic looking tears," Scott mutters. "Or maybe they were real waterworks because he's feeling guilty. We need to double check his alibi. If he says he was at the restaurant, there have to be plenty of people who saw him. Shall we do him after lunch?"

He checks his watch. "I've got an appointment at eleven with the best man, Kristien Fox. Do you want to tag along? Or I can drop you off at the station and I'll pick you up when I'm done?"

"Drop me off. I'll get the photo of the pendant blown up and send it around to the Pawn Shop detail. And once I get that done, I need to get ready for court tomorrow morning."

My boss glances up, then goes back to reading reports when I come into the squad room and settle at my desk. I can't decide if Ash likes me, tolerates my presence, or resents that I'm taking a spot from a more senior guy. Emphasis on 'guy'. The police service has come a long way with over forty per cent of officers now being female, but it's still a male-dominated organization.

Most are accepting of us, but there are the jokes, innuendos and comments that always work their way into conversations. I think most guys don't even realize their words and actions are inappropriate. It's only when you ask, "what would you do if that happened to your daughter or little sister?" that they realize boundaries were crossed. I rarely ask the question 'cause I don't want to get any more of a reputation than I've already got.

There are only a few bad apples in the bunch that truly harass. I'm lucky I've only had to endure one. Beavins.

I shake my head and get back to the task at hand. I've spent more than enough time over the past few years agonizing over what happened. I don't want to give any more power to the demons. Or to Beavins.

I see my desk and groan. "Oh God."

The guy at the desk closest to mine looks up and smiles sympathetically. "Someone from the file room dropped it off just a few minutes ago. I feel your pain."

Sitting dead centre, on top of the papers already littering my desk, is a Bankers Box. I suspect it contains files, evidence and the assorted detritus that comes with investigations. It's related to an old case that's finally going to court in two weeks. It has to do with a case I worked on while I was in Economic Crimes. Art, my partner at the time, was close to retirement. He'd been working for years with Customs and Excise on a cigarette smuggling ring.

I'll have to sort through these documents, a diversion from what I'd planned to do with the rest of my morning. I slit open the tape sealing the box and get to work. The office is quiet so maybe I can get through it by lunchtime.

Though I was transferred out of Economic Crimes and left Art alone to work the case, he never gave up. It took him another eighteen months, but he finally rounded up the ringleaders and gathered enough evidence to have them convicted for the theft. After Art passed away, it took the Excise guys months more to put together the tax avoidance charges, the real meat of the case.

The files in the Bankers Box are just as I remember, with Art's signature report style all over them. His death of a heart attack leaves me to give testimony on the tax avoidance charges. Art was a good guy and I wish he was still here to see the conclusion of his years of hard work.

I am putting the files back in the box when my stomach, as well as the clock on the wall, tells me it's time for lunch. As soon as Scott texts that he's at the back door, I grab my jacket and dash. It will feel good to see the sunshine, feel the fresh air, and shake off the memories of that last case with Art.

* * *

I'm munching on an uninspiring salad when I ask Scott, "What did the best man have to say?"

"Not much." Scott talks around his beef brisket sandwich. We are at Red's Diner, a Ramsay neighbourhood gem not far from the Stampede Grounds. "Fox confirms they were in Priddis on Saturday and Sunday. He could hardly wait to share his cell phone pictures. It looks like they hired a couple of girls to keep them company.

"Shark was the life of the party and Fox says there's no way he could have slipped away for more than a few minutes without everyone noticing."

"Did you get a feel for how reliable Fox is? Is he a party guy like Shark?"

My partner shakes his head. "He didn't come across as cocky as Shark. He's at least working for a living instead of living off his girlfriend. He works for Suncor as a geo-physicist. You can't be a slouch in that job."

Scott takes another bite of his sandwich while I take a French fry. He doesn't seem to notice.

"When I asked if he'd seen any friction or fighting between Maxwell and Sophia, Fox thought they got along fairly well, but he wondered whether the wedding was a good idea. He liked Sophia. He thinks she was smart about business, but when it came to Maxwell, she had blinders on.

"Fox says he's known Maxwell for a long time, and he's always been a player. Maxwell didn't seem ready to settle down, but when Sophia came along, she was too good a catch to let walk by."

My lunch salad will never keep me satisfied for the rest of the day, so I'm grateful for the fries. Maybe someday he'll tell me to order my own, but until then, I'll just take another couple.

He watches me dip them into some ketchup. "Fox thought Sophia might have been getting anxious, though. When he and Maxwell went out drinking or whatever, she'd often call, and he thought it sounded like she was checking to see who Maxwell was with and where they were. Fox wondered if she might be suspicious. And Maxwell whined that he and Sophia were bickering more than usual."

"It's a long way from bickering to murder."

"I know, but if Maxwell thought his sugar-mama was going to cut him off, you never know. And I've said it before, just because *he* was at the stag, he could have gotten someone else to do the job." He shrugs and rotates his shoulders, grimacing slightly at the movement.

"And Fox didn't have a name of anyone that Shark was stepping out with, either."

"What did he say about Maxwell's temper?"

"Said he could get chippy, but not so much that he'd be called a hothead. Fox figures Shark wouldn't want to get into something and risk getting his face messed up."

"I suppose that lends more credence to him getting someone else to do the job."

"True, but just like bickering, being chippy is a long way from murder."

* * *

After lunch, we settle at our desks. I put in a call to check out Corbin's alibi at the restaurant where he and his fiancée had dinner. The Manager tells me, "Yah, I know Bradley. Ya wanna talk to the guy who waited on him? He's in later this afternoon at four. Stop by before five, though. After that, we get busy, and he won't have a break to talk to you."

Al's report still isn't here, but the phone companies have complied with the Production Orders and downloads are here with cell phone records for Sophia, Maxwell, Corbin, and the restaurant.

I start with Sophia's records. I'll handle the texts and social media, leaving the telephone numbers to Scott.

He's finished cross-referencing the cars coming in and out of the parkade, and now he's scrolling through the cell phone records. "I'm finding calls from Barbara Stephens to Sophia, but none the other way, from Sophia to Stephens. At least, not on her cell. Didn't Corbin say Sophia often talked to his fiancée?"

"Maybe Sophia told him that to make him think they were buddies. Or maybe Corbin was lying to us."

Scott scratches the stubble on his chin. "Stephens called Sophia on Saturday night around Monica's TOD. It lasted just seconds. Too short for a conversation. Maybe, just time for voice mail to kick in."

I chew on the end of my pen. "Why would Stephens call Sophia? Didn't Corbin say she was in the states with her parents that weekend? And why didn't Sophia answer? Was she already incapacitated by then?"

"Maybe Stephens deserves a look." Scott's quiet for a few minutes, then pushes keys, and goes over to the printer. He comes back with a fistful of papers. "I just ran Stephens. The woman has a past!" He hands me the paper while reading off his screen. "There's a Criminal Harassment conviction in the '80s, followed by Common Assault and Assault in the early 2000s. Probation for all of them. No jail time."

I whistle. "Well, it would seem she has a temper. But nothing since 2010?"

Scott shakes his head. "Nothing that I found."

"Give me a minute. Let me poke around and check her social media."

It doesn't take me long. "Not much activity, as far as I can see. A few posts here and there."

"Maybe she's a lurker?"

I can empathize. I read what others post, but rarely do anything myself. "Could be. In any case, we need to have a chat with her. When's she supposed to be back from the states?"

"Didn't Corbin say the end of the month?"

My phone trills. The conversation is over in seconds, and I reach for my jacket.

"C'mon, Scott. That was Corbin's wedding planner. She's at the Pallisades and can talk to us now. Otherwise, she's headed out of the town tonight and will be away for a couple of weeks."

Scott reminds me, "We can kill two birds with one stone. Remember the Maid of Honour talked about some other bride wanting the same space for her wedding. We can ask the conventions manager about it while we're there."

* * *

The Pallisades is a jewel in the Canadian Pacific Railway chain of hotels across Canada. It sparkles along with other heritage properties like the Banff Springs and the Chateau Lake Louise in Banff National Park, built along the transnational railroad line. Since 1914, Queen Elizabeth, prime ministers and presidents, and film stars have rested their heads on its down-filled pillows. Today, purchased by another mega-accommodation chain, it is still one of the most sought-after hotels in the city. If there is a black-tie event, chances are it will be held at the Pallisades.

Street parking in front of the hotel on Ninth Avenue is scarce, but I pull the beige, unmarked Ford into the valet lane and show the parking attendant my badge. Scott and I leave the car without a backward glance.

At the top of the granite steps, an elegantly uniformed doorman, wearing immaculate white gloves, opens the grand glass, brass, and mahogany door for us. Despite renovations over the years, the lobby retains a gracious, historic charm. The front desk clerk, quietly dressed in a white shirt, dark green and black plaid skirt, standing behind the intricately carved front desk, gives us directions to the Convention Manager's office.

Leaving behind the elegant public areas, adorned with heavy oak wainscoting, opulent fabrics and crystal chandeliers and sconces, we pass through an anonymous door into the realm of staff-only hallways. The hotel has wasted no money on frippery down these impersonal and bland corridors. They are uncomfortably narrow and airless. I check for exit signs out of the warren, but they do little to assuage my anxiety. Some days, my claustrophobia is worse than others.

We finally come to a partly open door stenciled with 'Conventions Manager, Avis Mercury'. We pause before knocking and hear the tail end of a conversation.

"... yes Ms. Armstrong, I can confirm that the ballroom is now available for your reception on December twenty-first. .... Yes, I can meet with you next week to discuss details... Yes, I will wait for your call."

I knock, and the same curt, British-accented voice calls, "Enter".

It smells suspiciously like cigarette smoke in the cramped office, even though there's been a ban on smoking in workplaces since 2008. A portable air filter whirs away in the corner in a futile attempt to decontaminate the air.

Two women stare at us. The woman behind the desk is sliding an ashtray into the desk drawer and gives a brief smile. "Yes, how can I help you?" The office was never meant to hold four people, so I stand in the doorway, propping the door open, while Scott stands just inside.

The whip-thin woman in a guest chair interrupts my reply. "Avis, these must be the police. I told them to meet me here. I hope you don't mind." She turns to me. "I'm Vi Lance. I believe you wanted to talk to me about the Stephens/Corbin wedding?"

The wedding planner's makeup is flawless, giving the illusion of youthful skin and a chiseled jaw line. She could be any age, except her neck and exposed décolletage rat her out. The crepe-y texture makes me think of sun worship and someone well over fifty.

I nod. "Yes, thank you for your time."

While I pull out my notebook, I make introductions. "I'm Detective Janice Maidstone with the Major Crimes Unit, and this is my partner, Scott Amble. We're looking into the sudden death of Sophia Turnbull."

Both women nod with appropriately sombre expressions. The wedding planner speaks up. "Avis was just telling me about it. What a tragedy. I had the pleasure of meeting Ms. Turnbull several times, and she was a lovely woman. Can you tell us what happened?"

"I'm sure you understand that I can't discuss the details of her death."

She sighs and nods. "Yes, I do, although you're here asking questions so there must be something awry."

She's fishing, but I don't take the bait. Instead, I turn to the Conventions Manager. "This will take only a few minutes."

Vi Lance speaks up. "What would you like to know?"

"We are looking into the activities of many of Ms. Turnbull's contacts. This is routine in investigations. We would like to confirm the time her partner, Mr. Corbin, and his fiancée had their cake tasting last week."

While she pulls out a massive appointment binder and flips pages, she snipes at us. "You could have asked me this over the phone and saved yourself the trip." She finds the page she's looking for. "They came in for their cake tasting on Friday evening. The tenth." Her finger traces a line in the book. "Spiced pear with salted caramel, coffee and cognac, and earl grey with fresh figs."

She looks at the conventions manager. "You remember them, Avis? They're having their reception here up in the Penthouse Boardroom at Thanksgiving.

A lovely couple, though she's a little homely. Doesn't wear a stitch of make-up. Bradley is quite nice looking, however. Tall, lanky? Dark glasses?"

"Wasn't the cake tasting originally scheduled for Saturday evening?" I ask the wedding planner, getting her to focus back on my questions.

"Oh, yes, in fact, it was. I rarely schedule meetings for Saturday evenings, in order to leave them free for events, but Ms. Stephens was adamant, so I granted her request. Then, at the last minute, she changed her demands to Friday night."

The wedding planner pursed her lips. "I accommodated them, of course. One must be flexible in this business."

'Did Ms. Stephens give you a reason for the change?"

She shrugs. "No. Brides these days often expect their demands to be met, regardless of the inconvenience they cause to others. And it's my job to make them happy."

"Was there anything noteworthy about the appointment with them?"

She thinks for a moment. "Well, no. I can't think of anything. She seemed more invested in the process than he did, although there is nothing unusual about that. Grooms often give the impression they would rather be elsewhere. She was more interested in flavours that would impress guests, whereas he just wanted what he liked best. He mentioned chocolate was his favourite, but you will notice that chocolate was not even included in the samples."

"Uh huh," I nod. "I suppose you've spent quite a bit of time with the bride planning her wedding?"

"I have. When I first met her, I thought she would be a relaxed bride, but, especially lately, she seems quite anxious."

"Is that normal?"

"You mean normal for her? Or for brides in general? In this instance, if I have to say, I don't think it's the wedding she's worried about. It seems her concerns are more about her relationship."

"Can you elaborate?"

"Nothing specific, really. Just passing comments she's made, conversations with Mr. Corbin that I've overheard. Things like that."

It's like pulling hen's teeth to get the wedding planner to spit it out. "What sort of things have you heard?"

Ms. Lance shakes her head. "The spats have been about him working too much. Spending too much time at the restaurant. He's part owner of ..."

Her voice trails off.

I nod at Scott, and he takes over and addresses his questions to the Conventions Manager. "Ms. Mercury, I have a few questions regarding the wedding booking that Sophia Turnbull had with the hotel on December twenty-first. We have learned that you had a conversation with her in the days prior to her death about a booking conflict?"

Mercury nods. "Well, I wouldn't call it a conflict. But, yes, you must be referring to a request made by Erin Armstrong. We often get multiple requests for a venue, particularly on popular dates like the holidays, and the winter solstice happens to be one of those dates. We are often able to accommodate requests in one of our other venues, but in this case, Ms. Armstrong wanted the Crystal Ballroom and wouldn't take no for an answer when I told her it had already been booked."

She bestows a thin-lipped smile on us. "You see, the Crystal Ballroom is the premiere location in the city for special events. It is ideally suited because of its size and decor, and flexibility in set-up. And of course, our service and food quality are without equal."

She sighs. "In any case, she came in for an appointment shortly after Valentine's Day and became quite upset when she found the ballroom was already booked. She really should have known better than to come in with less than a year before her wedding. Venues book sometimes years in advance and to expect the ballroom to be available at that late date is quite preposterous. I tried to accommodate her in another function room, and, on the off chance that Ms. Turnbull's date was flexible, I even gave her a quick call. As I expected, Ms. Turnbull was firm on her date, and I relayed that to Ms. Armstrong."

Scott nods while taking notes, encouraging Mercury to continue.

"That's Erin with an 'e' and one 'n'. I was anxious to accommodate her if possible. She is marrying Arnold Rutland, an excellent client of the hotel." She pauses for a moment. "Ms. Armstrong did well to snag Rutland, but, and I probably shouldn't say this, since she'll be wife number four, who knows how long it will last? And he's old enough to be her father."

"Did you give her Sophia's name? Did she know that it was Sophia that had booked the space?"

Ms. Mercury shakes her head. "Gracious, no, I didn't tell her. That would have been very unprofessional."

"Can you tell me how your conversation with this other bride concluded?" Scott asks.

Avis Mercury looks at the wedding planner, as if to confirm the details. "In the end, I recommended other venues I thought would be suitable, but she would have nothing to do with it."

The Conventions Manager rolls her eyes. "It appears as though she's gotten her way in the end, though. Ms. Turnbull's fiancé called this morning to cancel, and I just got off the phone from letting her know the space is available."

* * *

Despite taking up half of the reserved valet parking space in front of the hotel for almost an hour, the uniformed doorman gives us a cheerful "have a good afternoon" when we get back to our car. He might not have been as friendly if the demand for his services would have been heavy. On a Wednesday, midafternoon, though, he mostly stands at the top of the stairs, hands quietly clasped in front, waiting for sporadic guests to arrive.

While pulling on his seatbelt, Scott asks, "What is it with all these brides in this case? First Turnbull, then Stephens, Corbin's fiancée is added, and now this Armstrong woman."

"I don't know. In the year after the COVID restrictions were lifted, there was a flurry of weddings because they'd been put off for a couple of years. But you'd think that backlog would be over by now."

I shoulder check, then ease into Ninth Avenue traffic, building with the afternoon rush hour. Turning right and under the railroad tracks, I take another right down Tenth Avenue toward Bonterra Trattoria. En route, Scott texts Nguyen with a request to do a records check on Armstrong.

I love Bonterra, though going there more than once or twice a year is beyond my budget. It's cozy, multi-level interior is softly lit, with plenty of wood and Italian accents. It's always richly perfumed with the mouthwatering aromas of freshly baked bread and roasted garlic. It's the outside patio I love the most, though. Despite being on the corner of two busy streets, it is surrounded by high concrete walls that are disguised behind vine-covered lattice. Little fountains, an outside pizza oven and fireplace, fairy lights strung over the tables and flowers festooning the pillars make the small patio a magical respite where the sounds and feel of being in the middle of a busy urban area are banished. Overhead heaters extend our brief summer outdoor restaurant season.

My mouth waters as soon as we walk into the rustic trattoria. It reminds me that all I have in fridge at home are tired leftovers. I push the disappointment aside, and corral the white-aproned fellow who served Corbin and his fiancée on Friday night.

He has no hesitation. "Yep, I had them in my section. They came in around seven. They're here lots. Maybe a few times a month? He's a pleasant guy, but he seemed off that night. They had wine, like usual, and a main course, but no dessert. They left around nine o'clock and they were arguing."

"What about?"

The young man shrugs. "I didn't hear much, really. To be honest, it's not the first time. He's easy-going but she can really light him up. And on Friday, she was on him hard. It could have been about him spending so much time with someone at work? I was slammed with other tables and really, I try not to listen to that stuff. No sense getting bummed by other people's problems, ya know?"

* * *

Sunshine is still pouring through high office windows when we get back after leaving the cocky waiter to his first tables of the night. I wish we could have stopped for a bowl of their Rigatoni Amatriciana; my taste buds tingle when I think of the hot chili flakes and red wine tomato sauce. Instead, we stopped at Tim's and grabbed subs to eat at our desks.

Between bites, we're tapping at our keyboards, delving into online archives. "Remember the headaches we'd get when we had to look through microfiche?" I ask Scott.

He doesn't take his eyes off his screen. "Sure do. Hated the stuff. But microfiche was better than digging through archives. Why is it that so many of those boxes had been sitting in basements that had been flooded?"

I shudder. "Uck. Which reminds me. Are we up to date on our hepatitis vaccinations?"

He nods, "I am. Don't know about you. Send a note to HR. They can find out for you," without even pausing his clicking and scrolling.

Not long, between social media sites and plain old Google, we have insight into our latest suspect, Erin Armstrong.

Born and raised in Alberta, her high school yearbook pictures show a chubby teenager with wild, frizzy red hair and heavy-rimmed glasses. Her classmates have smiles on their faces, but she's dead pan. Glum, or serious, it's hard to tell.

We find pictures of her on a university field trip. By then, the awkward teenager had ditched the heavy glasses, tamed the electric hair, and shed the extra pounds. Other photos show an outdoor loving girl hiking with friends, then a stylish urban dweller enjoying shopping and sidewalk patios.

She's a graduate of an interior design programme, and the website for her current employer has her showing stunning interiors and sharing glasses of champagne with delighted clients in their newly decorated spaces.

A dive into social media shows her attending fund-raising events, often on the arms of wealthy, usually older, men. Stunning designer gowns cling to her body.

I pause and look down at my serviceable khakis, as much a hallmark of the work I do, as the expensive wardrobe show-ponied by Armstrong. My washable pants and golf shirts are comfortable and practical, whether I'm hunched over my computer or a body, or running down a suspect.

Scott always looks sharp. His tall athletic body looks good in anything, whether it's jeans or a suit. He has a relaxed way of carrying himself, his movements fluid. I've seen photos of his Puerto Rican dad. Scott is lean, just like him. He got his dad's curly hair, too, but his mom's blue eyes.

Scott looks up and catches me staring at him. "What?"

"Just thinking that Armstrong's more likely to answer questions coming from you than from me."

"Yah?"

I nod. "You can flash your dimples, and she'll be like putty in your hands."

He flashes them at me. "Sure. It's my superpower. Ready to head out?"

"Yep. Just let me have Dispatch send someone past her house. See if she's home."

Dispatch relays an update from a patrol car just as we leave the station parking lot. "We drove past the house you wanted us to check. A car just pulled into the garage and a tall red head got out. Do you want us to stick around to make sure she doesn't leave before you get here?"

I key the mike. "Ten-four. We're on our way. If she leaves, can you keep an eye on her?"

"Sure. We'll park just down the block."

We take the fastest route to a ritzy part of the city where the multilevel concrete and glass house overlooks the Elbow River. There's not much beautiful about the design, but it certainly makes a statement. Driving past the marked patrol car, I wave and give them a thumbs-up. Immediately, they flash their headlights and cruise off.

It's a few degrees below freezing, cold enough that I shiver when we leave the warmth of the car and approach the house. I checked its Title documents before we left the office and they show the house is owned by Arnold Rutland.

The wind howls, typical late March weather. A bite in the air suggests more snow is on the way.

Scott reaches the door first and pushes the doorbell.

A tall redhead, barefoot but still in a maroon sheath dress, opens the door and glares at us. "Yes?"

Scott and I show our badges. "Good evening. Ms. Armstrong?"

She nods.

"We're investigating a matter that we hope you may be able to help us with. Do you have a few minutes?" Scott asks.

The woman stands her ground in the doorway, at first not acknowledging the wind, but when a particularly strong gust ruffles her hair, she steps back, "Please, come in."

She motions us to follow her across the entry hall, almost as large as my living room.

To our right, a wide staircase sweeps up to the second floor. On the left, the foyer opens up to a massive living room. We trail after her on a hardwood floor, featuring an intricately inlaid gold logo for Arnold Rutland Developments. I wonder if Rutland writes off his house expenses on his income tax as an advertising expense.

A series of built-in cabinets in the living room display crystal glasses, decanters, and liquor bottles, bathed in a soft golden glow from under-mount LED lights. I stop and nudge Scott with my elbow. From across the room, I see a distinctive green bottle of champagne. Moving closer to the cabinet, I confirm it to be Bollinger Extra Brut, the same type as we found in Sophia's condo.

Erin turns and puts her hands on her hips, impatiently waiting for us to catch up. When we follow her to the brightly lit commercial-looking kitchen, she gestures for us to sit at the polished concrete island, the size of a small driveway. The kitchen is mostly stainless steel and white, with a splash of colour coming from an extravagant bouquet of red roses.

She tells us. "I'm going out, and don't have much time. What would you like to know?"

I open my notebook and scrutinize the woman while she focuses on my partner. She's applied her makeup with a heavy hand. Her eyes are thickly rimmed with black liner and encased by heavy black lashes. I'm not sure if they are false, or extensions.

She gives Scott the once-over and likes what she sees. There is a softening in her face; her eyes widen fractionally.

Scott begins. "We are investigating the death of Sophia Turnbull."

He leaves some space for her to comment.

She nods briefly and comments with no inflection in her voice. "Yes, I heard about that. How sad."

"Did you know Ms. Turnbull?" Scott asks.

The redhead shrugs. "In passing. I knew who she was. We'd met a few times at various social functions."

Scott says. "We have learned that you and she shared the same wedding date. And that you wanted to use the Crystal Ballroom for your wedding, the same venue that she had already booked."

Her eyebrows arch. "Really? What a coincidence."

"Did you know that?"

She purses her lips. "I don't believe I've heard her name in relation to that. I mean, I might have heard it in passing, but I've been so focused on my wedding, well, it's quite possible I've forgotten."

She cocks her head to one side, a demure affectation, "You see, I've been planning my wedding for over a year, and somehow booking a venue had fallen through the cracks. I contacted the hotel, but unfortunately, the room had already been booked and although I tried to convince the hotel to rebook the other bride, they were not cooperative. Until today, that is. The hotel gave me a call and said they had a cancellation, and I could have the Crystal Ballroom. If they happened to mention her name, it just went right over my head."

She continues as if the death of Turnbull is of no significance to her. "The ballroom is the loveliest space of its kind in the city."

She fluffs her hair. "When that snippy woman at the hotel first told me it was booked, I was devastated. I pleaded with Arnold, he's my fiancé, to speak to the hotel manager about it."

We oblige her with a nod, and she continues.

"I didn't think he was going to, but then when the hotel just called to give me the space, I thought maybe he did. Except now you say that Ms. Turnbull has died."

I am taken aback by her apparent insensitivity to Turnbull's death, her desire for the ballroom, and our presence here asking her questions.

She leans forward to touch one of the magnificent roses. "I've pictured my wedding since I was a little girl. I know some might say I am a traitor to feminists who disdain the institution, but I can't wait to get married."

With thoughts of a perfect wedding, her shoulders have softened.

"I dreamt about getting married on the solstice. It symbolizes the rebirth of the sun, coming closer to the earth, like giving you a fresh clean slate to make a new life together as husband and wife."

She looks at me. Maybe I snorted. "Perhaps you think it sounds fanciful, but isn't it romantic?"

She waits for me to agree with her, so I do, giving a couple of head bobs.

"And Arnold has been supportive of my dreams. He wants that day just as much as I do. Of course, if we had to, we would have gone outside the city, but ..." She gives a shrug and her voice trails off.

Scott replies, "I know how important having the perfect day is for a bride. I'm happy it's working out for you."

He sounds sincere, but I doubt he has any idea what a bride wants. As far as I know, he's never been close to being engaged. It has never come up in our conversations.

Her phone, sitting on the table beside her, chirps. When she looks down to check it, Scott glances at me and I catch his wink. I hide my smile by finding something fascinating in my notes.

"Ms. Armstrong, let's go back to when you first found out there might be a problem getting the wedding venue you wanted. What was your reaction?"

She straightens one of the stems in the bouquet before answering. "I was disappointed, naturally."

"Did you ask who had the room booked?"

"I cannot recall. I might have done."

"For something so important to you, I'd think you'd remember who was standing in your way," Scott says.

She scowls.

"When did you find out who had the room booked?"

"Well, you just told me."

Scott waits for her to answer the question. He watches her, and at first, she stares back at him. She stubborn, and it takes a minute, but she drops her eyes. "Oh, I suppose it doesn't matter. The convention manager has a large calendar on her desk. I'm used to reading things upside down on blueprints and designs, so it wasn't difficult to read Turnbull's name on it."

"Did you contact Turnbull about changing her date?"

The designer pauses, then shakes her head. "It crossed my mind, but decided I'd be wasting my time."

"Still, it must have been upsetting." Scott continues. "What did you do about it?"

Erin shrugs. "There wasn't much I could do about it."

Scott leans forward. "What did you do last weekend? In particular, what did you do on Saturday evening?"

Erin cocks her head, looking puzzled. "Nothing in particular. Why?"

Scott shrugs. "With all the stress of planning your wedding and not being able to confirm the wedding venue you wanted, I wonder if you did anything special to relax. Did you go out or have company?"

"Well, although it's none of your business, I was at home."

She's not smiling now. "My fiancé had meetings in Banff, and he wanted me to go with him, but I didn't feel like it. He wasn't happy about me staying home, but I didn't really care."

"So, he went without you. What did you do then?"

Her posture stiffens and a faint flush appears on her neck before she answers with a question of her own. "Why does it matter what I did on the weekend?"

He doesn't bat an eye. "Just wondering. Did you go out on Saturday? Have company?"

"Again, Detective, not that it's any of your business, but I stayed in. Alone."

"Saturday night?"

The redhead has had enough. She stands and folds her arms. "It sounds like you're asking me for an alibi."

* * *

I'm tired, hungry and want to turn off my brain for a few hours when I finally get home after the Armstrong interview. Terry's texted multiple times throughout the day, asking if he can come over, and when he promised it will be just for a few minutes, I relented. *Ok, but just for half an hour. A quick beer.*

He's waiting in his car when I pull into the driveway. I curse. I suspect he's going to pout when I tell him I need to take Treacle out for a quick trot around-the-block. He's never happy when I put her first.

He gets out of his car carrying an armful of flowers. Huh. That's new. When was the last time he brought me flowers? Come to think of it, when was the first?

At the beginning of the year, when we started seeing each other, I enjoyed spending time with him. Lately, though, I'm wondering if the relationship is worth it. He's drinking my beer, watching my television, and waiting for me to cook dinner.

He complains about how much child support he has to pay for his two kids. Maybe this explains why he mooches off me, but for once, I'd like it to be all about me. I see the flowers and think, maybe something's changed.

"Hi babe. Here, I brought these for you."

He hands them to me while I'm still busy unlocking the door. At times like this, it would be useful to have three hands.

"Thanks, Terry." I hate being called babe and have told him so many times. I swear, the next time he does it, I'm going to whip out a package of diapers. Instead, I hold my tongue. "To what do I owe this lovely bouquet?"

"No reason. You've been working long hours lately, and I figure you'd like them."

"I do, thank you." I give them an appreciative sniff and hand the bouquet back to Terry. "Can you hold them for a sec while I unlock the door?"

I admit. I'm happier to see Treacle prancing around my feet than I am to see Terry. She's low maintenance, full of unconditional love and devotion, and I don't have to worry about entertaining her.

"Let me take Treacle for a quick walk, and then we can visit. Do you want to come with us?"

"Really? Does she need to go right now?"

"Yes, she does." I know my reply is terse. "Are you coming?"

"No, thanks. I'll get a beer and watch some TV."

"Okay then. There's leftover lasagna in the fridge you can throw in the oven. I haven't had supper, and I'm starved."

There's a chill in the air, but the brisk walk will keep me warm. Unlike most dogs, Treacle is more interested in keeping her nose to the wind than checking pee-mail at every corner. Her unadulterated joy when we go for walks always lifts my spirits, so by the time we get back after a detour through a neighbourhood park, I have a smile on my face and colour in my cheeks. I look forward to spending time with Terry, instead of curling up in bed with a book that will put me to sleep in about five minutes.

Unfortunately, there's no aroma of lasagna wafting through the house, and Terry left the flowers on the counter. I plunk them in the water jug sitting beside the sink and settle for a bowl of Cheerios. Terry's watching a hockey game, so I join him on the couch.

Careful not to spill my cereal and milk, I lean against the armrest on the far end and scoot my chilly toes under his leg.

"I haven't seen you for ages, it seems. What's new?" I ask him. I'm tired. If something's so important he had to see me, I'd rather he tell me sooner rather than later.

"I know, right babe? How's the case going?"

I clench my jaw, then shrug. "We're making headway. Have a few people we're looking at but nothing concrete yet. It's early days, and that means long hours."

"Mmm," he's distracted by the television. "Must be tough."

I watch him watching the game.

I'm slurping the dregs at the bottom of the bowl when he turns to me. "You know, I think I saw an old friend drive by the other day, but I'm not sure. I got the licence plate of the truck." He fishes in his pocket and hands me a piece of paper. "Would you check it out for me?"

Huh. So, this is why he wanted to come over so badly.

I don't even glance at the plate number on the paper. "You know I can't do that for you, Terry."

"Aw, why not? You could pretend you're looking it up for yourself. For an investigation or something."

"You know why. That would break like a kajillion privacy laws. If I'm caught, I'd be in serious trouble. I could even lose my job."

"How would anyone find out? I won't tell."

"I'd know, and anyway, it's not a chance I want to take." I try to hand the paper back to him, but he waves it away.

"Aw, come on, Janice." He scoffs. "Don't be such a stick-in-the-mud. I've never asked you for a favour before."

Except for wanting me to cancel the speeding ticket he got a few weeks ago. "Sorry, Terry. I won't do it."

He crosses his arms and turns back to the game. He's pissed. Shall I placate him, or let him simmer? I'm too tired to play games, but I feel a need to smooth things over. Why, I don't know.

"I can't do a records search for you, but you've tried looking for him yourself, right? If he's an old friend, do you have friends in common you can ask? You've Googled him? Facebook?"

"Of course I have. You think I'm a fucking idiot?"

This is a side of Terry I've not seen before. Belligerent. Mean.

"Whoa there. Why the attitude?"

"I thought you'd help me out."

"Still, if you know people in common..."

"All right, this guy. He asked me to do something for him, and I just want to know more about him. Before I do anything, you know?"

"Something illegal?"

"Nah, nothing like that."

"Why don't you just ask him?"

"I don't know. But, just this once, can't you do something for me?"

"Do something for you? You mean, like other than making dinner and sitting here while you watch hockey when you know I can't stand it?"

"I take you out plenty of times."

I don't want to say anything I'll regret or argue about anything tonight. I'm too tired.

While I'm trying to decide what to say, Terry snaps, "Anyway, never mind."

I'm not going to press. He can stew.

A few minutes later, he drains his beer and stands up. "Well, if you won't do anything, I'm outta here."

"Don't be like that, Terry. I can't get that information for you, but is there something else I can do?"

"I doubt it." He uses his fingers to make air quotes. "It might 'get you into trouble'."

Tossing the paper into the decorative ceramic bowl on the coffee table, I get up and follow a few steps behind him. Treacle had been stretched out, fast asleep, but she's on full alert now, sensitive to tension in the room.

Terry grabs his jacket from the rack at the front door. "See ya'". He jerks the door open and slams it behind him when he stomps down the sidewalk, leaving me standing in the hallway with my empty cereal bowl.

Chapter Seven

The Turnbull case is on the back burner this morning while I appear in Court of King's Bench on a case I investigated more than a year ago. Not the cigarette case with Art. No, this was a charge against a tow truck driver who'd assaulted an old man driving a beat-up Chev pulling a horse trailer. The tow truck driver lost his patience with the old man for taking too long to move out of a parking spot. A couple of extra minutes wouldn't have hurt the tow truck driver, and sure as hell wasn't worth popping the old man when he opened his window to argue back.

I've switched out my golf shirt and khakis for a blouse and coordinating pants and jacket. In my early days as a detective, I attended court when another detective showed up dressed casually. The judge kicked him out of the courtroom, embarrassing the detective and the rest of us observing the lecture. Though that particular judge was a notorious stickler for decorum, I never want to risk that the almighty one sitting at the front of the courtroom will make me do a similar walk of shame.

While I'm otherwise occupied, Scott will check Corbin's alibi, finish going through Sophia's phone records, and attempt to clear the piles of paper off his desk. Our department has a "clean-desk-policy", something that Scott ignores for as long as possible, until Ash issues the order to clean it up. I'm glad I'm not there to hear Scott grumble.

Waiting for my turn on the witness stand, I alternate between pacing the courthouse corridor and sitting on the incredibly uncomfortable benches placed in the hallway outside each courtroom.

The conversation I had last night with Terry keeps replaying. Did he bring me flowers hoping to soften me up so I'd cave to his request for information? And what sort of beef does he have with someone that would warrant him wanting to find out where they live? The way he acted has left a nasty taste in my mouth.

I realize I don't know him very well. During high school we hung around, sure, but his life after grade twelve is a mystery. He hasn't willingly shared, and I've not pried because I respect his privacy and figure he'll open up when he feels it's the right time. But the way he expressed his anger last night makes me uncomfortable.

I shrug off my thoughts about him and settle for watching the variety of people move past me.

Prosecutors, laden with files, sweep down the hall with their black robes billowing behind them like Dementors in the Harry Potter franchise.

The opposing counsel, high priced defence lawyers in expensive suits and shiny shoes, are accompanied by their lowly assistants weighed down by document boxes. Continuing the Harry Potter analogy, these would be Lucius Malfoy and Dobby, the house elf. It is easy to differentiate the fancy hired guns from the slavishly over-worked and underpaid legal aid lawyers who represent those who can't afford anyone else. They carry their own files, rarely having the luxury of assistants to act as beasts of burden.

Witnesses, both the professional, like me and expert witnesses, mix with the bewildered and anxious families and friends of both the accused and the victims. For so many, the outcomes of these trials will change the course of their lives, for better or worse.

And finally, feeding off the egos and swirling emotions are the media, rushing here and there with cameras, cell phones and microphones ready to thrust into unsuspecting faces.

I lower my gaze and focus on the feet. Trudging or strutting? So much can be told about a person by their walk, the shoes they wear.

A pair of worn, but polished cowboy boots move through my field of view. They remind me of Dad.

A woman wearing three-inch heels moves past and my mind slides to thoughts of the Turnbull case and the interview last night with Erin Armstrong. She'd wear these, I think. Flashy, but God, they must be uncomfortable.

Would Sophia have worn shoes like this? I recall seeing stilettos in her closet when Scott and I went through the condo that first day, but maybe they were from a previous time in her life. Was her personality expressed better by the heels in her closet, or by the pink kitten slippers she was wearing when she died?

Even though no cause of death has been determined, we're still treating this as a homicide. If Monica doesn't call today with a cause of death, I'll ask her tonight when we meet for wine.

I'm shaken from my thoughts when a hand touches my shoulder. "Hey Maidstone, quit daydreaming," the court bailiff teases me. "They're ready for you."

"They're moving quickly this morning," I mutter as I pass by. He mumbles something in reply.

Once sworn in, my testimony lasts only minutes. The defence counsel doesn't bother to grill me. On a superficial level, the lack of defence makes me feel sorry for the accused, but I get over it. I know the guy's a bully, and guilty to boot. We've got witnesses who saw the whole thing, and the old guy that was punched will give solid testimony on the stand.

* * *

Coming back into the office, I flatten against the wall when guys rush past me. I raise my eyebrows at

Scott when I make it to my desk. He reaches for the coffee, chicken sub, bag of chips, and another bag with donuts that I've picked up for him. "A body's been found at the end of the C-train line. They think the suspect is still in the area."

"Finding a body at lunchtime? That's unusual." I manage with a mouthful of cruller. I'm not distracted by the agitation in the room and turn my mind to our case. "Figure out anything while I was in court?"

He looks disgusted. "I went through the security camera footage with Nguyen. What a waste of time! The picture looks like it was taken under water in a storm drain. Why would a high-class building have such a lousy camera setup? It's useless. I sent a clip to Al's group, but I doubt they can do much with it."

I shake my head. "Damn. We'll have to canvas the building again just in case someone's remembered something."

"I think anyone remembering anything is pretty unlikely." He glances at the clock. "We could do it today, but more people will be home on the weekend. Why don't you ask Marshall to check it out first thing on Saturday?"

"I will. It's a trade-off. The longer we wait, the more likely people are going to forget, but yah, more people will be home on Saturday. Marshall's not going to be happy about knocking on doors. Isn't he planning on heading out with his trailer?"

Scott shakes his head. "No. He's on the roster for Saturday, so he might as well work on this case as one of his own."

"And I suppose you want me to tell him."

"You're the boss."

"Yeah, right. Now, anything else happen while I was out?"

Scott shakes his head. "The crime scene report's still not here. There's no point in calling Al again, though. Pestering won't get it here faster."

I finish licking cruller glaze from my fingers. "No, not at all. He gets testy when he's bothered."

Scott finishes his sub and starts in on the sour cream glazed donut. "I've been working on the champagne angle. The distributor shipped thirty bottles to Turnbull's restaurant over the last six months. I also ran down the bottles sent to liquor stores." He slides a piece of paper across to me. "We got lucky here. Not that many bottles were sold, and I got copies of the receipts for the purchases. Look who bought not just one, but two bottles."

I skim, and halfway down the page, I look up and return his smile. "Arnold Rutland. And Erin Armstrong's his fiancé."

Scott stretches and puts his hands behind his head. "We saw one bottle in her house last night. Where did the second one go? Is it tucked away in a cupboard, or did it end up in Turnbull's condo?" He grins. "Maybe we need to have another talk with Ms. Armstrong."

"It will be an interesting conversation, unless she decides she needs to lawyer-up."

"There's no way we'll know unless we try.

Scott tosses the wrapper from his lunch into the garbage can. "How was court this morning?"

"About as I expected. Closing arguments will happen this afternoon. How did it go with Corbin's alibi?"

"The evening shift manager confirms Corbin came back to the restaurant to reboot the POS system, then disappeared into his office for the rest of the night. Said he didn't want to be disturbed. As far as the manager knows, no one went into the office, but he walked by at one point and heard Corbin laughing. He figured Corbin was on the phone.

"He was out for smoke break a few times but never saw Corbin's car move from its usual spot. While I was talking to the manager, the Chef was in and out of the office. He piped up and said he saw Corbin's car, too, every time he went out."

Scott checks my lunch bag, hoping I had something else tucked away. "By the way, I left another message with Stephens in Montana to call. I haven't seen anything from Monica with COD. Are you going out drinking with her tonight? You going to see if she's made any progress?"

I nod and watch the Desk Sergeant stride into the squad room with a legal-sized envelope. He makes a bee-line for our pod, and hands me the package.

It's from the Crime Lab. I check my email and see that an electronic copy is waiting for us, too, hyper-linked to explanations of technical terms, and applicable tables.

"Good ol' Al." I smile. "He always delivers." My phone dings and I glance at it. A text from Al. *Just sent the Turnbull forensics over. I'm around all afternoon when you want to talk.*

I open the envelope and hand Scott part of the contents while I start on the rest.

The fingerprints found in the condo were of people normally expected to be there. Sophia, Maxwell, the personal assistant, and housekeeper. Except for one partial, smudged print on the champagne bottle. Not enough detail to match it with anyone.

A section of the report details the contents of the trash cans throughout the condo. Since the housekeeper was there on Saturday morning, I expect there won't be much to go through. What there was, though, gives me pause.

"Hey Scott, there's a list of stuff they found in the garbage. Not much, an apple core and wrapper from a protein bar, which probably came from the box we saw in the pantry, but this is interesting. A handful of bleach wipes. And a tissue with what appears to be saliva."

"Whose saliva?"

I shake my head. "Al doesn't say. And any DNA that might be there would be destroyed by the bleach. But the wipes lend credence to the idea someone was there and used them to remove any trace of their DNA."

"Did you notice any containers of the wipes? I wonder if the killer used some that were already in the condo, or they thought to bring their own? If they brought their own, that shows premeditation."

I search the list of items the crime techs took from the condo. "No container listed here. We can drop by the condo later today and check. If we get a warrant to search anyone's place, we'll want to be on the lookout for the same type of wipes Al found.

"Lots of trace on the pillow from the sofa. Hair and skin, looking like it came from Sophia and Maxwell. No surprise there. Also, evidence from others. If we find a suspect that claims they were never in the place, we might be able to place them there if any of it matches them. No blood. Semen, but not recently deposited."

I go over the other results with Scott. Two additional bits of evidence raised our eyebrows. The first was the mink eyelash extension, still attached to the original eyelash. Al sent it off to the specialized DNA lab.

The second was from the Sharps container. All the syringes were the same kind, which was to be expected, but one didn't have the needle cap replaced, so the needle was exposed. Being unusual, they examined the syringes for fingerprints. All had Maxwell's prints, except the one without the needle cap. That barrel had been wiped clean.

I'm thinking out loud. "What are the chances that someone other than Maxwell would drop a used syringe in the container? There was a vial of insulin that, according to him, was missing. Who else would have used it? And then wiped off fingerprints?"

Scott finishes reading. "Good question. An insulin syringe with no prints and an errant eyelash. What in the hell are we going to do with the syringe, and how do we track down where the eyelash thing came from? Salons should have client lists, right? If we find a suspect who's also on a client list, that would be fantastic. And look here, Al even gave us a brand name. Can you imagine the weird databases he must have access to?"

I laugh. "Why don't you call and ask him? He's in all afternoon."

Scott just snorts his reply.

I tap the pages. "I don't know if Armstrong was wearing extensions. She had thick lashes, but whether they were false or extensions, I couldn't tell."

Scott interrupts. "They couldn't be her own?"

I shake my head. "Those caterpillars? Doubt it. Anyway, we don't have enough cause right now for a warrant for DNA or fingerprints unless we can put her in the condo."

Al's findings about the syringe prompt me to thumb a quick text to Monica. *Any chance insulin could have played a part in Turnbull's death?*

I start an email to Nguyen and Marshall to bring them up to date on Al's report, and to ask Nguyen to do a Production Order for Armstrong's credit card transactions. I also break the news to Marshall that we want him to canvas the condo building on Saturday morning.

Scott nods. "Armstrong better come up with an alibi 'cause right now, even though all of this is circumstantial, she's looking good for this. She has a bottle of the same champagne in her house AND has a motive."

"True." I run my fingers through my hair, making a mental note to make an appointment for a haircut. "But I'll feel a lot better about all of this when we get a COD. I'd hate to be wasting our time if it turns out Turnbull died of natural causes."

I send off the email to Lance and Marshall, then glance at the clock. "Thursday night, Scott and I'm done for the day. Monica's going to be wondering where I am."

I transferred out of uniform into plain clothes about seven years ago. I was happy to leave midnight shift rotations behind, and with the promise of civilized hours, I wanted to expand my circle of friends beyond fellow cops. When the city's annual Wine Festival rolled around, I decided to go and see if I could meet new people, as well as sample the wines. Two birds with one stone sort of thing.

Lines of eager oenophiles were lined up at most of the booths when I arrived on opening night at the Telus Convention Centre, the major convention facility located in downtown Calgary. I finally inched my way to the front of one line serving a Washington state pinot noir, I was rewarded with a minuscule sample. A dark-haired woman beside me took a sip from her glass at the same time.

"Ugh, this is awful," I muttered, looking for the handy bucket into which I dumped the rest of my glass.

The woman at my side caught my eye and similarly grimaced. "I hope this isn't an omen for the rest of the evening."

We shouldered out of the throng and meandered to the next exhibitor, making idle chitchat. After jostling through a few booths, the novelty of tasting unfamiliar wines wore off, and we agreed to forgo the rest of the free tastings in favour of a single glass of great wine in the relatively quiet wine garden. Conversation flowed easily, and eventually, tentatively, we wound around to talking about our occupations. Revealing that I am a police officer is sometimes a catalyst for complaints, and I've found budding friendships wither when I'm asked if I can fix a ticket, and I say no. Similar, I guess, to the reaction I got from Terry last night.

Over the years, drinking wine with Monica on Thursday nights has become a regular occurrence. Our favourite spot is a cozy wine bar in a small urban neighbourhood, a little off the beaten path.

Her work persona is startlingly different from the one I see on Thursday evenings. In work mode, she's serious, intimidating, and as demanding of herself as she is of everyone around her. Off the clock, she's witty and warm.

At first, when Scott only knew her as Dr. Patel, he couldn't understand why I'd willingly spend time with the aloof pathologist. Then one evening, he and one of his dates ran into us at the wine bar. Teasing, laughing, and engaging, Monica charmed them both. Scott leaned across the table and whispered in my ear, "Is she the same person?"

On this Thursday night, Monica already has a glass of wine in front of her when I rush in. The Barrel, identified by a decades-old sign carved out of old wine casks, is on a side street in trendy Kensington. Its front door leads four steps up to a restaurant, and four steps down to a cozy lounge. Low ceilings, flickering wall sconces and a concrete stamped floor evoke the ambiance of an old-world wine cellar. A collage of wine corks covers one wall, while old casks provide thematic, but uncomfortable perches around high-top tables. We only endured them once, deciding we prefer the well-padded chairs around the regular height tables.

"Sorry to keep you waiting, Monica. I had to go home and take Treacle for a quick pee."

"Don't worry about it," she says, shaking her head. "I haven't been here long." She waits with a Cheshire cat grin on her face until the server comes over and I order my usual zinfandel. Then she leans forward. "I know we don't usually talk shop, but I've got news that I can't wait to tell you."

"Really?" I raise my eyebrows.

Even with the cover of Frank Sinatra crooning in the background, she lowers her voice. "Thanks for the heads up about the extra syringe in the Sharps container." She pauses and takes another sip of wine.

The server momentarily interrupts and places my wine in front of me. As soon as he is out of earshot, I hiss at Monica. "Well?"

"The tissue sample from Turnbull's back? The results came back just before I left the office. We found traces of insulin."

I squint. "And so?"

Monica sits back, assuming a professorial attitude. "Insulin is, of course, naturally produced in our bodies, so it rarely raises any alarm bells if it's found in lab tests. And it's metabolized quickly. But an overdose is an effective way to kill someone."

She shakes her head. "Once I thought about it, it seemed so obvious! Turnbull was killed by an overdose of insulin."

Before my mind can become preoccupied with suspects and scenarios, I touch my glass to hers. "Great news, Monica. You're my favourite medical examiner."

She laughs. "Yeah, whatever. I don't think you even know any other medical examiner."

I just shrug and laugh back.

With her bombshell news out of the way, we get on to the business of our lives. Monica tells me she's been asked out for dinner this weekend.

"Good for you. Where did you meet?"

"In the line-up for coffee at the Foothills Medical Centre. She's got a lab up there doing stem cell research."

"Cool," I say, but I have no idea what that means. "Do you want to explain it to me, or will it be over my head?"

Monica laughs. "At the very basic level, a stem cell is an undifferentiated cell that's capable of developing into a different type of cell. We start out as an embryo, which is basically a collection of stem cells. Ultimately those cells differentiate and become organs, bones, tissues. There are incredibly exciting avenues of research that are showing us new ways of treating and healing our bodies using these cells."

I sip. "Thank you, professor."

She continues, "I don't know exactly what Shira's doing, but it's high level. Fascinating."

I smirk. "I look forward to hearing more."

Monica smirks back. "I look forward to it, too. I'll keep you updated. But I don't plan on rushing into anything, especially since she has kids." Monica grimaces. "You know me. I'm not sure about them."

She sits back. "Now, tell me what you and Terry have been up to."

"Not much, especially with being so busy." I take a sip and grimace. Not at the wine. "But he showed up last night with flowers."

"You make flowers sound like a bad thing," Monica observes.

"Well, he's never brought them before, and I think he just wanted to butter me up. He asked me to trace a licence plate and get an address for him."

She shakes her head. "I hope you didn't say yes."

"I told him I wouldn't, and he got pissy about it. He up and left, wouldn't even tell me what it was all about, except that he has a beef with this guy."

"What do you think?"

"I don't know. There's a lot I don't know about Terry between the time I left the ranch, and when he suddenly turned up at the grocery store and asked me for coffee. It's a nice connection to old times, but red flags are starting to poke up."

"Like what? Is he okay with you working so much? With Scott?"

"Well, he gets frustrated with the hours, and he's not keen on Scott. Not so much that I spend so much time with him, as that he just doesn't like him."

"Why?"

"Maybe he's jealous 'cause Scott played pro-ball? Or 'cause Scott's so easy-going and everyone likes him? Or because Scott doesn't like him either. The other day, Scott asked me if Terry has ulterior motives. He said it like it was a joke, but it's got me to thinking."

"Well, do you think Scott's right?"

I take a drink to give myself time to think. "At first, I thought, no. But Terry didn't seem too surprised when we ran into each other in the grocery store. And he was pretty quick to ask me out. At the time, I was flattered, but now I'm wondering if it was all planned. And he's asked me to fix a speeding ticket, and now this week, to track down a license plate."

I shrug. "Maybe I'm being paranoid, but I'm pretty sure he's rifled through my desk and tried to log into my computer."

"Have you confronted him?"

"No, I don't feel like having a confrontation about it, and since I'm not planning on getting serious with Terry anytime soon, does it really matter? If he's being either disingenuous, or dishonest, it will come out in the end."

"As long as you've got your eyes open, and you don't have anything at home that he shouldn't see."

"Don't worry."

Monica gives a satisfied nod. "Okay, I won't. Now, talking of Scott, isn't ball season starting up?" The woman loves baseball and finds his near brush with MLB stardom intriguing.

"Yep, practices started this week. He's optimistic about some of the new guys who've signed up this year. The first tournament of the year isn't too far away, so we'll find out. If the weather isn't bad, maybe I'll go watch a game. I'll let you know if you want to tag along."

"Thanks. What else is going on?"

I sigh. "Guess who made an appearance in the office yesterday?"

"Huh, you've got to be talking about sleaze-ball Beavins. What did he want?"

"I don't know. To schmooze with the guys, maybe. He smeared his greasy self around, walked unnecessarily close to my desk, and generally made me want to vomit."

I shudder. "He spent some time in Ash's office. Ash is taking time off next month, so Beavins is probably going to be our acting boss."

Monica nods slowly. "That won't be very comfortable for you."

"It sure as hell won't be. But at least I won't be stuck one-on-one with him anywhere."

"Thank God for your partner, huh?" Monica says.

"Yes. I know I can handle Beavins on my own, but it's nice to have Scott around. Beavin's not likely to whip out his dick if my partner's there."

Monica screws up her face in disgust. "Want to borrow a scalpel, just in case?"

I laugh. "I know you're teasing, but..."

She laughs along with me, waggling her eyebrows.

"The thing is," I take a serious tone, "the man is seriously a genius when it comes to finding needles in a haystack. He may be a prick and a pervert, but he's also damn smart and a good investigator."

I shiver. "And he makes my skin crawl."

"Don't let him get to you, Janice."

I take another gulp of wine. "Do you think he does it on purpose? To get under my skin?"

I've told Monica the bare bones of his weenie wagging escapades in the unmarked surveillance car. She was disgusted and encouraged me to make a formal complaint. The incidents happened over five years ago though and I figured it was too late to go to HR. At the time, heck even now, it would be his word against mine.

"Of course he does. He likes to make you squirm. I'm sure he's still trying to intimidate you, so don't give him the satisfaction of letting him. Besides, people aren't blind. Or stupid. They may not know the details, but they know something went down."

Monica pushes a plate of gyoza my way, then continues. "There are plenty who would be on your side, even if they may not come right out and say it. The brass aren't oblivious to his reputation, either. He won't get another promotion or get moved to another division. He's tapped out where he is."

She continues, "I heard he had eyes on a promotion to the Chief's office, and he's pissed he's not going to get it.

"You know this for a fact?"

"Yep." A sly smile appears on her face. "I have my sources, you know." She pops an olive stuffed with blue cheese into her mouth.

"Yeah, I know you do. You guys in the OCME office have connections all over the city.

She touches her glass to mine. "Touché.

"Now, enough about him. He doesn't deserve our time. How are your mom and dad? What's happening out there on the prairie?"

Monica never fails to ask about my parents. Hers passed away a number of years ago. They always stayed back in Toronto, their first port of entry when they immigrated. They'd left their professional lives and home country to give Monica the advantages of life in the West. She's told me of their sacrifices so she could go to medical school without worrying about finances. She had been so proud to give back to them once she graduated and she often talks about them. I never tire of hearing stories of when she was a little girl and watching her mom in the kitchen. I wish I could have tasted her mother's cooking.

I relay the latest news.

Monica jokes. "Maybe you'll go back and become a rancher."

When I don't laugh and pooh-pooh her idea, her dark eyes bore into mine. "No, don't tell me you're considering it.

"I just don't know, Monica," I sigh. "At the moment, nothing's off the table."

Chapter Eight

I'd planned to leave The Barrel at a reasonable time last night, but my good intentions evaporated after the second glass of wine. I could blame Monica, but it is as much my fault as hers. Consequently, I'm moving slowly on Friday morning. Scott is no more chipper.

I flop into my office chair and mumble, "How was ball practice?"

He grunts. "Too cold so we ended up in the bar and I stayed way too late." He yawns and rubs his eyes. "How was wine with our favourite M.E.?"

"I should have gone home earlier, too, but Monica let me know Turnbull's cause of death, so there was reason to celebrate."

I ignore my headache and grab the marker for the whiteboard.

Scott looks up from resting his forehead in his hands. "Oh really?"

"Yes, really. Remember, I told you she'd taken some tissue samples from Turnbull's back? Lab results came back finding traces of insulin."

Near the top of the whiteboard, I write 'COD: INSULIN OVERDOSE'

"Now she's trying to narrow down what kind of insulin so we can tie it to Shark's supply."

His usual grin returns. "So, we're looking for someone that Turnbull was comfortable letting into the condo, and someone, in addition to Shark, who had access to a particular kind of insulin and syringe."

"Right, and presumably whoever has the insulin would also have the know-it-all to inject it."

Scott scratches his chin. "I doubt that takes a brain surgeon."

He leaves his desk and returns in a few minutes with a couple cups of coffee. "When I got in this morning, I called Corbin's fiancée again. Again, no answer, so I emphasized, *call us, or else* sort of thing."

He follows my gaze to the persons-of-interest on the board. "In the meantime, let's talk to Rutland, Armstrong's fiancé. See what he will tell us about Erin and her beef with Sophia."

Scott reaches for his notes. "I've got his number here."

I glance over at the boss's office. "I'll let Ash know about the COD. Media Relations may want to do an update. Keep your fingers crossed we don't have to show up at a press briefing."

* * *

A property developer, Arnold Rutland makes money by bulldozing wide tracts of expansive foothills and rich farmland to build oversize houses for others who make more in one hour than people who hold menial jobs make in a month. Driving past the city's largest homeless shelter on the way to his office illustrates the vast gulf between the rich and the poor.

The marble mezzanine in the Rutland Developments building features an inlaid, gold, company logo, similar to the one we saw in the foyer at his house. His assistant asks what type of coffee we would like, listing an impressive menu. I settle for a regular. Just plain.

We wade through thick wool broadloom to sit on comfortable, upholstered chairs in Rutland's inner sanctum. His office looks west to the mountains; his credenza displays photos of his children and polo ponies. I don't see a picture of Erin. He stands to shake our hands. "How can I help our city's finest officers?"

The sleeves of his crisp white shirt are neatly rolled to just above his elbows. The man's short, so he looks me straight in the eye. His handshake is firm and dry. He motions for us to sit facing his desk, and at an oblique angle to the windows, just as his assistant delivers our coffee, along with biscotti and crystal glasses of water, on a silver tray. Rutland's beverage is mounded with white froth.

Rutland says, "Thank you, Marcus. That will be all."

I wait until the door closes. "We appreciate your seeing us on short notice, Mr. Rutland. Erin may have already told you about our conversation with her about the booking of your wedding reception at the Pallisades."

He looks puzzled. "Erin and I haven't spoken more than a few words in the last couple of days. She's busy with work at her firm and planning the wedding, and I'm burning the midnight oil with deadlines on my current project. So no, I didn't know you'd talked to her. But if this has to do with the wedding, you should know I'm not involved in its planning. It's all in Erin's hands. I just pay the bills and show up when she tells me to." He sighs and rolls his eyes. "It's her big day. I've endured the whole wedding rigmarole before, and I'd be just as happy to get married in front of a marriage commissioner with a couple of witnesses."

Although I am not inclined to believe that his fiancée didn't mention an interview with the police, if what he says is true, I look forward to his unrehearsed reactions.

"I don't think we'll stump you with any of our questions, Mr. Rutland."

"Well then, go ahead." He nods, glancing at me before letting his eyes drift to the view out the window.

"You're getting married on December twenty-first?"

"Yes, that's the date going on the invitations."

"And as far as you know, everything is going smoothly?"

He shakes his head and brings his focus back into the room and onto me. "Oh, good Lord, no. Erin is in a perpetual tizzy about something. If it isn't about her dress, it's about the flowers, or about the colour of the bridesmaids' dresses."

He clenches the muscles in his jaw. "I'm going to marry the girl, but good God, she's spoiled. Figures she should get whatever she wants. Never takes no for an answer. There were even problems with the venue, and she kept nagging for me to intervene, something that I sorely didn't want to do."

Then he grins and taps the table with his well-manicured hands. "But it turns out that my intervention isn't necessary after all. It's resolved itself and she's got the space she wanted."

"What problems was she having with the hotel?"

He pulls on an earlobe. "It was so bloody important to her to have the Crystal Ballroom. But it was already booked. As far as I'm concerned, there are plenty of other suitable places. But she said she had to have it. And the date, too. The winter solstice."

"What did she want you to do?"

"As I said, she wanted me to go to the General Manager and apply pressure. I wasn't about to do that, and to be honest, I would rather have the reception at the Country Club."

He pauses. "But she told me the hotel called and said it was available if she still wanted it."

I file away the fact that they've spoken enough that he knows she recently heard from the hotel about the venue being available, yet she didn't mention a visit from the police. Did she not tell him? Or is he not telling us about it?

"Do you know why it suddenly opened up?"

"I'm sure she said, but I can't remember." He sighs. "I'm in the middle of negotiations on a new development. I don't have time for wedding nonsense."

With these next questions to confirm Erin's whereabouts on Saturday night, I could lose Rutland's cooperation, so I tread carefully.

"We are investigating an incident that took place on Saturday and are confirming the whereabouts of a number of individuals on that evening. If the hotel had tried to contact you on the weekend, Saturday evening, would you or Erin have been home to take the call?"

"I wouldn't have been. I was at a fundraiser in Banff." He pulls out his phone and looks at his calendar, as if he needed to confirm what he was doing just a few days earlier. Something catches his eye, and he taps and scrolls.

"Was Erin with you?"

He pauses scrolling for a moment. "Uh, no, she didn't go. She usually enjoys going to these things, but she decided to stay home. She'd been out of sorts all afternoon and I have to say, I was relieved. She wouldn't have been good company."

"What did she do instead?"

"She said she was going to stay in, watch movies, get groceries, and run some errands. Catch up on sleep. Typical weekend things."

His phone pings, and Rutland takes a look, scrolling through a text, apparently.

I glance at Scott. He gives a slight nod of encouragement. I have my poker face in place when Rutland put his phone down, face up on the desk in front of him.

Scott returns to quietly taking notes.

"Ah, where was I? Oh yes, I left the city late afternoon on Friday. I stayed the night, had a few meetings on Saturday, and went to the event. If Erin had been with me, we would have stayed another night, but since she wasn't there, I came back to the city."

"That was on Saturday evening? What time did you get back?"

"Yes, Saturday. I left as soon as the speeches were over, so I got home about eleven."

"Erin was home when you got back?"

"Oh yes, she was home. She was still in a foul mood. I'd hoped that having the day to herself would cheer her up, but if anything, she was worse."

I'm surprised Rutland has shown no disinclination to answer my questions. He is either distracted, or he doesn't have a care in the world about having the police talk to him.

His reputation as a shrewd businessman is at odds with how congenial and chatty he is being with us. "Mr. Rutland, do you and Erin drink champagne?"

He cocks his head, looking puzzled at the abrupt change of subject, but answers readily. "On special occasions, of course. Not frequently. Erin might drink it more often. You'd have to ask her."

"We're following up some details. Would you have purchased two bottles of Bollinger Extra Brut Champagne last week?"

"No, I didn't, but Erin might have." He reaches for the phone. "I can call and ask her if you'd like?"

"No, thank you. That's fine."

He shrugs and settles back in his chair.

I continue, keeping my fingers crossed and voice light, hoping he'll continue to freely answer my questions. "You said Erin was angry about the ballroom being booked. Do you know who had booked it?"

He answers without giving the question much thought. "No, I don't." Then he looks out the window for a moment. "Ah, yes, I think Erin said it was Sophia Turnbull. I could be wrong."

"And you know Turnbull?"

"Yes. We've met at the restaurant. I've also run into her at some charity functions. I know her well enough to say hello, but that's about it."

"Does Erin know Sophia?"

"Peripherally, definitely, from dinners at the restaurant, but I don't know if they know each other socially. Again, you'd have to ask her." His phone pings, and he glances down at it, attention again drawn to the device.

Out of the corner of my eye, I see Scott shift in his seat, waiting for the reaction to my next statement.

"Actually, Mr. Rutland, were you aware that Sophia Turnbull has been murdered?"

Distracted by his phone, it takes a moment for this to sink in, then his head pops up, slightly cocked. "What did you say?"

I repeat myself.

"Oh my God. How? When? What happened?"

"Saturday evening."

His posture changes as the implications of our questions sink in. His friendly, forward leaning body slowly straightens. Almost delicately, he puts his phone face-down on the desk, no longer interested in the messages pinging. "How do Erin and I fit in with this?"

I pause. "Did you speak to Erin when you were out of town on Saturday night?"

"No," he shakes his head. "I mean, why would I? And why do you care?"

"Do you know if she was home alone?"

"We don't have any staff in the house, so unless she had someone over, she would have been alone." His lips form a thin line as he looks at Scott and me. "Does Erin need a lawyer?"

Rutland's good-natured cooperation ends when he senses Erin is a person-of-interest in our investigation. He stalks over to his office door and yanks it open. He stands to the side, and I assume we are being asked to leave. I thank him for his time.

Scott leaves first, and just as I reach the door, I turn, Columbo-style, "Mr. Rutland, it slipped my mind. Are you or Erin diabetic?"

I am close enough that I smell his coffee-tainted breath when we're told to, "Fuck off."

Deep in thought, I trail Scott back to the Ford. "Interesting conversation, wouldn't you say?"

Scott starts the car, then looks at me. "Yah, he went right to asking if she needs a lawyer. What would your first reaction be?"

I snort. "I don't count. I'm a cop. First, I'd deny everything. Then ask for a lawyer. But then, I know if I'm being asked about it, I'm being fingered for it."

Scott laughs. "Yah, me too."

I stare straight ahead, thinking about the interview. "I should have waited until after we got the insulin question answered before I started digging around for alibis. That was a rookie mistake."

Scott tries to make me feel better. "At least we know Erin was in town. Now we need to put her in the condo."

He shoulder-checks and pulls into traffic. Scott drives and I stare out the window. It's a blah day, matching my mood.

When Nguyen sees us walking into the bullpen, he gathers papers from his desk and meets us at the whiteboard. Marshall yawns and slowly pushes to his feet. Is he actually reluctant to work on this case, with me as the lead, or is he putting on a show for his buddies?

Once both are leaning against my desk, I tell them. "The boss texted me. There's a press conference at 4 PM. I have to be there, but Ash is giving the rest of you a bye. We'll announce the Turnbull death as a homicide. Timing is such that it can make the evening news. Wayne, tips should pick up."

He loses the vacant look and nods. "Yep, probably. I've had a few calls come in, but nothing actionable. I'll hang around until the news is over, just in case. Then I'll have the front desk route calls to the guys I've lined up for the rest of the weekend. If anything sounds time sensitive, they have my number. I'll re-canvas the neighbours in the morning. If anything pops up, I'll let you know."

I make eye contact with Nguyen. "Anything more on backgrounds? Pawnshops?"

He shakes his head. "No, and I doubt anything will come this late in the day. And probably nothing over the weekend either. Pawn shop detail got back. No necklace has shown up so far, but they'll continue to monitor.

"I popped into the scene like you asked and checked for any containers of disinfectant wipes. There was a container of bleach in the laundry room, but I couldn't find any wipes."

"Thanks, Lance.

"Anyone see any problem with releasing the scene back to Shark?"

I wait to see everyone shake their heads. "Right then, I'll let him know he can go home. Anything else we need to talk about before the weekend? If not, then see you guys on Monday."

They nod, leaving Scott and me at our desks.

I pull up Shark's number and dial. The call goes to voice mail. "Maxwell, this is Detective Maidstone. You are free to go home. If you notice anything missing, or have questions, please don't hesitate to call me. In particular, if you find Sophia's aquamarine pendant, let me know right away."

I follow that up with a call to the office coordinating the watch on the condo door, letting them know they can pull off the security tape.

That task completed, I scribble on the whiteboard and end up putting reminders for next week in my phone. Scott had been writing up his notes, but now he's got his feet on his desk, texting someone, probably lining up a drink.

I'll take some time for myself this weekend instead of working. That time won't include Terry. He texted me yesterday with a terse apology for being a dick on Wednesday night, but I'm not ready to let bygones be bygones. And I'm definitely not in the right frame of mind to have it out with him yet.

It's difficult to find good dating material. Looking for someone on the police service isn't a good idea. Dating a cop would mean never getting away from work. And besides, my ex-husband was a cop and look how that turned out.

Scott interrupts my thoughts. "Hey, I'm heading out for drinks with a couple of guys from the ball team. Wanna join us?"

"Huh?" I'm not usually included in his social plans, so I'm immediately suspicious about his intentions. "No, I've got the press conference."

"You can always come by after. Those media things never last long."

I squint. "Have you forgotten that I'm dating Terry?"

"No, and it doesn't mean you can't come out for a drink after work with me and my friends. Unless things have changed, you two aren't exactly serious." He glares at me. "Are you?"

"No, we're not." I'm over-tired and chippy, so I snap back. "But what if we are?"

"I don't know. It just seems sudden."

"Sudden? We've been seeing each other for months now. And we've known each other since we were kids."

"Not that I'm keeping track, but you weren't seeing him last Christmas, so you've been with him for, what, four months? How much do you really know about him?"

I shrug. "Enough, I guess. Like you say, we're not exactly serious. No one's planning a future together."

"Good."

I must be in a real crappy mood 'cause I'm not willing to let Scott off the hook. "What does that mean?"

"I don't know. It was just something to say."

"Come on. I know you don't like him. What's the problem?"

Scott shakes his head. "It's none of my business. Let's just drop it, okay?"

Part of me wants to get things out in the open and find out what Scott has against Terry but now is not the time. I don't want to argue with my partner, especially about personal stuff.

"Okay. No problem. But are you trying to set me up?"

He feigns being hurt and furrows his brow. "Of course not."

"Scott," I growl. Why am I defending a relationship with Terry? I'm uncertain about this guy, so why aren't I jumping at an opportunity to get to know someone else? And why am I jumping down Scott's throat?

"Well, maybe. One of the new guys, Dave, is single and seems like a nice guy. He just moved here from California. I just thought maybe…"

"Nope. Wouldn't feel right." I shake my head but smile to let him know I'm not pissed.

* * *

The press briefing runs smoothly and Ash stick-handles the few questions from reporters in the first row like a pro. However, they pay little attention to Turnbull and show more interest in how crowds will be handled if Calgary advances in the hockey playoffs. I feel a pang for Sophia. Tonight's headlines will cover the latest high-profile trades in the hockey world, shenanigans of a spoiled and self-indulged reality star and a dog who rescued a kid from a storm pond. Surely Sophia's life deserves more coverage.

I mope on the way home but shake it off when I walk through the front door. I savour the silence, interrupted only by the mantle clock marking time, and Treacle happily panting and tippy-tapping on her black and white paws to greet me. When I first brought her home from the ranch, I worried she wouldn't adjust from being a working cow-dog to a city-house dog. She had a few tentative days, anxious about the strange noises coming from outside, but she's smart and figured out the new routine quickly.

She had a conniption the first time I took her to the groomer. The only baths she'd had in the past were swims in the river and dugout or runs through tall grass after a rain. She didn't know what to make of the tubs and sprays at SuperPups. Her drooping ears and tucked tail conveyed her embarrassment. When the humiliation of the experience ended with lots of belly rubs and a cube of real cheddar, though, she had a change of mind and pranced proudly out to the car.

I kneel down and give her a hug and scratch. "Just give me a minute, old girl, to get changed, then we'll go for a walk."

Treacle's tail is wiggling back and forth, excited about the prospect of supper when we get back from our walk around the park. I pour nuggets into her bowl, and she's finished by the time I've poured myself a glass of wine.

For a moment, I gaze into a photo I've framed and put on the wall beside the fridge. It's of me and my favourite mare, taken not long before I left to join the police. I've got on my old work coat, the one that's warm enough to wear in the dead of winter when the wind is driving snow across the prairie. It's not a pretty photo, but one that feels like home. I look at it now and wonder how I'd feel if I was back in the old house.

I perch on one kitchen stool and put my feet up on the other as I flip through the mail. As usual, it's mostly junk, except for a letter from my sister, Emily. Every week she sends something. Whether a note, card or letter, it's always hand-written and upbeat. Though I left the ranch almost two decades ago, she says she still misses having me live just down the road.

She's a chatterbox, even on paper, filling me in on town gossip. Between the news she harvests at the hospital, and the scuttlebutt her plumber husband brings back from his coffee buddies, she has all bases covered. She passes along enough that I know about everybody's business. If I have to go back and take over the ranch, at least I'll be up to date on the lowdown.

I should give lip service to cleaning my house tonight, but when my dog whines and glances over at the couch, I agree with her.

"Good idea, girl. Let's watch a few episodes of Bridgerton and have that leftover lasagna."

I fall asleep with the empty plate on my lap, and her at my feet.

Chapter Nine

Media vehicles are parked up and down the street when I get to the office off Westwinds on Monday morning. I push through the crowd of reporters milling about in front of the building, keeping my head down so those that recognize me don't mob me for comments on whatever reason it is that they're here.

In the normally tidy and subdued squad room, desks are littered with abandoned coffee cups. Garbage cans overflow with pizza boxes and take-out containers. Noses are glued to computer monitors; terse, tight-jawed conversations replace casual banter. The few that look up and give me a tense 'Morning' have the telltale blood-shot eyes of not enough sleep and too much screen time.

In contrast, Scott's fresh and relaxed, skimming through the weekend crime report, stopping periodically to actually read the contents.

"What's up?" I motion to the surrounding atmosphere.

He marks his place on the screen with a finger. "Triple shooting southeast of Glenmore Trail. Probably happened on Saturday night but discovered yesterday afternoon. One dead and the others critical. Looks gang related. Also, a home invasion last night. Homeowners were roughed up and one is in the hospital in serious condition. They're not sure yet, but there could be a connection between all of this and the shooting on the C-train line last week."

I shrug off my jacket and settle into my chair, turning on the computer and pulling notes out of my desk. "That explains the media out front."

"Yah. They're getting a briefing at nine.

"Ash pulled Nguyen and Marshall in on it. I talked to them before they left for the scene, though. Marshall's got a couple of civilian members to help out with tips when he's away. And he went back and canvassed the condo building on Saturday. Nada. No one saw or heard anything.

"Atkin's left us a spreadsheet of all the orders and warrants issued and requested. It's all but spit-polished. It's on the shared drive, but I printed a copy." Scott points to a sheet of paper on his desk.

"Give me a few minutes then we can get out of this madhouse and go for a coffee."

"Sounds good," I mumble. Nothing in my in-basket requires an immediate reply, so I turn to the social media accounts for the key players, including the restaurant itself. Condolences continue to pour onto the Sophia's on Seventeenth accounts. Mixed in with the genuine and tasteful expressions of sympathy are social media junkies posting overwrought lamentations of grief, and trolls making rude noises. I'm looking for something out of the ordinary which might be a clue to a grudge resolved: a 'she got what she deserved' comment. I check her DMs, hoping to find a mention of her pregnancy to someone. If she told anyone, I haven't seen it.

Scott sits back from his monitor. "Let's go."

I pull myself out of the rabbit hole of on-line platforms.

We duck out the back of the building to avoid the media scrum. Right across the parking lot, there's a local beanery. It's got a reasonable noise level — loud enough that we're comfortable discussing work, but quiet enough we can hear each other without yelling. We find a table in the corner and sip our coffees.

"We need to re-interview Shark," I say.

"Agreed." Scott scrapes the thick glaze off his cranberry scone. "He's got the strongest motive to get rid of her, especially if their relationship was on the rocks and he was afraid of getting turfed. Or, if he knew about the pregnancy and wasn't the father, that might have fueled the idea that he was going to get pushed aside. The thing is, I'm not getting bad vibes from him. At least as far as murder goes, anyway."

"I know. I agree. He's got motive but nothing about the trace points to him. And talking about trace, I'll call around to the manufacturer of the eyelash extension today. See if they have a list of places using that brand."

Scott finishes his coffee with one gulp. "I'll help later, but I'm going to run out and follow up some details the prosecutors want on my hit and run from last month. It shouldn't take long."

"No problem." I say.

We head our separate ways: me back through the back door to the office, and Scott to the parking lot.

I've never been a fan of desk work. Who is? Today, with little hope of quickly tracking down the salons who applied the extensions, is going to be a long one.

Al's provided the name of the eyelash extension manufacturer in his report. I find the number for the Canadian distributer, but when I get someone on the line, I get bounced from one person to another when I ask for a list of the estheticians in the area using their product. I sigh with relief when someone finally knows what they're talking about. "Yes, I can send that to you right away."

Within five minutes of hanging up, I hear a ding from my in-basket. Once downloaded, the list of salons using the product is over a page long. I print it out and start to dial.

I'm only part way through by the time Scott gets back. I give him half the remaining numbers and grumble. "After all the effort we're putting in over this stupid eyelash, we better find someone with a direct connection to Sophia."

We work the phones until lunchtime, when Scott stretches and tosses a crumpled piece of paper my way.

"I'm going for lunch with a friend. You can join us if you want."

I rub my computer-weary eyes. "Where are you going?"

"The buffet at the Indian place next to Pengally's."

I'm torn. I brought my lunch today, but the sound of butter chicken is too good to pass up. The cheese and pickle sandwiches will keep until tomorrow, so I yank my jacket off the back of the chair. "Let's go."

Chapter Ten

We're on our way to re-interview Maxwell Shark, ten days after he found his fiancée's body. We haven't told him we're coming.

A middle-aged man and his beagle are at the main entrance when we arrive at the condo building. The dog is friendly, sniffing our shoes while his owner gives us a suspicious up-and-down as we approach.

I flash my badge. "Good morning, sir. We need access to the building."

The man takes a moment to study first mine, then Scott's identification. "Sorry," he says. "You can never be too careful."

"No need to apologize," I say, as he holds the heavy front door open. Scott reaches for the door and nods for the man to proceed into the building.

To pass the time while standing in front of the elevator doors, I say, "This is a beautiful building. Have you lived here long?"

Now that he's established we aren't here to rob the place, he's eager to interact. "Yep. Almost ten years." He looks down at the beagle. "Charlie was just a puppy when we moved in."

I hunker down. "May I give him a scratch?"

"Oh, by all means."

I love how dogs communicate without artifice. Charlie doesn't hesitate but leans into my hand while his tail does the windshield wiper thing.

"You're a sweetheart," I croon.

The man beams. "Yes, he is. I don't know what I'd do without him. He gets me out walking first thing every morning and keeps me fit as a fiddle."

The man's attention isn't solely on his dog. He chews the inside of his lip, and his eyes flick back and forth between Scott and me. No doubt, he's bursting with curiosity, just not sure if he can come right out and ask what we're doing here. He licks his lips, about to open his mouth and ask us, when the elevator door opens.

He and Charlie are expecting us to get into the elevator with them, but Scott and I step back.

Scott tells him, "You go ahead. We'll wait for the next one."

We don't want to add to the building gossip by pushing the button for the seventeenth floor.

* * *

Scott knocks on Shark's door. His hand is poised to knock again when the door opens.

Maxwell's come to the door wearing blue plaid pajama bottoms slung low on his hips. I could do laundry on his washboard abs.

Black stilettos lay a kilter beside the door and a Coach handbag rests on the quartz-topped entrance table. The rich, smoky aroma of freshly brewed coffee tickles my nose, and mellow jazz fills the condo with a lazy vibe.

Shark notices my glance at the women's shoes and steps in front of them so they're partially hidden. He barks. "Have you found out who killed Soph yet?"

It's interesting that he's asked who killed Sophia, and not what killed her, but since I have no intention of letting him lead the conversation, I ignore his question.

"We have a few more questions for you, Mr. Shark."

He rolls his eyes, but motions for us to sit at the glass top dining table. "Excuse me for a moment," he says, and heads back to the bedroom. We pick the chairs with our backs to the light coming through the window.

From down the hall, we hear murmuring, and the sound of a door gently closing. He stops in the kitchen and returns with a cup of coffee. He doesn't offer us one. "Ask away."

The more I'm around Shark, the more I dislike him. He's arrogant, and having female company so soon after his fiancée died is disgusting. How committed could he have been? This makes it easier to suspect him, but that still doesn't mean he actually did it.

I don't waste time with pleasantries. "Who has access to your condo?"

"I already told you when you first grilled me. Me, the maid and personal assistant."

"No one else has a key?"

"Oh, well, Corbin does."

"Anyone else?"

"I don't think so. Sophia gave me a key when I moved in, and I've never had it copied."

He thinks for a moment. "Unless the building manager does."

I pepper him with more questions. Most of them, I've asked before, but we'll compare his responses and see if his story matches up. Can he think of anyone who had a grudge against Sophia? Did he know of anyone who may want to get back at him through hurting Sophia?

"How well did Sophia and Bradley Corbin's fiancée, Barbara Stephens, get along?"

He gives a one-shoulder shrug. "I don't know. They both come from old money in the city, so they knew each other through connections. Both members of the Glencoe Club and Ranchman's Club. At least their dads were."

"The last time we spoke, you told us that Barbara is sometimes difficult to get along with. Did she and Sophia have issues?"

"Uh, no, not really." He partially closes his eyes in thought. "But now that I think about it, there was a time when Bradley and Sophia were standing next to each other at a function, and it seemed like Barbara pushed between them more forcefully than was necessary. I didn't think anything of it till now."

"When did this happen? Can you remember?"

Shark nods. "For sure. It wasn't that long ago. It was a fund raiser reception for the zoo. Bradley and Barbara were there. They were standing at a high-top with drinks, and Sophia and I came over. Soph stood next to Bradley, and Soph was wearing really high heels. I remember that because she didn't usually wear them 'cause they hurt her feet. Anyway, Barbara went around and shoved between Bradley and Soph. Like pushed her way in between them hard enough that it knocked Soph off balance. She spilled her drink and probably would have fallen, except I caught her.

"Other than that, I can't think of anything in particular. Why?"

"Bradley Corbin seems to think they talked regularly."

Shark shakes his head. "No, I'm pretty sure they didn't."

"Did Sophia mention to you she was pregnant?"

Shark huffs. "Don't you remember any of my answers from before? No. Soph did not tell me she was pregnant. That's not something I'd forget. But I didn't want kids, and she knew it, so maybe that's why she didn't tell me. Maybe she was just going to get rid of it and didn't think she needed to discuss it with me."

"And you would have been okay with that?"

He snorts, "Her body. Her decision."

I glance over to Scott, who's sitting at the head of the table, at right angles to both Maxwell and me. His lips tighten and his head gives a miniscule shake. This is a topic that's come up in our conversation. We both agree with the idea that it was a woman has the right to make her own decision, but Shark is coming across as an uncaring moron.

I bite my tongue and nod. "You lived together — you didn't notice that she'd missed a few periods? She didn't have any morning sickness? Nothing to make you wonder?"

Maxwell starts to shake his head, then pauses to think. "Well, it didn't even cross my mind. Why would it?" He sits back. "There were a couple times she turned down wine, and I thought that was weird. But pregnant? Nah."

I probe. "Now that you've had some time to think about it, if you're not the father of the baby, who would be?"

He shakes his head. "No idea."

"What would you have done if you'd found out she was pregnant?"

"Ah," he carefully answers my question, "She knew I couldn't have kids and always said it didn't matter 'cause she didn't want them either. If she was pregnant, I don't know what I'd do."

He shrugs. "I wouldn't have been happy, but I woulda gone along with whatever she wanted to do. I mean, I wouldn't have broken up with her over it. But I'd want a paternity test. I'd want to know if I can father a kid. After all this time of thinking that I couldn't, it would really blow my mind."

He's slow to continue. "And, if there was someone else, I'd want to know."

I nod at Scott and let him take over the questioning.

He leans forward, resting his elbows on the table. "I can't help but notice you have company."

Maxwell looks up quickly, first at Scott, then at me.

Scott pointedly looks down the hall, and continues, "I have to be honest with you, Max. It seems awfully quick to have company, so soon after Sophia has died."

Maxwell just shrugs.

Scott presses. "Is this someone you've been seeing? Or is this someone new?"

"Not that it's any of your business, but she's an old friend. She came over to give her condolences, and we had a couple drinks. One thing led to another. You know how things go." Maxwell doesn't look like he has any regrets.

"Mind giving us her name?"

"Why d'ya want to know? She hasn't done anything wrong." He's riled at Scott's question.

"No, I'm not saying she has. Do you have a problem with us knowing who she is?"

"Well, no, I don't. I think it's an invasion of her privacy."

I stand up. "I'll just go ask her myself."

"Ah, no," Maxwell quickly says, "no reason to bother her."

I want to check Maxwell's story before he's had a chance to coordinate it with the woman in his bed. "Sit down, Maxwell. You and Scott can chat, and I'll be right back."

Maxwell doesn't look happy, but slumps down in his chair.

I tap on the bedroom door, "Janice Maidstone with Calgary City Police. May I come in?"

"Ah, yes, just a minute." There's a moment of fabric rustling, then, "All right, come in."

Sitting in bed, with the covers tucked high around her waist, and wearing what looks to be a man's shirt, an attractive woman looks flustered. In the morning light, her cheeks seem unnaturally pink. She's about Sophia's age, I estimate.

I start by saying, "To set you at ease, you're not in any trouble. I would like to ask you a few questions, though, if that's okay with you."

She relaxes slightly, colour fading to a more natural shade. With a quick, nervous smile, she says, "Oh, uh, I have to admit I'm a little embarrassed. It probably doesn't look very good for me to be here. I mean, Sophia's gone, and well, you know..."

"Don't worry, I'm not here to judge. What's your name?"

"Tanya Wilson. I'm a friend of Sophia and Maxwell."

She volunteers, "I came over last night to offer my condolences to Maxwell. In hindsight, I should have met him someplace else for coffee or something."

"Why do you say that?"

She picks at an imaginary loose thread on the duvet. "Well, it looks pretty skanky to get all dressed up, and come over here in the evening to just say sorry-about-your-loss, doesn't it?"

I have to agree with her, but don't. Instead, "Again, Ms. Wilson, I'm not here to judge. Can you tell me, did you have a prior relationship with Maxwell, or was this just a one-off situation?"

She touches her cheek, "Oh my God, no. Maxwell and I never... I mean, I was more friends with Sophia. And I, well yes, I've always found Maxwell attractive, but I never, ever thought about sleeping with him. I truly came over to give my condolences, but after a couple of drinks, well, let's say I had a lapse of judgement."

She looks over to her clothes tossed on the dresser. "Trust me, this will never happen again."

I nod, encouraging her to continue talking. "Tanya, you said you were more friends with Sophia. Did she say anything to you about a disagreement with anyone? Someone she was afraid of?"

"No, she didn't. But you know, we were casual friends, and to be honest, we only talked or got together a few times a year. The last time I talked with her was probably New Years."

I'm satisfied with the woman's answers and don't think she has much to offer the investigation. "Thank you, Tanya. I'll leave you be."

I leave the room and behind me, I hear her scrambling out of bed. I wonder if our visit here has cut short the intimate morning Maxwell might have planned.

He and my partner are discussing baseball when I get back to them. We bid him good morning, and when in the elevator, I say to Scott, "Maxwell's quite the guy."

Scott's still shaking his head when we leave the building in the bright sunshine. He drops me off at the station for a lunch of the left-over pickle and cheese sandwich from yesterday, while he heads back out for more palatable fare. He doesn't bring his lunch from home nearly as often as I do.

I'll use the time to prepare for our afternoon interview with Armstrong. She made googley-eyes at Scott the first time we talked to her. Flirtatious. Maybe she feels more powerful and in control when expressing her sexuality, and would prefer to talk to Scott, but we want her on the back foot. I'll ask the questions this time.

* * *

Erin Armstrong is a design consultant in a boutique firm with a reputation for exclusive interiors and commensurate prices. It occupies two floors in a recently built sandstone structure along Tenth Avenue. We tell the receptionist at the polished steel front desk that we have an appointment with Ms. Armstrong. He assures us someone will be with us in a moment.

We cool our heels for over fifteen minutes before an assistant arrives, slightly out of breath. Her pencil skirt is wrinkled and twisted, with the back seam well off centre. Bright sunshine coming through the large windows emphasizes dark circles under her eyes.

Did Erin make us wait to impress us by how busy she is?

We follow the assistant down an interior staircase and along a hallway with deep, plush carpet. Through open office doors, I see drafting tables and side credenzas piled high with rolls of blueprints, fabric swatches, tile samples and flooring of all kinds. Occupants hunched over their work don't glance up, absorbed by the telephones pasted to their ears and eyes glued to design specs.

The assistant leaves us at an open door and scurries away. Erin's office is tidier than the others, with materials neatly stacked in distinct groupings on the side credenzas. A diorama of a housing development, with an inlaid gold Rutland Developments logo, occupies most of the floor space.

Erin acknowledges our presence. Her mouth moves a fraction. It could be a smile. She doesn't bother to get up from her chair or offer any apology for keeping us waiting.

Her navy suit looks couture. The V-neck shell worn underneath the jacket dips low enough to show cleavage, but not so far as to be provocative. Her red hair is loosely tied back, giving an appropriate business-like appearance for the pretentious design firm. Deep red matte lipstick looks freshly applied.

I feel her cool appraisal as she takes in my utilitarian golf shirt and khakis, sensible shoes and makeup-free face. I am dismissed. Scott, however, receives a warm, somewhat sultry smile, showing lots of very white, very straight teeth. For a woman about to be married, she gives off predatory vibes.

"I have a meeting with a client in a few minutes. What can I help you with?"

We sit down in the two client chairs across from her desk. She purses her lips, not impressed.

Although she directed her question to Scott, it's me who answers. "When we spoke a few days ago…" I look down and make it appear that I'm checking my notes, even though I know every detail of that conversation.

"You said you had discovered it was Sophia Turnbull who had booked the same wedding venue."

Ms. Armstrong drags her eyes away from Scott. "Correct."

"Did you contact Ms. Turnbull to discuss this?"

She doesn't answer my question, nor does her expression change, but her eyes dart, ever so briefly, to the door and back to me. "Why do you ask?"

I pause, expecting her to fill the silence.

She doesn't.

"You were upset she had booked the hotel ballroom for December twenty-first."

"Yes, but I don't understand how that had anything to do with her death." Armstrong argues.

I let my question hang in the air, unanswered. To let her think I'd forgotten it. And then I introduce a completely different topic. "Have you recently purchased champagne? Specifically, Bollinger Extra Brut?"

"I buy it occasionally," she admits.

"When was the last time you had occasion to purchase a bottle?" Her eyes flick to the door again.

"I cannot recall. Perhaps a couple of months ago when I had friends over."

"Just one bottle?"

Her heavily lined and shaded eyes narrow. "I can't remember."

I now go back to an earlier question, the one that she tried to avoid answering. "Did you contact Sophia Armstrong after you found out she had booked the reception venue on December twenty-first?"

Maybe she thinks she can avoid an out-and-out lie by just shaking her head.

"Are you sure?" I ask, then pause for a moment before adding. "We found a bottle of Bollinger Extra Brut in her condo."

She hesitates before answering. "What does that have to do with me? It wouldn't surprise me if she also liked it."

I persist. "You're sure you didn't take a bottle over? We have a receipt showing you purchased two bottles the day before her murder, and then a bottle of the same champagne shows up in her condo."

She lifts her chin slightly when she answers. "I'm sure lots of people purchase that champagne. Just because I did, it doesn't mean I had anything to do with her death."

"What would you say if we found fingerprints on the bottle? Would you be concerned they could be yours?"

She purses her lips, narrowed eyes darting from me to Scott. Is she wondering if she failed to wipe the bottle clean of prints? I hold my breath. Surely, she's going to stop talking to us and demand legal counsel.

She pushes back from her desk and stalks over to the office door. After she's softly closed it, she returns to her desk and snaps at us. "I have nothing to hide, so alright, yes, I took a bottle over, but I didn't hurt her."

I keep my expression neutral, but my heart rate doubles.

I switch to using her first name. "Thank you, Erin. What happened?"

She licks her lips. There's little left of the freshly applied red lipstick. "I, uh, found her address and went to her condo."

"How did you get her address?"

She hesitates. "It is in a file here in the office. The firm did design work for her."

"What happened then?"

Her shoulders sag. "I thought that if we could talk about it, I could get her to understand how important the solstice and the ballroom are to me. I can be very persuasive and knew I could convince her to find another place for her wedding."

"How did you get into her building?"

"It was easy. I waited outside the doors, pretending to talk on my phone. It didn't take long until someone was leaving, and then I slipped in before the doors closed. No one really cares, you know. If you act like you belong, most people assume you do."

"What time was this?"

She looks up at the ceiling for a moment. "Around seven."

I nod. "And when you knocked on her door, Sophia welcomed you into her condo?"

"Well, not at first. She was reluctant, probably because she thought I was there to sell her something, but I said that I worked with Sarah, who designed her restaurant, and through her I'd found out that we were getting married on the same day, and thought we should celebrate."

The designer shrugs. "I acted like we'd met a few times and was really friendly. I said, you know, that we could talk about our plans and that sort of stuff." Erin smiles. "After all, what bride doesn't want to talk about her wedding?"

I give what I hope she interprets as a sincere smile. "And then what happened, Erin?"

"At first, she was confused, like she didn't recognize me." Erin pauses. "And to tell the truth, I knew it was a long shot. I mean, we'd only met in passing, so it wasn't surprising that she didn't remember me." Erin looks down at her desk, re-stacking a column of flooring tiles. "I didn't mention the ballroom, though. I wanted to save that until after I'd gotten her to like me."

"And you drank the champagne?"

"Yes. I had it in a gift bag and I said I'd brought it because I thought people who were going to share the same wedding day, especially on the winter solstice, should celebrate it together. I told her I didn't know anyone else who had the same date planned, and I wanted it to be an extra way to celebrate my," she corrects herself, "our special day."

I had to ask. "What would you have done if she wasn't at home? Or if she didn't let you in?"

Unfazed, the redhead waves a hand. "No skin off my nose. If she wasn't home, I would have come back the next day or something."

She anticipates my next question, "And if she hadn't let me in, I was going to leave the bottle as a gift, anyway. You know, to lay the foundation for getting together some other time."

"Wasn't she suspicious?"

Erin nods. Her lips look dry and chapped. "She was, at first. But she warmed up once we got to talking. And then I opened the bottle. I was kinda disappointed when she said she didn't want any of it, but I poured her a glass anyway. She took a sip, then put the flute back on the table."

I still expect the young woman to clam up at any moment, but until she does, I've got plenty of questions. "Did you convince her to change her wedding venue?"

She shakes her head and frowns. "No."

"What happened?"

She sighs. "I had a few glasses while Sophia just sat there. She was pleasant enough, relaxed. Laughing at my jokes, you know, and I thought she was getting me. Like she understood where I was coming from.

"By then, we had our feet up on the coffee table and were having a good time. Things were going really well, and I thought it was time to ask if she would change her wedding venue." Erin stops, deep in thought.

I wait. "And...?"

Erin's eyes focus back on me. "She said no. And then she laughed at me."

"She what?"

"I know, right? I couldn't believe it either. She laughed at me. She said, and I quote 'Hell no!' It pissed me off. I mean, she didn't have to be mean about it. She said nothing about the date being really special. Or that the ballroom meant anything to her. She was just being spiteful. What a bitch."

Erin's not actually shouting, but she's getting there.

I risk a quick glance at Scott. His eyebrows lift, just a titch. He's enjoying her reaction. He likes it when suspects lose their cool.

Erin continues. "I told her again how the ballroom was so special to me, you know, because it reminds me of when I was a little girl and pretended to be a princess. And I was dancing with my prince."

She takes a deep breath. "You have to understand, my wedding is something I've dreamed of ever since I was little. I wasn't going to let her take it away from me."

This woman is out of touch with reality. Even the simple idea of asking another bride to change her wedding date, or venue, is farfetched. But though it sounds crazy, it's not the first time I've seen desires obfuscate rational decisions. Motives for murder are often emotionally driven, even by outwardly rational individuals. How far would this woman go to maintain her wedding fantasy?

Erin's makeup is too heavy for me to see her face flush, but where the makeup ends beneath her jaw, red blotches mar her neck. She's angry, that's obvious, but she takes a deep breath to calm herself. "She didn't have to laugh at me. I admit. I lost my temper."

"I agree, it does seem a strange reaction to laugh at you," I say.

"I know, right?" Erin says and continues. "When she kept laughing, it just made me angrier."

I ask, "How angry?"

She glares at me. "Not enough to hurt her, if that's what you're asking."

I give Armstrong a moment. "Why do you think she responded that way?"

"How the hell should I know? I didn't think she was one of those mean girls. I had enough of them in high school." Erin purses her lips. "But maybe she was. Anyway, there was no point in continuing our conversation. I figured I'd give her a call and ask her for coffee this week. Maybe be more convincing. After she laughed at me, I didn't want to waste any more of my time on Saturday night, so I left."

"She was fine when you left?"

"Yes, of course, she was fine. She was already reaching for a piece of pizza and her book when I left."

"And you left when?"

"Probably eight-thirty? I'm not sure of the exact time. No later than nine, though."

"Did anyone see you leave?"

"No, I don't think so. At least, not that I noticed."

The redhead thinks and repeats slowly. "When the hotel called me and said that I could have the ballroom, I just thought she'd changed her mind." Erin pauses and meets my eyes. "I didn't even know she was dead until you told me."

I let her last words sink into the thick carpet in the well-appointed office for a moment before switching topics again, keeping her off balance. "Are you a diabetic, Ms. Armstrong?"

She blinks and looks at Scott before looking back at me. "Huh?"

"Diabetic? Are you a diabetic?"

"No. Why would you think I'm a diabetic?"

I leave her question hanging.

She looks at me like I've got two heads. The question threw her, but I'm not sure if it's because she's feeling threatened and guilty, or if I've confused her.

I toss a few throw-away questions her way before ending the interview. "I think that's it for today. Do you have anything you want to tell us? Anything you need to share? Anything at all about you and Sophia?"

She shakes her head.

"Well, if something comes to mind, call me." I push a business card across her desk.

Just as I'm leaving the office, I turn around. "Oh, one last question, Ms. Armstrong. Do you wear eyelash extensions?"

She shakes her head, partly in confusion, partly in answer. "No, I do not."

* * *

Getting settled back in the car, the interview plays in my mind. I hit the ignition and turn to Scott. "If Armstrong did it, would she be so open to talking to us?"

Scott pulls on his seatbelt. "I find it hard to believe she'd admit to being there if she killed Turnbull." He shakes his head. "But she's got a temper and even told us she lost it when talking with Sophia. I don't know if we can rule her out."

"Okay, for argument's sake, let's say she did it. Why would she take the champagne, and then also have the insulin? Was the insulin her back-up plan? No, if Armstrong did it, it would have been a spur-of-the-moment thing. It's more likely she'd have smashed the champagne bottle over Turnbull's head, than to have the premeditation to inject her with insulin."

Scott sits, staring out the window. "So, if we believe her, then we have Turnbull alive and eating pizza about nine. Who else visited her that night? Corbin's fiancée?"

"Maybe. Why hasn't she called us back?"

"I'll get on it. In the meantime, I've got an interview with a witness on another file. Drop me off at the station and I'll get another car."

"No need. You can take this one. I've got calls to make and need some desk time."

* * *

Reports. The bane of my existence.

190

I'm still at my desk and it's after five. Ash's light is on, so he's still here, but otherwise the room is empty. I look up when I hear footsteps. He's walking toward me with a box in his arms. He plunks it on my desk.

"Janice, would you mind taking this down to the file room? It's labeled and all you have to do is put in on the clerk's desk for tomorrow morning."

It crosses my mind that he has two legs and could take it down there himself, but he's the boss. "Sure thing." I save the report I'm working on and put the screen to sleep for security, especially important since the boss is watching, and we just had a lecture last week about securing our computers when we are away from our desks.

"Thanks." He turns and stalks back to his desk.

There's no point in grumbling, so I heft the box and head to the elevators. The file room is four flights down in the basement.

I press the down button with my elbow and the door opens almost immediately. Beavins.

Like sticking my finger into an electrical socket, a shock runs through my body. I recognize it for what it is, a primitive urge to run and avoid another encounter with him. It's a foolish reaction, but one my body makes without consulting me.

Scenarios race through my mind. *Please God, make him get off the elevator on this floor.* My next thought: *wait for the next elevator.* Then, ridiculously: *put the box down and shoot him.* And finally: *don't be silly. Get on the damn elevator.*

He conjures a smarmy smile. "Hello Janice. What a pleasant surprise. That box looks heavy. Can I help you with it?"

"No. I've got it." I don't bother to smile back.

The main floor button is illuminated. I don't make a move to push the button for the basement, just in case he decides to follow me down there. I'll let him get off first.

The doors slowly close and he stands unnecessarily close to me, his aftershave making me want to hurl. "I haven't seen you around much. You been keeping busy?"

I nod. "Yes."

"We'll have to go for a drink and talk about it. Catch up on old times," he suggests, all but doing a wink, wink, nudge, nudge.

White noise pulses in my ears. I put aside the polite-girl manners my folks drummed into me.

"No, we will not have to go for drinks, coffee, or catch up on old times. Just fuck off."

He's been a cop for a long time so he's pretty good at keeping a deadpan expression, but I see a slight pull back of his chin. His eyes widen, then narrow. I feel a tinge of regret, realizing I've set myself up for retaliation down the road. But in this moment, I figure it's more important to draw a line in the sand.

"I'm sorry you feel that way, Janice. My experience and years on the force could benefit your career."

The doors slide open on the main floor, and he steps out. I swallow the stress in my throat and push the button to the basement, willing the doors to close more quickly. There's a threat in his words.

What is it about the situation with him that makes me feel powerless? If he had punched me those years ago, I would have reacted immediately by hitting him back or even filing charges. But because it was a sexual assault, I felt an unwarranted sense of shame or guilt, and it still haunts me. I have sympathy for victims of sexual violence who are reluctant to come forward. How can I tell a victim to be brave, yet not be able to internalize that message for myself?

The elevator door slides open into the well-lit basement. A file clerk is still hanging around, so I hand off the box to them.

Back at my desk, the squad room is still empty and even Ash has gone for the day. I wish someone was here so I could shoot the breeze, letting the stink of Beavins wear off.

I rake my fingers through my hair, then shake my arms loose, letting the nastiness drip off my fingers. Facing bad guys is easier than confronting the Beavins-demons.

Telling myself to get it together, it takes a few minutes to refocus on work and stop wondering what sort of pay-back the man will put in action. Whatever it is, he'd better bring his A game, because I'm not going to be his victim anymore.

Chapter Eleven

Investigations are like junk drawers. Bits and bobs of evidence, and conversations with suspects and witnesses accumulate. You remember the big pieces; they stay in front, and you see them every time you open the drawer. But some stuff gets pushed to the back and forgotten. Since sometimes it's those bits that are the most valuable, periodically we need to empty the drawer and look at what's in the dark corners.

I stand, tossing a red marker from hand to hand. Scott's at his desk, thumbing through his notes. Nguyen and Marshall have pulled chairs over.

Statistically, people are most often killed by their domestic or business partners. Our top two suspects are Maxwell Shark and Bradley Corbin. We've interviewed both guys and they have strong alibis.

I've written Erin Armstrong's name under Corbin and Shark, but my suspicions as her being the killer are fading.

I ask Scott, "Have you heard back from Stephens?"

Scott nods. "No. I tracked down a number for her parent's place in Whitefish, though. Someone answered. A friend of theirs. Apparently, her dad's just had a heart attack, and she's been at the hospital with him and her mom. I asked the friend to pass along the message to call us. Said it was important."

"Thanks, Scott. Have any of you heard rumbling about grudges against Sophia or even the restaurant? From social media, tips, anything?"

There's a chorus of shaking heads, so I move on. "Lance, did we get Shark's bank and credit card statements?"

He nods and flips back in his notes. "I went back six months. Nothing jumped out. No big purchases on the credit card except a new TV, and something that looks like entertainment..."

He glances at me. "And by entertainment, I mean escort service. Imagine what the fiancée would have done if she'd seen the credit card statement?"

I shake my head. "Is he dumb, or did he just not care if she found out?"

Scott says, "I put a check in the dumb column. If a guy's going to screw around on his lady, he can't be putting that stuff on the credit card."

I ask, "If Maxwell didn't bother to hide the cost of the escort agency, was it because he was careless, or dumb, or was it because he knew Sophia wouldn't be around to check?"

Scott scrunches his mouth back and forth. "Good points. I'll ask the best man to see if this was a regular thing." He searches his notes to find a number for the best man, and while he's on the call, Lance speaks up.

"As far as Shark's bank account goes, nothing jumped out at me. No big withdrawals."

It's not long before Scott hangs up. I perch on the desk.

"Well?"

"Fox says they used the same entertainment service last Thanksgiving for a guys' night."

Nguyen jumps on it and ruffles through the file and pulls out a sheaf of paper. "Yeah, here's the November and December statements. And..." he runs his fingers down the charges "... yep, here's a charge for five hundred bucks, just like this time."

I shrug. "Darn. Well, it was worth looking."

I slump in my chair. "How about Corbin, then? Did you look at his records?"

Nguyen nods. "He has a pattern of significant cash withdrawals from his bank account. I went back two years. Ten grand a month, and transfers in from his investment accounts whenever the bank balance gets low.

"Kind of unusual, but he's been paying by cheque to a holding company. I checked the company out, and they lease and sell used aircraft.

"His credit card shows hefty charges to Shell, which could be for aviation gas if he's filling a plane's tank. Other than that, nothing pops out."

"We're assuming neither of them has secret bank accounts or credit cards. Under different names, for example?"

Nguyen nods. "I ran them both using social insurance numbers and different spelling of their names and went back ten years. It's easy enough, though, to set up an account or credit card in an assumed name."

Scott picks up the baseball on his desk. It's a stress ball that comes in handy when he needs to think. "That would add a layer to this, implying the murderer has been planning this for a long time."

We think about this, oblivious to the office noise around us.

I say, "We're assuming that Sophia knew, or at least trusted, whoever it was, because she let them into the condo, and then get close enough to her to inject the insulin without a struggle."

Marshall mutters. "You know what they say about assuming anything. And don't forget, Sophia didn't know Armstrong but still let her into the condo."

"But both Erin and Rutland said they'd met, at least in passing. Sophia might have thought Erin looked familiar enough to let her in."

"True enough," Marshall admits.

I tap the white board column heading "Means. The insulin."

I go back to my chair, temporarily setting aside the red marker, already well-gnawed.

Scott summarizes. "We think, again assuming, that the insulin came from Shark's inventory because he says some is missing. The syringe might have come from his stash, too. At least it's the same kind. As far as access and means, it points to him."

I rock back and forth. "But that sounds too convenient. I mean, though I don't think Shark's a rocket scientist, I can't believe he'd be dumb enough to use his own stuff."

Scott tosses his stress ball in my direction. Occasionally I miss, but today I'm expecting it. I catch it and lob it back.

He raises his eyebrows to acknowledge my prowess, then says, "The batch number on the syringe tells us it comes from a US distributor."

"Is that where Shark buys his needles? Did we ask him?"

I shake my head. "Nope. Make a note to follow up with him."

Marshall argues, "But it's easy enough for anyone to get a syringe. Any pharmacy or even Costco, not to mention Amazon and all the on-line suppliers. Or it could come from someone else's personal supply 'cause Shark sure ain't the only diabetic in the city. Or it could have been filched from any of a thousand places all the way from hospitals, care homes and even vet clinics, to a friend or co-worker's supply. Frankly, I don't see how we can trace it."

"But," he jabs his Yeti coffee mug at each of us, "Tracing the insulin is a different story. You need a prescription for it, and we can trace it down to the dispensing pharmacy."

Nguyen pipes up. "As soon as we get the manufacturer from the lab, we can track it. Once we get to the pharmacy level, we'll have to get a judge to give us a General Warrant for a list of patients."

"Good plan," I say. "The last update from Al says they're still waiting for the analysis to confirm it's the same kind as Shark uses."

Leaning back in my chair, I realize I've picked up the marker again, and it's in my mouth. It's a bad habit.

More than once, these things have leaked red ink. I'm pretty sure the stuff is toxic, but I think better when I chew.

I take it out of my mouth long enough to add. "We have Corbin at the scene, for sure, until around noon. Then he's alibied at the estimated TOD. But the designer admits to being there in the evening."

Marshall shakes his head. "She's got a motive, but jeez, it sounds trivial. I mean, come on. A place to have a wedding? Worth killing over? Nah."

Scott shrugs. "Maybe, maybe not. And don't forget the whole jealousy thing with Corbin's fiancée."

We mull the facts in front of us. Scott tosses the ball back and forth, from one hand to the other. I keep an eye on it, just in case Scott sends it back to me. I'd hate to miss and ruin my record for today.

I talk around the marker in my mouth. "I checked up on the past boyfriends. Just as the Maid of Honour said, one of them is in South America. The other's in Toronto. Doesn't look like there's been any contact with either of them except a quick email at Christmas. You know, 'Merry Christmas' and that's about it."

Nguyen speaks up. "Something we haven't talked about, really, is the missing necklace. What's the significance of it missing? Was it a robbery? Maybe someone killed her for it. Or was it a spur-of-the-moment grab? Did it have significance to the killer? Maybe they'd given it to her as a present and wanted it back? Maybe jealousy 'cause she was getting married to Shark? Or did she just lose it somewhere, and the necklace has no relevance?"

Scott says, "Shark says she had it before they started going out. He thought her dad might have given it to her but doesn't really know. The Maid of Honour didn't know either."

"Maybe it's from a secret admirer?" Marshal posits. "Or maybe not a secret admirer, but someone she wanted to keep on the down-low?"

"Or maybe she just really liked the necklace, and it didn't matter who gave it to her. Maybe we're putting too much significance on it."

Marshall, often good for an off-the-cuff remark, presents another idea. "Could it have been taken as a trophy?"

I shudder at the thought. "Oh God. Going through unexplained deaths looking for overdoses where an item is missing – I can't even guess how many instances we'd find. If we don't clear this pretty soon, we may have to go that route."

My comment elicits a chorus of groans.

Scott looks at Marshall. "How about tips? Anything of consequence?"

Marshall pulls out his notes for the first time. "No, mostly quiet. I dunno, maybe the home invasion and murders on the C-Train have diverted attention from Turnbull. There were a couple of calls I followed up on, though. One caller said she saw Turnbull out with some guy on the night in question. It turns out she confused Turnbull with the owner of the chicken place down the street. And the other caller got the dates wrong. He saw Turnbull grocery shopping, but when he checked the date on his grocery receipt, it was for the week before."

Marshall flips his notebook closed. "That's it for me. Wish I had something, but I don't."

I shake my head in frustration. "Well then, let's look at this from another way. What about Opportunity?"

Scott sighs. "Armstrong admitted she was there."

I add. "Shark was in Priddis. Corbin was at the restaurant."

Scott pouts. "And... we're back where we were an hour ago."

"You're right."

I go back to my desk, eyeing the clock on the wall. I blow out a heavy sigh. It's too early for lunch.

"Let's run through this one more time."

Scott puts his elbows on the desk and rolls his eyes, no more enthusiastic to cover the same ground than I am. Marshall slumps in his chair and grunts; Nguyen crosses his legs, glancing at his desk, longing to get back to his own files and the mounds of paper.

"Does the pregnancy factor into this?" I ask, "If Corbin knew she was pregnant, would he have brought champagne, knowing she probably wouldn't drink it?"

"But we've already established that Armstrong brought it."

"Oh, right." I say.

"How about access, then. Even accounting for all the keys, it could have been as simple as Sophia opening the door to someone who knocked, as she did with Armstrong."

Scott shakes his head. "If only the lobby security camera had been functioning properly. If only there were cameras in the elevator cars. If only..."

Our eight eyes stare at the board. Scott finally suggests. "What about outside cameras?"

I nod. "It's a fairly quiet street, so chances are there wouldn't be much traffic in and out of the building. We might get lucky and see someone go into the building who said they were someplace else.

"Is there a back entrance?"

Nguyen perks up. "I'll send the order over to the city to get access to all the cameras." He's off like a shot to his desk. I'm not sure if he's enthusiastic about the job at hand, or he's relieved to be out of our meeting. We've come to a standstill for the moment and when it seems the meeting's over, Marshall meanders back to his desk.

* * *

I've just hung up after speaking to the condo building manager when Nguyen gets back to us with the location of, and authorization to access, all city-owned cameras in the ten-block radius of Turnbull's condo. I thank him, then Scott and I open our browsers and get to work.

Later on, I tell Scott, "The building manager says there's a back entrance, but it's for egress only. There's no hardware on the outside, so unless it was propped open, no one could come in that way. And he said it's unlikely anyone would have propped the door open since there are often vagrants in the alley, and residents are conscientious about keeping the door secure.

I tap on my monitor. "We've got a traffic camera a block away from the building. I'll go through the footage later, but since it's almost noon, why don't we canvas the neighbourhood for private cameras. If we find any, we can get Nguyen on the warrants for the footage."

By lunchtime, in a bitter west wind that's whipping up dust, we've walked both sides of the street. We are not rewarded for our persistence. Only the two convenience stores relatively close to the building have cameras, but neither of them shows details of outside traffic.

We trudge into a deli in the next block and commiserate over bowls of hot soup. "I'm not looking forward to wading through all the traffic camera footage," I whine to Scott.

He's busy slurping his pho but eventually replies. "Me either, but if Nguyen helps, it shouldn't take too long. At least the time frame we're looking at isn't during rush hour!"

He pokes around the bottom of his bowl for some chicken scraps. "I've been thinking about Armstrong. If she only recently found out Sophia booked the same venue on her preferred date, would she have had time to orchestrate the murder, get the insulin and syringe? She may have been in the condo, but she didn't kill Turnbull. If we believe what she says about timing, though, she left the condo about nine o'clock. If that's the case, we're looking for someone to have administered the insulin between nine and midnight, Monica's estimated TOD. We need to check cars going through the intersection from eight to midnight."

By five o'clock, I'd love to head home for the day, but Scott and I are on a training course tomorrow and Friday. We'll have to stay tonight until we get through the camera footage.

The Police Service emphasizes training and education, and we've been assigned to a two-day workshop on cultural awareness and diversity training. The timing isn't great for us, but we already postponed our attendance last quarter. We can't miss this one without having a mark on our personnel file.

Chapter Twelve

Treacle has her dancing shoes on when I come through the front door. I drop my briefcase, grab her leash, and head right back out with her quick-stepping at my side. She's not the only one who needs fresh air. Two days sitting in a classroom was torture, and I'm looking forward to my weekend. There was a time when I probably would have trudged back into the office, but nowadays, I recognize the need to take time and recharge my batteries.

After the brief catch-up with Beth in the Medical Examiner's office last week, I feel the urge to give her a call.

She answers on the first ring and sounds delighted to hear from me. "I was hoping you'd call. Can you come out for a ride?"

I smile. "That's why I'm calling."

"How about this afternoon?"

"Ah, about one?"

"Absolutely. The weather should be perfect. Are you bringing Treacle?"

"She'd feel hard done by if I didn't." I laugh and look down at my dog. Her tail is wagging, as if she's already looking forward to trotting alongside a horse.

"And if you don't have plans for supper, I've got a roast ready to go into the oven."

"Supper sounds great!"

I hang up and scratch Treacle's ears. "What do you think, girl? Want to go out and play with the horses?"

She channels my enthusiasm and is instantly ready to go. I hurry so I don't keep her waiting.

"That was wonderful." I push back from the table. "Let me help you clean up, then Treacle and I need to head back to the city."

"Oh, forget about the dishes. Let's have tea instead. I'll tackle the dishes later."

We sit with steaming cups of herbal tea in the glassed-in porch of Beth's old farmhouse. The two-story structure is far larger than she needs, but it's been in her family for generations and she's reluctant to tear it down and rebuild.

Sneaky drafts curl in around the windows and make the flames of the candles dance and flicker. Through the windows and falling darkness, we can just make out mares and their foals stretched out on convenient piles of straw in the pasture.

I sigh, rubbing my foot on Treacle's belly in front of me. "Beth, have you always lived here? I noticed some photos on the wall in the hallway. It looked like you in front of Toronto City Hall."

"Yes, that was me. So many years ago!" Beth smiles gently. "I was born here, but went to U of T. Then I landed my dream job and found a great little apartment a stone's throw from Yonge. I loved the inner-city life."

"And yet somehow you ended up living..." I sweep my arm in front of me, "on this acreage."

"Yes, I did." She took a sip. "When I first went down East to university, I couldn't wait to come back to the Prairies, but I fell in love with the energy in Toronto. The dating scene. The convenience of my neighbourhood.

Then, when Dad got sick, I had to come back and help him. Once he got back on his feet, he still needed help, and I realized I had to make a choice to either go back or stay and help him and raise horses."

"That couldn't have been an easy decision."

"No," my friend admits. "I was in my late twenties and resented leaving the excitement of single life in Toronto behind. But coming home turned out to be the right thing. Not just for Dad and the horses, but for me, too."

"How long did it take you to figure that out?"

Beth chuckles. "Though I wasn't thrilled with it, even from the beginning I knew it was the responsible thing to do, so I made up my mind that I'd make the best of the situation."

We sit, the crackling of the fire in the pot-bellied wood stove in the corner filling the silence.

"You don't miss it?"

"I did, but not anymore."

At the risk of prying, I ask, "Why not?"

She laughs. "I missed my friends in Toronto, and the things we did together. But I realized it was up to me to keep the legacy going here. This place has been in my family for generations and I didn't want to be the one to let it slip away. This place is in my genes, and jeans too, for that matter. And I've come to love it."

"You're probably wondering why I'm asking all these questions."

From the corner of my eye, I see her nod. "I figure sooner or later you'll get around to telling me why. Does it have something to do with your family's spread in Saskatchewan?"

I startle Treacle with my sigh. "Yes, it does. Maybe you remember me telling you that my older brother Richard has been running the ranch since Dad's dementia has gotten worse?"

"I seem to recall, yes."

"Richard has decided to leave the ranch and go to The Island to raise llamas."

"Llamas?" Beth laughs. "Sorry, but it's a stretch to go from range cows to llamas. And from cactus and short-grass prairie, to Douglas fir and salal. Is he going through a midlife crisis?"

"I had the same reaction when I first heard his plans. It could be a midlife thing, I guess. He's restless, but it's mostly getting away from his ex-wife and her new boyfriend."

"Ah. I guess I can see that."

"Yah, well, even though I can understand him wanting to put distance between them, it puts me in a pickle. If I don't go back and run the ranch, I don't know if we have any alternative but to sell it."

"And what does this new man in your life have to say about it?"

"Terry? I haven't made it a point of discussion," I admit. "Honestly, his opinion won't have any bearing on my decision. We've had fun going out, but it's not going to last much longer. I'm definitely not making plans with him in mind."

Beth and I talk well into the evening. She understands both sides of my dilemma and is a good listener. Though I appreciate she doesn't spout tired platitudes, unfortunately, she doesn't offer any solution, either.

That's okay. The day with her, horses, and country air has been good for me. I'm exhausted in the best possible way, and when my head hits the pillow, I'm asleep before Treacle starts to snore.

Chapter Thirteen

Over the weekend, the drama of last week's triple shooting and home invasion was resolved when a couple of gang members stabbed each other and ended up in the hospital. Weapons found in their possession tied them back to the homicides. The knuckleheads were even wearing some of the stolen jewelry.

Guys trickling in on the day shift greet each other with fist bumps and high fives. It doesn't take long, though, until the office environment returns to normal with the murmur of voices occasionally being interrupted by outbursts of good-natured arguing and laughing.

I love the feeling of kinship in the police service. We may bicker and grumble, get involved with gossip and innuendo, but like most families, we have each other's backs when the going gets hairy.

Nguyen, Marshall, and I are having coffee when Scott comes in. He pulls up his chair and we continue to shoot the breeze until Ash walks by, looking pointedly at his watch. Time to get to work.

Scott gives us an impish grin, so broad it crinkles his eyes. I wait for a moment to see if he will break first before I ask the question he's waiting for. "Okay, you look like you swallowed a canary. What's up?"

He leans back in his chair and puts his hands behind his head. "Well, Barbara Stephens finally returned my call. She's agreed to come in to talk to us on Friday when she's back from Whitefish."

He pauses, "But I've got more. Guess who else I got a call from?"

I play along. "Let's see. You got a call from the Pirates. They're looking for a fielder." I know he still dreams of playing professional baseball, even though he's more than a decade past his prime as an athlete.

"Ha Ha, hilarious," he snaps back, but with enough singsong in his voice that I know he hasn't taken offense. "No. I'll give you one more guess."

Nguyen and Marshall are about to join in the guessing game, but I beat them to it. I try one of the other 'P' teams. "The Padres?"

This time, he rolls his eyes. "Well, better team, but still no. Because you three will never guess..." He makes a show of pulling out his notebook. "I want to make sure I have the details correct." He touches his forefinger to his tongue, then flips a few pages back and forth, dragging out the suspense. "I got a call from, drum roll please, the lovely Stephanie Campbell."

I lift my eyebrows while Marshall drawls, "The neighbour across the hall from Turnbull?"

"One and the same."

Marshall teases. "O-o-o-o, did she ask you out?"

"Pfft," Scott shakes his head. "Nope. Well, kind of." He gives a crooked smile and shrugs his shoulder. "She said she remembered something about the night Sophia was killed and wondered if we could talk about it over coffee."

"Ah ha!" I point my finger at him. "I knew it. Her eyes got all twinkly when we showed up at her door. Did she make a move on you?"

His cheeks take on a pinkish hue. "No, she was a lady. And I was a gentleman. I'll grant you, at first, I thought it was just an excuse to call me. But she really did have something."

"Do tell." I lean forward and tent my fingers. I draw out my words, still teasing, but he's got our undivided attention.

He rolls his eyes at me. "It turns out she popped out of her suite after she got home from book club to take out her garbage. The garbage chute is in a room next to the elevator. She was just leaving the room and she saw a woman get on the elevator."

"Interesting. What did the woman look like? Was it Armstrong?" My heartbeat quickens.

"No. Stephanie said the woman was a bit plump. About her height, so that would be about 5'4". Caucasian. Wearing a dark kangaroo jacket with the hood pulled up so she didn't get a good look at the woman's face."

He shrugs. "So, while the physical description doesn't tell us much, other than it doesn't sound like Armstrong, what she was wearing stood out. Stephie remembers the hoodie had a logo on it. It said 'Meadow Lake'."

I nod. "Saskatchewan?" I'm familiar with the small town in the northern part of the province. "Anything else?"

"Yes. When the woman reached out for the buttons in the elevator, Stephanie saw a bright yellow bracelet."

Marshall scowls, "Why did it take her so long to come forward with this? Didn't you talk to her the day of the murder?"

Scott nods. "Yah, we did. I asked why. She had salmon this week, and it triggered her memory. She said she had fish on that Friday, too. The day before Turnbull was murdered. She'd thrown the leftovers in the garbage, and it was stinking up her condo."

I shrug. "That sounds plausible. Too bad she didn't come forward sooner."

Scott nods. "True, but at least we have it now."

Marshall drawls, "Now we have to find a woman wearing a dark hoodie with a Meadow Lake logo and wearing a bright yellow bracelet. Should be a piece of cake." He snaps his fingers.

"So, let's go back to the building CCTV with that time stamp. See if we can pull anything off and enhance the image. Also, do any of our suspects have ties to Meadow Lake? But until that mysterious woman falls in our lap, we..." I circle my index finger to indicate all four of us, "should finish going through those license plates. And Nguyen, do the paperwork for Stephen's phone. Let's see who she's been calling while she's been ducking our calls."

As we look down at the long list of licence plate numbers in front of us, I can't resist needling Scott, "Well, when are you meeting up with Ms. Campbell again?"

Chapter Fourteen

My phone pings with an email. From Tiffany Meldrum. I read it, then share it with Scott. "The necklace? The Maid of Honour says she went through old high school photos, and didn't see it in any of them."

Scott says, "Good to know, but it doesn't help us much. It's still something she could have gotten from her dad. Or she could have bought it herself, and we have no way of knowing where or when she bought it, or if she paid cash. Or someone could have given it to her. Back to square one with that."

I'm checking the list of clients at eyelash salons, while Scott's taken over the mind-numbing task of matching plate numbers to the registered owners of vehicles going through the intersection only a block from Turnbull's condo building.

Nearing the end of the day, he grunts and heads off to the printer. He hands me the paper when he comes back to the desk. "I've got a Tiguan that came through the traffic light on Saturday around seven. It's registered to Barbara Stephens."

"When did you say she was going to come in for an interview?"

Scott puts the printout down. "She's back Thursday night. I told her to be here at 9 AM on Friday. If she doesn't show up, we'll go looking for her."

I look at the whiteboard with its list of unanswered questions. They're written in red, and it seems they pulse like heartbeats, waiting for answers.

Scott finally rubs his eyes and looks at me. "Finished going through the plates. Only interesting one was Corbin's fiancée. Any objection if I head off to ball practice?"

I shake my head. "No, go ahead. I'm going to finish up going through the list of lash clients, then I'm heading home, too."

Two cups of coffee later, and I'm only halfway through the last page when my eyes screech to a stop. I pick up my phone and dial. When I don't get an answer, I grab my coat and trot out of the office.

* * *

I pull up to the softball fourplex in the northern part of the city. Picking Scott out of the scruffy assortment of guys bundled in heavy jackets on the four diamonds is going to be a challenge. There are some wearing ball caps, but most have toques, a smart idea in this wind. I wish I had one on, too.

I walk down the paved main walkway separating the diamonds and hear the musical thwack of an aluminum bat hitting a softball. It's immediately followed by someone shouting. "Heads Up!"

Since I don't see any other spectators, I assume the warning is for my benefit. I cautiously glance up and see a pop-up fly coming my way. I could step aside and let the ball drop on the ground in front of me, but that would mean I'd have to lean over and pick it up in order to throw it back onto the field. It seems easier if I just catch it. No big deal, although I admit my hand stings.

I throw the ball back onto the field into the waiting glove of the shortstop. He catches the ball and does a double take.

"Bumper?"

"Scott? You're just the person I'm looking for."

He tosses the ball to the pitcher and jogs over the chain-link fence, yelling to the guys, "Go ahead without me."

212

A fellow from the dugout trots out to take Scott's position at shortstop, while Scott and I walk, him on one side of the fence and me on the other, to the gate. The brown grass in the field is starting to show patches of green, but the benches, bleachers, and fences are covered with a thick coat of red shale dust.

"Okay, what's so important that you had to come out here?"

"I tried calling you, but ..."

"I leave my phone in my ball bag."

"Yah, okay, no big deal. Anyway, I was going through the list of clients with eyelash extensions?"

"And?"

"There's a name you'll find interesting."

"Enlighten me." Scott enjoys foreplay.

I tell him. "And there's something else, too."

"Be still my heart," he teases, "Don't keep me waiting!"

"I gave more thought to the hoodie Stephanie saw on the woman in her hallway."

Scott nods.

"It had Meadow Lake on it, right? I'm from Saskatchewan, so I automatically thought about Meadow Lake, Saskatchewan. But here's the thing. There's another Meadow Lake. Guess where?"

His smile broadens, and waits...

"There's a resort just outside Whitefish, Montana."

He claps the sides of his head. "Of course! And that's where Corbin's fiancée has been."

"So, we have her driving in the general area of Turnbull's condo, we can place her in the building, she has lash extensions made by the same manufacturer as the one found on the body, and she has access to both insulin and syringes because of her brother's diabetes."

Scott and I discuss strategy as we sit on the bleachers, our shoulders touching, hunched against the chilly westerlies kicking up fine red dust from the ball diamonds. At least he's blocking the worst of it with his bulky jacket.

Later, just before I walk back to my car and leave him to drink beer with his buddies in the parking lot, he punches me in the shoulder. "Good shag on the ball when you came into the park, by the way. I'm impressed."

I look at him, "What? You think I grew up in small town Saskatchewan without learning how to play ball?"

"I never thought about it," he admits. "You never mentioned it."

"You never asked."

Chapter Fifteen

I wait for Barbara Stephens in the reception area of the police headquarters on Westwind Drive. It's also our office. When she comes through the heavy double glass-front doors, I have no trouble recognizing her from the photo on her driver's license. It has depicted her well.

Ms. Stephens is plain. Ordinary. Most people wouldn't look twice if passing her on the street. I'm not saying that's a bad thing. Most of us are unremarkable. Her mousy-brown hair is straight and unstyled. Though she's wearing no make-up, her lashes are remarkably long and feathery.

When I introduce myself and shake her hand, I find it unpleasantly clammy. Perhaps it's because it was cool outside, or is she nervous? While we walk back to the interview room where Scott is waiting, I engage her in small talk, trying to make her feel more at ease, at the same time as wiping my hand on my pants.

"Good morning, Barbara. Did you have any trouble finding the building?"

She shakes her head. "No, I used my GPS."

"That was smart. The streets around here are a bit of a maze."

She responds with a brief, timid smile.

I keep talking. "We're heading back to one of our interview rooms. My partner, Scott, is waiting for us."

She nods. "How long will this take?" She unzips her khaki anorak but doesn't take it off.

"Oh, not long," I lie.

She nods once when I introduce her to Scott. He's casual and excuses himself. "I'm going to pop out to grab a cup of coffee. Can I get you one, Barbara? How about you, Janice?"

"Thank you, Scott, I'd love one."

Barbara shakes her head. "No, thank you."

"Maybe a water then?"

"Oh, sure. Thank you." Barbara is still standing, not sure what to do with her hands, first clasping them in front of her, then putting them in her pockets, and then crossing her arms in front of her chest. When she crosses her arms, the sleeves on her jacket pull back slightly, showing a flash of yellow on her wrist.

I smile.

"Please sit down and make yourself comfortable, Barbara. Is it warm enough for you? I can turn up the thermostat if you're chilly."

In fact, the thermostat is only for show. The actual temperature control is on the other side of the one-way mirror. Observers can jack the heat up or down to keep guests comfortable or make suspects shiver or sweat.

"No, I'm fine, thank you." She sits down in the chair I've pulled away from the table.

I sit across from her. "Just let me know if I can get anything to make you feel more comfortable."

Scott and I discussed our strategy for the interview. He's going to give me a few minutes to chat with Barbara so I can tease out apparently trivial information. During this interview, however, every question has a purpose.

"I hear your dad recently had a heart attack. How is he doing?"

She flashes a brief smile. "Thank you for asking. He is doing okay, thank goodness. He had surgery and the doctors say he's out of the woods."

"It's worrisome, isn't it? Having older parents."

"Yes," she agrees. "Especially when they are so far away. It's hard to visit them as often as I would like. But my brother lives with them, so that helps."

"That must really take some of the worry away. Is this the brother that has diabetes?"

Barbara raises her eyebrows, probably wondering how I knew. "Yes, he's had it since he was a baby, and there have been complications so he needs care. Living with Mom and Dad is a good arrangement. Mom makes sure he eats right, and he helps around the house."

"Gosh, if he grew up with diabetes, he must have to take insulin. I've always thought it would be a challenge to have injections every day."

Barbara gives a non-committal shrug. "He doesn't make it a big deal."

"I don't suppose you've ever had to give one of his injections, have you?"

She shakes her head. "No, never, but if he can do it, anyone can. He's a klutz."

I obligingly laugh. "And it doesn't hurt?"

"I don't think so."

"I've heard that diabetes supplies are terribly expensive in the States. Is that true? Does he come back up here to buy his supplies?"

She shows no reluctance or hesitation to answer questions about the drug.

"For sure it's cheaper here. And his doctor is here in Calgary, so this is where he fills the prescription. But he gets his syringes wherever it's cheaper. Online, mostly, I think, 'cause I've seen the box from Amazon."

With these nuggets, I start lobbing simple questions related to her fiancé, the restaurant, and Sophia. She's still fidgeting, but answers willingly.

Yes, she's engaged to Bradley. Yes, she knew Sophia. No, Bradley knew Sophia before Barbara met him.

Scott comes back into the room and puts a bottle of water in front of her.

"Bradley and Sophia worked closely together. Did you have any problems or concerns with that?"

She shakes her head, but the pitch of her voice increases when she answers. "No, I didn't mind."

She clasps her hands in her lap so tightly that her knuckles turn white.

"Not even the late nights at the restaurant?"

She shakes her head again, a little more forcefully. Her lips pale when she tightens them before she answers, "No, it was just work."

I nod. "You're very understanding. Not everyone would be, you know."

She shrugs. "Well, Bradley's a great guy."

She picks up the bottle of water and tries to open it, but her fingers keep slipping.

Scott notices and smiles. "Can I help you?"

She smiles shyly. "Thank you. I must have put too much hand lotion on this morning."

He opens it and hands it back to her. She blushes.

Just then, her phone rings. She glances at the display, but lets it go to voice mail.

"It's Bradley." She explains. "I'll call him back later."

I lean forward, detouring again to the 'just exchanging girl-talk atmosphere'. "Pardon me for asking, Barbara. You have beautiful eyelashes. Can I ask, are they extensions?"

She nods, cocking her head slightly, looking confused at the change of subject, then relaxes her shoulders, perhaps relieved that I'm not continuing to ask about her fiancé and Sophia working together. "Yes, I have a sensitivity to most makeup. My eyes get red and itchy when I put on mascara."

The reprieve of girl talk about eyelashes is over.

"Barbara, you know we want to talk to you about the murder of Sophia Turnbull."

Of course, she knows what she's here for, but her eyes widen. She swallows. "Ah, yes, I suppose so."

"Two weeks ago, you and your fiancé were at a cake tasting at The Pallisades. Is that correct?"

She nods. "Yes, on Friday night."

"And then you went for dinner at Bonterra?"

A small smile. "Yes, that's my favourite restaurant. After Bradley's restaurant, of course," she qualifies.

"Of course."

She continues. "He suggested it, and I thought he might use the occasion to tell me where he's taking me on our honeymoon."

She giggles. "He's kept it a secret, but I think I figured out, anyway."

She pauses, obviously waiting for me to ask. I oblige. "Where do you think you're going?"

She beams. "I think he's going to take me back to Belize!"

"What makes you think that?" I ask.

"Well, we went there a few years ago and loved it. Especially Bradley. And the other day when I was taking out his recycling, I noticed some notes about a resort on a piece of paper."

She beams. "I can't think of anyplace I'd rather go."

I let her bathe in the rush of happy endorphins before continuing with my questions.

"But you and Bradley had an argument at the restaurant."

Her smile disappears, and she picks at a hangnail on her thumb. "How did you know?" She sneers. "Was it the waiter? It was, wasn't it? He's served us before, and I don't like him. He's not as good as he thinks he is. I mean, Bradley's restaurant wouldn't even hire him to bus tables!"

I remind her. "Your argument?"

"Oh, well, we had words. Nothing serious, though. You know, I guess you could say I have wedding jitters. And I had way too much sugar after tasting all the wedding cake samples. It made me hyper." She shifts in her chair, crossing then uncrossing her legs.

I repeat. "What was the argument about?"

She stops worrying the hangnail and waves her hand. "I can't really remember. Nothing important."

She clasps her hands in her lap, but it's not long before she's back picking at the hangnail.

Her phone rings again. She glances at it, but makes no move to answer it, allowing me to probe into the reason for her argument. "Could it have been about how many hours Bradley was working? That he was spending too much time with Sophia?"

Barbara shifts in her chair. "I can't remember."

I leave the argument for the moment. "What did you do after you finished at the restaurant?"

"I was tired and leaving to see my parents and brother early the next morning, so Bradley took me home."

"You and Bradley don't live together?"

"No."

"And you left to see your parents on Saturday morning? What time did you leave?"

"Maybe seven o'clock?"

"Where do your parents live?"

"They live in Whitefish, Montana."

"What border crossing did you use?"

"Carway."

"What time did you cross the border?"

She pauses for a moment. "I don't really remember. It usually takes three hours from here, so maybe ten o'clock?"

"Are you asking? Or are you telling me it was around ten o'clock?"

She's irritated and snaps at me. "I'm telling you, okay? It was around ten o'clock."

"And you were with your parents and brother on Saturday evening?"

I keep asking questions and with each answer, her pile of lies mount. She's going to find them toppling over before long.

Her eyes widen a fraction, a sign to me she's searching for an answer. Looking for something that will satisfy us. Then she tries to change the subject. "These are a lot of questions. I don't understand why you're asking me."

"We are establishing where Sophia's close contacts were on Saturday evening."

Barbara reaches for the water bottle to take a sip but finds it's already empty.

She laughs, but it sounds more like a snort. "I wouldn't call myself a close contact. I didn't know her all that well. We were hardly more than acquaintances, you know. We rarely spoke."

I change the subject. "When did your father have his heart attack?"

She frowns with the abrupt change of subject. "Ah, on Monday, a couple of days after I got there."

"You must have been very worried."

She nods.

"And that's why you didn't return my partner's telephone calls?"

She nods again.

"You weren't curious why the police were asking you to call?"

She pauses. "Well, yes, but I was so worried about my dad. And I didn't think it was important."

"Barbara, why do you think that? If I got a call from the police asking me to call, I'd at least be curious."

She shrugs. "I don't know. And anyway, like I said, I was busy with my dad and mom."

Opening the file in front of me, I pull out a piece of paper and run my finger down a list of numbers.

"I can understand you being busy with your mom and dad, but we've taken a look at your cell phone records. Guess what we found."

I pause before answering my own question. "During the time you said you were too busy to return a call to us, you sent and received 34 text messages and made nine long-distance telephone calls. Many of the texts and calls were made to Bradley, which would be expected, since you might want to get support from your fiancé at a difficult time. But there were also calls and texts to Lash Delight, your wedding planner, and Ticketmaster. Were all of them more important than returning a call to us?"

She blushes.

"Any explanation, Barbara?"

"Ah, no. Well, you see, I didn't think it was important."

"Do you so often get calls from the police asking you to return their call that you're not curious enough to follow-up?"

"No, I don't think I've ever had the police call me. But..." she looks down at her hands. "I sorta wanted to talk to Bradley about it first."

"Why?"

"Well, I thought he might know what it was about."

"The two of you exchanged text messages and phone calls during that time. Didn't you think about bringing our call up then?"

Her chest is rising more quickly with the intensity of my questions.

"No, well, yes, I was going to bring it up, but I didn't want to get into it on the phone and wanted to wait to see him."

"Get into it, Barbara. What do you mean by 'it'?"

"I don't know. I just meant that whatever you wanted to talk to me about, I thought he might know about it."

"In any of these conversations with Bradley, did he tell you that Sophia was pregnant?"

She freezes. Then her eyes narrow. "What do you mean? Pregnant? Is this a trick?"

I shake my head. "No, Barbara. Sophia was three months pregnant."

"Really? Well, I guess that's really sad then. You know, that whoever killed her also killed a baby. And no. Bradley did not mention it to me."

"Who do you think the father of the child could be?"

She shrugs. "Maxwell, probably. Who else would it be?"

"Just probably? You don't sound very sure."

"Well, they were living together and getting married, so I assume it would be his." She adds a throwaway line. "But I guess you never know. She could have been sleeping around."

"Why would you say she might have been sleeping around? Do you have any names you want to throw out? Any suggestions as to who the father might be if it wasn't Maxwell?"

She back-pedals. "That wasn't a nice thing for me to say. I have no reason to believe she would have been seeing anyone else."

"Is it possible that the baby is Bradley's?"

Barbara sputters. "Absolutely not. Bradley would never do that to me." She looks back down at her hands and twists the large diamond solitaire, avoiding my gaze.

"What would you do if you found out he was unfaithful to you?"

She whispers, "Well, he never would be." Then she looks at me. "But if he was, I would call off the wedding. Absolutely."

"Does he know that?"

"Yes, he does. He knows how I feel about infidelity."

"So, when you didn't call us back after we left repeated messages for you, it was because …?"

"I suppose it was just because I feel better when I'm around him. He is always so calm and levelheaded. I feel safe. I didn't know what you wanted to talk to me about, but I thought that whatever it was, he would give me good advice on what to say."

"Why would you need advice? Wouldn't you plan on telling the truth?"

"Yes, well, I would. But still, I wanted to be with him."

She sighs and looks at Scott. "I'm sorry I didn't call you back right away. Really, I am."

"Let's get back to Saturday night. You spent that evening with your parents in Whitefish? If we call, they will confirm this?" I bring her attention back to me.

She nods. "Yes, I went to Whitefish."

She doesn't specifically answer my question. "You know, we can check the records at the border to find out what time you crossed."

Her eyes dart to the door, to Scott, and back to me. Finding no escape, she says, "Oh all right. Please don't tell Bradley, but I didn't go to see my parents on Saturday morning. I didn't go down until Sunday."

"Why did you tell him you went on Saturday?"

"I just wanted some time by myself." She drops her head. When she speaks, she attempts to look at me but can't hold my gaze. "Planning the wedding is so much more stressful than I thought it would be, and I wanted Saturday to myself. To think, without Bradly wanting me to do something, or my parents needing something done. I just wanted quiet."

"Ok, you didn't leave the city until Sunday morning?"

She shakes her head.

"What did you do on Saturday?"

"I went shopping and, ah, mostly stayed home."

"What did you do in the evening?"

She fidgets, picks up the water bottle and tries to peel off the label. "Watched television."

"Can anyone confirm that? Did you see anyone? Talk to anyone?"

Her thumb is bleeding where she's yanked off the hangnail. She notices it and rummages through her purse for a tissue. She's buying time; thinking of a reasonable response.

Finally, she speaks. "Um, of course not. I said the reason I stayed in the city was to have some alone time."

"And you stayed home all evening."

She nods, setting her lips firmly.

"Are you sure?"

She jumps when her damn phone rings again. "Bradley again. It might be something important. I have to take it."

I intervene. "I would prefer you turn off your phone. You can return his calls when we're done."

She pouts but does as I ask.

"I was asking if you're sure you stayed home the Saturday evening?"

"Yes. I did."

"Do you drive a 2021 Volkswagen Tiguan?"

She is slow to answer. "Y-Y-Yes."

"Well, I'm wondering, Barbara. Would there be any reason for your car to be at the intersection of Seventeenth Avenue and Tenth Street Southwest, an intersection near Sophia Turnbull's condo on Saturday evening?"

I toss her a bone. "Maybe you forgot, and you went out to pick up a snack?"

Her chest rises and falls faster. She licks her lips. Her eyes dart to the door and back. "Oh, yah, I forgot. I got the munchies when I was watching the movie, so I ran out to get a bag of chips."

"You live in Rosedale, don't you? That intersection is quite a drive from your place. Aren't there any convenience stores closer to where you live?"

"Well, yes, I just like going to different places sometimes."

"Where did you stop this time?"

"I don't really remember. It was someplace along 17th."

"Can you be more specific?"

She rattles off the name of a small convenience store I'm familiar with.

"Did you stop anyplace else?"

"No."

"You went from your place to the convenience store, then straight home?"

She crosses her arms. "Yes."

"You didn't stop anywhere else?"

"No."

From somewhere, she finds resilience to stick to her story about going for snacks and then going straight home. Despite repeated questions, she doesn't admit to anything else.

I take her back through her story, now with the revisions she made about the delay in her trip to Sunday. She's sticking to it and doesn't budge.

I wait until her gaze drops to her hands almost hidden under the desk, then catch Scott's eyes. I quickly tilt my head to the door. Scott nods.

"Excuse me for just a moment."

Scott stays behind to watch her when I head out the door.

I text Nguyen. *We need an eyelash from Stephens. Can you get a judge to sign an order? How soon can you get it?*

Almost immediately, he replied. *On it. Give me 30.*

I return to the interview room with a bottle of water and a uniformed officer.

"Scott and I have to attend to a matter, Barbara, but if you don't mind waiting a few minutes, we will be back to ask you a few more questions." I nod my head at the officer I brought with me. "Jeannelle is here to keep you company, and in case you need to go to the washroom, she'll show you where it is. I'm sure you understand you can't just wander around the station on your own." I smile to show I'm a nice person, but Barbara doesn't seem to notice.

* * *

Scott and I relocate to the observation room where, through the one-way glass, we watch Barbara struggle to relax. She fidgets with her hair, checks her hangnails. She wipes perspiration from her upper lip but still doesn't take off her coat. When she pulls out her phone, we turn up the volume on the microphones to listen in.

She punches in numbers, then turns slightly away from the officer standing at the door.

"Hi Bradley. Sorry I didn't answer earlier. I'm here answering questions from the cops. What's up?"

"...No, I don't know what they want. They're asking questions about Sophia, and how we got along, and what I was doing on the night she died."

"...Well, I told them the truth, of course! I went down to see my folks. Remember?"

She rolls her eyes. "...I told them I got along fine with her. You know that..."

"...What else did they ask me? Well, about our dinner at Bonterra. That's weird, right? Why would they be interested in that?"

"...And why were they so interested in what we were arguing about?"

She listens for a moment. "Did you know that Sophia was pregnant?"

"...She didn't tell you?"

"...Do you think Maxwell was the father?"

"...Yes, I assume he was, but, you know, you spent a lot of time with her, and I thought maybe she would have said something. Maybe she mentioned some other guy she was seeing."

She lowers her voice and glances at the officer in the room before replying, "Of course I trust you, honey. You know I love you..."

She sighs. "...I don't know how much longer. They say they want to ask more questions, but they've left me just sitting here." She lowers her voice and does a poor imitation of Bart Simpson. "They probably went out for doughnuts."

Jeannelle, standing at the door looks detached, staring at a spot on the floor, but the corner of her mouth twitches.

Barbara isn't finished with Bradley. "And why would you tell her my brother has diabetes?"

A scowl crosses her face. "...Whatever! We can talk about this later."

She ends the call, slams the phone down on the table, and folds her arms. Then she picks it up to check the time. She glares at the officer in the room. "How long am I going to be here?"

"I'm sorry ma'am. I don't know."

Barbara sits back with a huff and continues to glare.

* * *

Scott's leaning forward, nose almost touching the glass and elbows on his knees, watching Stephens.

I swivel my chair to face him. "She's lied to us about going to Whitefish on Friday night; she's lying about it to Corbin. What else is she not telling us?"

"Do you think she knew they were having an affair, or just suspected it?"

I think about Scott's question. "She's damn naïve if she didn't at least suspect."

"So, maybe she went to confront Sophia. Maybe even had the idea to kill her and brought the insulin with her."

"Or she's been in the condo before and may have known where Maxwell keeps his insulin. Maybe she took some out of the fridge and had an opportunity to inject it into Sophia. Sophia wouldn't have been expecting it, right? Barbara isn't very big, but she could have held Sophia on the sofa with the pillow, if we got that scenario correct."

Scott sits back, putting his hands behind his head. "Either scenario can work. And if Barbara did it, she'd probably leave trace on the pillow."

"Yes, but she's probably been in the condo in the past, or since Bradley's been there numerous times, it could be trace transferred from him to the pillow."

My partner nods. "Every little bit of evidence helps, though. But back to her phone conversation with

Bradley just now. She told him she was out of town on Saturday night. She's lying to him, and trying to cover her tracks, so can we assume they didn't work the murder together?"

I shrug. "Hell if I know."

My partner suggests. "Let's poke at her and see if we can get her riled up. Maybe we can get her pissed off enough that she tells us something she doesn't want to."

Nguyen slips into the observation room and hands me a document. "Here's the Order. I gave Ident a call. They're sending a tech to do the collection."

"Thanks. Can you stick around until the tech gets here? Let them know we'll give the high sign when we want them to come into the room?"

"No problem."

Scott cranks up the temperature from the working thermostat in the observation room. I wonder how soon the heat will drive her to take off her coat.

"Ready?" I ask Scott.

He nods and opens the door. "Thanks, Jeannelle." He dismisses the officer standing just inside the room.

She nods and leaves Barbara alone with us.

My face is deadpan. This time when I sit across the table from Barbara, she won't get a comforting smile; Scott won't bring her a bottle of water. We won't ask if she's comfortable.

She senses the change. Her nostrils flare slightly with each rapid, shallow breath, like a horse about to bolt. Her eyes flick to the door as the latch softly snicks closed, and she swallows hard.

"Ms. Stephens," I emphasize her last name. "Care to tell us about your Criminal Harassment conviction?"

She quickly blinks twice. For an instant, I think she's going to deny it, but then, she shrugs. "It was all a misunderstanding."

I wait for her to continue. It is quiet except for the hum of the overhead lights and the sound of fabric rustling when Barbara's knee bounces up and down.

Most people feel uncomfortable in the void, and rush to fill it. She is no exception.

"One of my profs thought I was following him. And I wasn't. Not really. But the cops took his word and didn't believe me." She tries again to convince us. "It was all a misunderstanding."

I let that incident go, and bring up the next. "What about the Common Assault charge?"

"Oh, well, that was an accident. You see, I tripped and fell against a classmate. They said I pushed them, but I didn't. Not really. I didn't mean to."

"What was your relationship with this person?"

Barbara scowls. "I didn't have a...relationship... with them. I was dating someone else. I thought this other person was making a move on my boyfriend, and I wanted her to stop. And then, while I was talking to her, I lost my balance and knocked her over. She wasn't hurt or anything." She crosses her arms. "But oh no, the bitch said I pushed her on purpose. And I was just charged. The charges were dropped."

I nod. "Any other incidents you think you should share with us?"

She looks at Scott and back at me, weighing the chances of lying to us. She makes a wise decision.

"Um, yes, there's this other thing."

She tells us about the third charge, again for assault. Again, she tells us it was just a misunderstanding.

Scott speaks up. "Well now, Barbara. It sounds like you're often misunderstood. Or do you have a bit of an anger management problem? Were you, by any chance, angry with Sophia? For working long hours with Bradley? Did you think they were lovers? Did you know about the pregnancy and was afraid Bradley was the father? That he'd leave you for her?"

She vigorously shakes her head. "No. Absolutely not. Like I said earlier, I trust Bradley."

He persists, "Or maybe you decided to go and confront Sophia? Did you go to her condo with plans to kill her?"

She's shaking her head like a metronome, back and forth. "No!"

I take over from Scott. "Barbara, let's review what you've told us." I pause to let my words sink in.

"You told us you went to Whitefish on the Saturday Sophia Turnbull was murdered. When pressed, you admitted you didn't go until Sunday morning. But that wasn't your only lie." I don't allow her time to answer.

"You said you stayed home on the Saturday evening and watched television. But you changed your story and admitted you drove to Sophia Turnbull's neighbourhood.

"Is this correct?"

Her lips tighten, then she gives a small nod.

"You have a history of stalking and assault. It makes me wonder if you were so worried about her relationship with Bradley that you confronted Sophia. Wanted to get rid of her."

I open my hands, "Barbara, I think you were jealous of Sophia, and you went to her condo and killed her."

"I didn't do anything to her, I swear."

"Come on, Barbara. Convince me you didn't."

"I don't know what to tell you! I didn't hurt her. I didn't even see her that night," she whines.

I scoff. "That's not very convincing."

She glares at Scott. He used to be her ally, bringing her water and helping her open the bottle. He's usually friendly and warm. Now he's hard. Cold.

Barbara gives a quick, tight shake of her head. "I have nothing to say."

I look over to the observation window and give a nod. Seconds later, the door opens, and a technician walks in. He puts what looks like a small tackle box on the table. Barbara's eyes laser-focus in on the contents when the box is opened.

Inside it, there are little vials, glassine envelopes, and an assortment of instruments and small containers of liquid and powders.

The tech pulls on a pair of blue latex gloves and selects an instrument. Stephens presses back in her chair.

The tech stands and waits.

I open the file in front of me. "Is there a reason one of your eyelashes would have been found on Sophia's cheek?"

Her eyes widen in surprise and spots of red appear high on her cheeks. "No." The word comes out high pitched, almost a squeak. "Absolutely not."

"Barbara. I want you to think carefully about my next question before you answer." I pause. "Is there a reason someone would say they saw a woman, who looked like you, in the hallway outside Sophia Turnbull's condo on the night she was murdered?"

"People tell me I have a common face," she says, her mouth so dry the words sound sticky.

"This woman wore a hoodie with a Meadow Lake logo on it. What are the chances that a woman, looking like you, wearing a hoodie with a Meadow Lake logo, would be in that condo building?"

She tries to be nonchalant. "I don't know." Her hand shakes when she brushes a strand of lank hair out of her eyes. She uses the opportunity to wipe beads of sweat from her upper lip and forehead.

Just as it did earlier when she crossed her arms, the sleeve on her jacket pulls back, and I see her watch strap. I nod toward it. "The woman was also wearing a bright yellow bracelet."

The mousy woman pulls her sleeve down. "That doesn't mean anything."

Switching to my angry-Janice persona, I rise halfway out of my chair and pound the table with my fist. "Enough! We know you were there, Barbara."

She rears back with the violence of my tone, and in a tiny meek voice says, "But I didn't do anything wrong."

I sneer. "You've been lying to us at every opportunity. You have a history of stalking and violence. Why should we believe you now?"

I nod at the technician who's been standing patiently beside the table. "We have a warrant to take one of your eyelashes, Barbara, to compare it and your DNA to the eyelash found on Sophia's body."

The technician steps forward. At first, Barbara rears back, as if she's going to refuse to cooperate, then thinks better of it. She huffs and glares at me with narrowed eyes and clenched jaw.

An open glassine envelope is laid on Barbara's cheek. Then using a spoolie brush, the technician very gently sweeps her lashes. He glances into the envelope, satisfied that a lash has fallen inside, then places the brush inside with the lash and folds the envelope closed. He labels the envelope, and places it in the toolbox. He then breaks open a paper sheath containing a cotton swab and motions for Barbara to open her mouth. She complies, but her glare in my direction never wavers.

When done, the tech steps back. "Anything else Detective?"

"No, thank you."

He turns and leaves the room. All this time, Stephens hasn't said a word.

I look at her. "We know you were in Turnbull's condo building. Was Bradley there, too."

I give her a theory to grasp; a validation of why her lash was found on the body. "Maybe he planted one of your eyelashes on her. Tell us what you know. No more lies. We will find out what happened. You might as well save us time and help yourself."

She glances at Scott. He gives a glimmer of a smile and a nod, encouraging her to speak. He's much kinder than I am. "Barbara, I know you're anxious and upset, but I promise, you will feel better if you come clean."

Her eyes shift back and forth, weighing her options. Her lips tighten to a thin line.

Scott says, "Think of how your parents are going to feel when we charge you with murder."

That's enough. The flood gates open and tears stream down her face.

I leave the room and come back with a box of tissues, then put my phone on the table in front of her and hit the record function. The activity is already being recorded by the video equipment built into the room, but I want my own record until a transcript can be prepared.

"Barbara, Under the Canadian Charter of Rights and Freedoms, you have the right to remain silent." I give her the required warning, and continue, "This is the statement of Barbara Stephens concerning the death of Sophia Turnbull on the night of Saturday, March 13, 2023."

Barbara sops up the tears and blows her nose. She swallows a couple of times, draws a shaky breath, licks her lips and begins. "Honestly, I'm telling the truth. I didn't kill Sophia. I never even saw her that night."

Barely audible, she starts. "I thought Bradley and Sophia were having an affair. I asked him a bunch of times, and he always laughed and said of course not. He and Sophia were just friends and business partners, he told me. Really good friends, he said, but nothing that I should be worried about. He said I was being paranoid."

She looks at Scott and back to me. Her voice is stronger now, with a hint of whine. "But I was, you know, worried. She was so pretty and popular.

"I'm not stupid. I know I'm not pretty or vivacious. Sometimes I think the only reason Bradley is with me is because of my money, but she had lots of money, too. Not as much as I'm going to have when my parents die, but she had other things going for her. She always knew what to say and what to do. I can't blame Bradley if he wanted to be with her. I was terrified that someday he'd wake up and wish he was with her instead of me."

She shakes her head. "This had been bothering me for a long time, and finally I decided I had to confront them."

She looks at me, head up and jaw set. "I told Bradley I was going to see my folks. I suspected that as soon as I left town, he'd hustle over to Sophia's. He'd already told me that Maxwell had a big party planned with his buddies down in Priddis, so I knew she'd be alone that Saturday night."

Words tumble out of her mouth.

"I knew Bradley was going over there for their usual morning meeting and if I confronted him about the time he spent with her in those meetings, he'd just shrug it off as business. Nothing for me to get bent out of shape over. But he wouldn't be able to brush me off if I caught him over there in the evening. He'd have a hard time coming up with an excuse for that.

"I went over and parked where I could see the entrance to her building. I tucked in behind another car on a side street where Bradley wouldn't see me if he drove up."

Barbara pauses for a few moments. "It felt like I waited forever, and I started to worry that he wasn't going to show up, then about ten-thirty he walks right past my car! I thought he would be driving, but it's really not that far from the restaurant so I guess he walked. He went up to her building. He didn't even have to buzz up, so he obviously had his own key fob."

She looks at Scott then back at me before continuing. "I waited about half an hour, maybe a little more, because I was going to go up and confront them, but before I had the chance, he came back out. He was walking really, really fast with the collar turned up on his jacket and his shoulders hunched up around his ears. He was on the other side of the street, and he didn't notice me then, either."

Barbara stands and walks to the one-way window in the room, staring at her reflection. She doesn't primp. "I waited a few minutes, wondering what I should do, then decided I'd go up and confront Sophia."

Barbara turns and paces back to the table. Before she sits on the edge of her chair, she shrugs out of her coat. An acrid smell of nervous sweat wafts from her. "At first, I was worried I couldn't get into the building, but I waited until someone was leaving, and I slipped inside before the door closed.

"I went up to Sophia's door and knocked. She didn't answer, so I knocked again. And again. I hoped she'd think it was Bradly coming back, but she didn't answer.

"I used my cell phone and tried to call. I heard the phone ringing inside, but she didn't pick up."

Barbara looks back and forth to Scott and me. "I got a weird feeling. I wondered, you know, maybe she wasn't home and that's why Bradley hadn't stuck around. But if she wasn't at home, why did he spend as long as he did in the building?

"As I was getting in the elevator, I remember seeing a woman coming down the hall towards me. I didn't do anything wrong, you know, but I didn't want to talk to her. And Sophia had asked us for dinner a few times and I didn't want to take the chance this woman might recognize me from before."

"What did you think Bradley did to Sophia?"

She shakes her head. "Don't know."

"Do you think he could have harmed her?"

Barbara refuses to meet my eyes and continues to shake her head. "I don't think so. I don't know. I really don't know."

I run her through her story again to clarify the details, then have her write it all down. Once she signs and dates the statement, she's as limp as Mr. Roger's grey cardigan. She only sniffled a few times while writing the latest version of her activities that evening,

but without distraction, her emotions bubble to the
surface. Before long, she's reaching for more tissues.

Chapter Sixteen

Given what Barbara told us, we are going to arrest Corbin, but we are concerned that she's going to pick up her phone and warn him that we're on our way. We don't have grounds to take away her phone or arrest her, but I make it clear to her that she's to keep her mouth shut.

"You must not let Bradley know about this conversation. Do not contact him. If you, in any way, warn him or cause him to flee, we will consider you a 'party to an offense'. That means, whether or not you had anything to do with killing Sophia, if you help Bradley, you can also be charged with the murder."

I wait a moment to let it sink in. "Do you understand me?"

She bites her lip, looking up at me. "I think I do?" Her voice trembles.

Scott adds to my warning. "If we even have a hint he knows we're coming, we'll check your phone records, your texts, and your emails, to see what you've been up to."

She savagely scrubs the remaining tears from her cheeks. "I won't call him. Why would I?" She lifts her chin. "Why should I? He cheated on me. Who knows what he did with her that night? Why would I let him get away with it?"

Maybe there's more to mousy Barbara than I first thought.

Scott and I are about to head out the interview room door when I turn. "Barbara, does Bradley have guns? Any weapons?"

"Uh, no, I don't think so. I've never seen a gun, and he's never talked about one. But it's never come up in our conversations."

On the one hand, it's nice to have her tell us he doesn't have an armory stashed in his basement. On the other, we'd be foolish to discount the possibility he has something that he hasn't told her about. We're not stupid.

"Thank you. Hold tight here. Do you need to call anyone at work and let them know you won't be back?"

She looks exhausted, slumped with her elbows on the table. Her head rests in her hands like it's too heavy to hold up without support. "No one's expecting me. When I left, I told them I had an appointment, and I wouldn't be back today."

"I'll have someone check on you. Bring you something to drink."

She just nods, staring blankly at the empty bottle of water in front of her.

* * *

Scott and I race to the parking lot. Barbara promised she wouldn't call, but we don't want to take a chance on her changing her mind. Or Corbin getting spooked after their earlier conversation.

Before we jump in the car, we rummage in the trunk and pull out the tactical vests.

"Call for backup?" Scott asks.

"Probably a good idea. We don't need to bring a crowd into the restaurant, but we should have a car close by just in case."

As much as I'd love to embarrass Corbin by dragging him past a crowd of lunchtime diners, we're going to do this low key. I don't want a phalanx of wanna-be photojournalists recording the drama. I mean, I wouldn't mind photos posted of him shuffling out of the restaurant in handcuffs, but I'd rather my mug doesn't show up.

At the podium just inside the entrance, we're met by the hostess. She's lovely and greets us with a pleasant smile that disappears when she sees our tactical vests. I wave my badge under her nose so she knows we're not looking for a romantic table for two.

"Is Corbin in his office?" Scott takes the lead as we head down the hall.

The hostess is wearing a tight black skirt and three-inch heels but manages to trot alongside us. "Yes, but he said he didn't want to be disturbed."

I position myself to one side of the door and use my arm to push her behind me. No sense standing in front of it in case Corbin has a shotgun. I try the knob first. It's locked.

I pound the door three times with my fist. "Bradley Corbin, this is Detective Janice Maidstone."

I give him a few seconds, then yell again. "Bradley, unlock the door."

Scott's on the other side of the hallway with his ear cocked, trying to hear if anything's going on behind the door.

He shakes his head. No response.

The hostess hovers behind me. "He should be there. I didn't see him leave and I've been at the front all morning."

"Do you have a key to the office?"

She thinks a bit. "Yes. I think so."

She just stands there, until I bark. "Then get it."

She whirls away and runs to the kitchen, surprisingly agile on those incredibly uncomfortable looking heels. I hear her yelling "Chef! I need keys!"

We shift our weight from one foot to the other, but I'm not patient. When our eyes meet, Scott moves in front of the door.

I pull my gun out of the shoulder holster.

If the emergency response team was here, they would have a fancy battering ram, but Scott has a

Vibram soled boot, and it's a fine replacement. He lines up, and with a sharp kick, hits the door beside the doorknob. If it was a steel door, or solid core, it might have offered resistance, but this simple, hollow-core, passage door flies open. Splinters fly and it crashes against the wall, embedding the doorknob in the drywall.

A quick peek around the door jamb shows us the office is empty.

The hostess comes trotting down the hall. Her face falls when she sees the trim around the door frame hanging. Between a thumb and forefinger, she holds up a key on a red curly coil. "Ah, here's the key."

Scott is in the office first, checking any spot where someone could hide.

I slide my gun back into the holster and turn to the young woman. Adrenaline is firing sparks through my body, but I keep my voice as pleasant as I can. "You said he went into the office, and you didn't see him leave?"

She nods, and points to the back of the office. "But he could have left out the back."

"Where does he park?"

"Sometimes out front, but usually in the reserved spot in the alley."

When we burst into the bright afternoon sunlight, even through my squinted eyes, I see there's no car in the parking spot with bold lettering on the wall in front of it. RESERVED.

Scott scans up and down the alley. He kicks out at a nearby dumpster. "Fuck!"

I ask Dispatch to find out what Corbin drives. When they tell me it's a silver Audi S3, I ask them to put out BOLO for it, and to send a car past his house.

It's pointless to drive up and down the streets looking for Corbin. Adding us to the dozens of marked cars who will have the description won't make a difference.

We are assuming he's not just out on an errand, but instead, he's running. Barbara is in big trouble if she called him. In the meantime, he's got a head-start, and the best use of our time is to go through his office. Maybe we can find something that will give us an idea of where he's heading. If we can't find anything, we'll hightail it over to his residence.

Scott's still cursing under his breath while we rummage through the office. He takes the bookcase and filing cabinet when I take the desk.

Nothing jumps out at me, but when I jiggle the mouse, the screen lights up. Still displayed is a weather report, but not for the city. It's a weather service for aviators, showing conditions for a flight plan to Central America.

I whisper under my breath. "Sonofabitch, he's running."

Scott takes a look over my shoulder. "Looks like. Remember the charges to that aircraft lease place on his credit card?"

I shrug. "Time to have another heart-to-heart with Barbara. If he's leaving her behind, she won't be pleased about it. Whatever she knows, she'll spill."

* * *

The quickest way back to our car is through the restaurant. Late-lunch diners pause with forks part way to their mouths when we thunder past.

The trip back to the station is fast. Scott pays lip service to traffic lights; my head is on a swivel checking intersections and crosswalks. Our siren breaks through heaters on high, and radios blasting the latest hits, when I toggle between whoops and every toddler's favourite, the nee-naw.

"Watch it, Scott. This trucker isn't even slowing down," I yell as we are about to cross the main artery into downtown. I brace my hands against the dash.

Scott lays on the horn and the brakes at the same time. Our car fishtails when the gravel truck barrels past in front of us, so close I can see the driver's eyelashes. At least I could if his hand with a one-fingered salute wasn't in the way.

I call the station and ask if Barbara is still in the interview room. When I'm told that she is, I yell, "For God's sake, don't let her leave."

We don't bother pulling into a parking space, but double park in the alley outside the back door. I yank repeatedly on the door handle, frustrated by the seconds it takes for the electronic locks to clunk open. When they do, we race through the maze of hallways to the interview room. Barbara yelps in surprise when we burst in.

She's worse for wear. Her hair hangs in strings, and her face is red and puffy from crying. I don't think she had anything to do with the planning or execution of Turnbull's murder. Her role has been limited to not coming forward with what she knew, likely because she was afraid of losing Bradley, maybe the first guy to pay attention to her. I feel momentary pity for her, but that doesn't mean I'm going to give her a bye.

"Barbara, Bradley wasn't in his office. Where would he go?"

I'm breathing heavily. My pity fades when she stares at me with a blank expression. I snap, "If he was trying to run, where would he go?"

Her lips tighten and her eyes dart. She hasn't had a change of heart, has she? Did she call him?

Scott pipes up. "The way I see it, you just might be thinking that if Bradley gets away, he's going to call for you. Then you can trot to wherever he's holed up, and you can make a happy life together." Scott is uncharacteristically harsh. "I hate to break it to you, but you're not part of his plan."

Stephens doesn't want to listen and turns away from my partner. He continues a little more gently, "Come on, Barbara. I'm a guy and I know how guys think. He's going to let us charge you with the murder and he's getting away free as a bird."

I pipe up. "Did he involve you in his plans to go to Central America?"

She snaps her head around, making the leap from the mention of Central America to the country she thought was going to be her honeymoon destination. "Belize? What are you talking about? We were going together after the wedding!"

Scott presses, "Does he have a plane at his disposal? Where is it?"

She holds a closed fist to her mouth, forehead furrowed. Scott puts a hand on the table in front of her and leans in. "Barbara, it's time for you to stand up for yourself. Where is he?"

Whispering, she says, "He leased a Beechcraft King Air a few months ago. He keeps it at Springbank."

Leaving Barbara staring at her hands on the table in front of her, we are out the door at a dead run. One thing about the station is that if you're running and yell 'out of my way', no one asks why. People flatten against the walls.

We're heading to the reliever airport twenty-six kilometres west of Calgary

*　*　*

Scott's driving again. He's aggressive, making the Ford howl on the straightaways. During the COVID years, rush hour was non-existent, but since people are back in their downtown offices, it's back with a vengeance.

Ahead of us, traffic is bunched at a light. Scott dekes through back alleys, dodging delivery trucks, dumpsters and potholes. At the best of times, the Springbank airport is about forty minutes away from the station, but Friday afternoon traffic heading out of town, and major construction projects on some of the main routes mean detours and terrible congestion. Corbin's got a massive head start, with plenty of time to get in the air.

When we alert the RCMP that we're in pursuit of a suspect in their jurisdiction, they reroute their closest patrol car to give us assistance. It is southeast of the city, but they're on their way.

I call the airport to talk to the Control Tower but get caught in an automated voice mail system. A real person finally answers, and though I identify myself, they hem and haw about connecting me. When being cordial gets me nowhere, I yell, "Connect me to the God-damned tower!"

It works and the Controller in the sky-box gives me the information I need. He agrees to deny Corbin permission to take-off. "We'll hold him on the apron, ma'am, but if he ignores us, we have no way of keeping him on the ground."

I acknowledge, then hang up.

In case he hasn't heard my conversation over the engine noise and siren, I fill Scott in. "Corbin's filed a flight plan, heading to Bozeman, Montana. If he takes off, we'll need Ash to contact someone to pick him up down there. Who has jurisdiction?"

Scott shrugs. "I have no idea. Bozeman police? State Troopers? Homeland Security? FBI? The closest air force base is Malmstrom near Great Falls. But who says he'll even follow the flight plan? Once he takes off, he can head west into the mountains, fly low through a pass right into Idaho, or who knows where. There are plenty of red-necks and folks living off the grid who'd have no issue with assisting someone running from the law."

Scott's right. For that matter, Corbin doesn't even have to fly across the border. He can land the plane here on the Canadian side and drive across one of the smaller border crossings or slip across on a back road. He has almost unlimited options on the interlacing of old trails and dirt roads used by bootleggers, past and present, and ranchers to check for strays. It's imperative we get him before he takes off.

Not familiar with the maze of roads at the small airport, we can't find our way onto the tarmac. Finally, fed up and stuck behind a low fence, we abandon the car and head out on a run through a man-gate to the twin engine King Air on the hanger apron.

Sunlight reflects off the windscreen so we can't see if anyone's in the cockpit. Rounding the nose with our weapons drawn, Scott hangs back and watches for movement through the windows along the fuselage. I approach the stairs leading into the fuselage.

I identify myself. "Detective Janice Maidstone! Bradley Corbin, you're not going anywhere. With your hands up, come to the back of the plane. Lace your fingers together and place your hands behind your head."

There is no movement, so I repeat myself. "There's no way out, Bradley. Come to the back of the plane."

I glance at Scott. Seeing no movement through the windows, he shakes his head.

I slowly climb the stairs until my next step will put me in full view of Corbin if he's lying in wait for me. Like a trapped animal though, I know he could make a last-ditch effort to escape. I'm counting on him not to make a stupid decision that could end up with one, or both, of us getting shot.

Then, from my higher perspective on the stairs, my eyes catch movement on the far side of the hanger apron. Corbin isn't in the aircraft. Instead, he's on the other side of the hangars, running toward a parking lot. Was he tipped off, or did he see our flashing lights coming down the road and put two and two together? Regardless, he's abandoned his plan with the plane. Or abandoned his plane with another plan.

He's moving quickly, a small duffle in his hand not weighing him down.

"Scott!" I point. "It looks like he's heading back to his car."

"Shit! We'll never catch him from this distance on foot..."

In the distance, I hear sirens.

Scott's legs are a lot longer than mine and he beats me to our car, but not by much. He starts the car and reaches across to throw my door open.

He slams the car into gear and we're accelerating even before I've got my door closed. Corbin's Audi is flying down the road on the other side of the airport and we're going to have to go the long way around to catch him.

* * *

Our car fishtails when we swerve onto the gravel behind Corbin. He's got a head start, in a car with a lot more juice. It makes me long for the days in traffic when the cars had real guts under the hood and suspensions to match.

Just when I think we've lost him, I glimpse the silver Audi almost a kilometer ahead, floating over the top of a hillock, before disappearing into the dip on the other side. Scott is merciless on the Ford, pushing it through tooth-rattling washboards and ruts. Thank God for my sports bra.

At each intersection, I check both ways to see if Corbin's left the main road, wishing the gravel was dry so dust plumes would lead us to him.

Scott's not taking his eyes off the road, leaving it to me to use our GPS on the unfamiliar maze of back roads. With more turns than a rattlesnake's back, there are T intersections and blind corners. We need to be careful lest we sail off into the heavy brush. My phone's mashed to my ear as I struggle to hear dispatch when they relay the Mounties' progress. They're either driving a bullet or have an excellent driver. Probably both. I'm told they're already on the road parallel to ours. It's in better condition, so they figure to make time and will cut Corbin off before he reaches the highway.

Scott's ready to turn either left or right at the next blind T-intersection, waiting for my directions. I'm still wishing for a dust plume to tell us which way Corbin's gone, but it turns out I don't need the dust. At the end of the T, the silver Audi is nose-down in the ditch, almost windshield deep in a murky-looking slough.

Scott stands the Ford on its nose, and before he's slammed it into park, I'm out running to the Audi. The airbag has deployed and hangs like a sad, dingy pillowcase from the steering wheel. The driver's door's open, but Corbin's nowhere in sight.

I call across the car to Scott. "Which way do you think he went?" It's a pointless question except maybe he can see some footprints that I haven't noticed. Unless... I ask, "You think he might be in the water?"

The water is the colour of strong tea, and rafts of soggy fallen leaves float among the brown fingers of old cattails edging the shore.

Scott shakes his head. "If he was unconscious, wouldn't he be floating? And it's probably only a few feet deep."

He looks into the heavy underbrush and aspens around the slough. "Nah, he's running, but I'm not going in there after him unless I have to. Let's call for a dog."

Corbin picked a lousy place to make a run for it. This area is pockmarked with depressions and hillocks, leftovers from scouring glaciers thousands of years ago. They've filled with water to make little lakes and bogs. Wild rose bushes, burdock and tangled branches make moving through the underbrush almost impossible. On the other hand, they also provide great places to hunker down and hide.

A K9 unit's on the way. ETA ten minutes. We let the Mounties know. They'll park their car at the top of a hill on the other side of the swampy area. From there, they can watch down the long stretch of road, waiting in case Corbin comes out of the woods and crosses in front of them.

When the K9 car pulls up, Duke's going batshit crazy in his kennel in the back. We've seen this mahogany German Shepherd work before. He lives to find people, and if they happen to run and he gets to chew on them, so much the better.

Randy, Duke's handler, comes over to us for details.

"We're looking for a male, about six feet. Caucasian. Brown hair. Name Bradley Corbin."

I point to the Audi. "Came out of the car probably fifteen minutes ago. We haven't touched anything."

Randy nods. He's a man of few words, preferring to work with Duke instead of people.

We back out of the way and let the team do their thing.

Randy takes the dog over to the car and lets him sniff around. And then, away they go; the dog on a long line and Randy running behind when Duke's nose pulls them along.

Scott and I stay back so we don't interfere with the scent field. When Duke finds Corbin, we'll hear it.

I call Dispatch and ask for a tow truck to take Corbin's car into the impound yard. Without much to do, we lean against our car and take in the late afternoon sunshine while we wait for Duke to catch his man.

Slowly, my heartbeat returns to normal as the adrenaline works itself out of my system. I help it along with a few deep breaths and a roll of my shoulders. The bush is full of spring sounds. Chorus frogs are peeping from every pond, competing with the chickadees and white crowned sparrows in the trees.

"It's been a long time since I've been in a chase," I say. "It got my heart racing."

Scott holds out his hand. It's still trembling. "Yah, I know what you mean." He pauses. "It's fun though, ya gotta admit."

I nod. "It is. Especially when the only scratches are on the other guy's car."

He laughs. "And you'd know about that, right Bumper?"

I laugh along with him.

We enjoy the quiet. It's a pleasant change from the bedlam of the chase through the city with siren whooping and radio blaring. Time slows down, then in sequence, we hear Randy yelling. Duke barking. A man screaming. That's our cue.

We wade into the bush. Within a few steps, we're muddy and wet almost to our knees.

As we get closer, I make out the screaming.

"Get 'im off! Get 'im off!"

I shake my head when I hear Corbin begging. Randy always warns people not to move, and I don't know why anyone would refuse to obey. No one can outrun a dog.

By the time we slog through the mud to the trio, Corbin has stopped yelling. He's face down in the mud, though, cursing about the bites on his leg and ass. Randy's got a grip on Duke's collar, but the dog remains hyper-focused on Corbin.

I stand back with Randy and Duke while Scott hauls Corbin to his feet. His nose is swollen, with blood oozing from both nostrils. Amazingly, he still has his glasses, but they're sitting crooked on his face. Maybe the air bag broke the frames, or maybe the frames are fine, and it's the broken nose that forces the glasses out of position.

His white shirt, the colour of tea after being soaked in the slough water, clings to his body.

Corbin moans and complains. "Take it easy, will ya. Fuck." His posh, precise way of speaking has disappeared.

Scott's short on sympathy when he puts the cuffs on Corbin and clearly outlines the reason for the arrest, and his constitutional rights to remain silent.

Corbin glare speaks volumes.

Scott asks, "Can you walk?"

Corbin takes a few, limping steps. "Yah." He snarls at Duke. "Keep that fuckin' dog away from me."

Randy ruffles the shepherd's ears. "Don't give me a reason to let him go."

Duke's eyes are riveted on Corbin, and he quivers with excitement, hoping for another chance to chase.

With all the blood and mud, there's no way I want Corbin in the back of our car. Besides, he probably should go to the hospital to get fixed up. On the trek back to the road and vehicles, I call dispatch and ask for an ambulance to haul his sorry, muddy, chewed-on ass to the hospital.

* * *

It takes about six hours before the over-worked healthcare workers in the Foothills Hospital emergency department pack Corbin's nose and put in a few stitches before releasing him back into our custody. Helping him into the back seat of the unmarked car, I get a close look at his face. His angular face is almost unrecognizable with swelling and bruises. His lips sport stitches and the splint on his nose does nothing to improve his looks. Although cleaned up somewhat for examination by the medicos, mud still cakes his hair and clothes. What was probably a crisp white shirt when he left for work this morning is torn and filthy. No amount of bleach will ever get out the blood and mud stains. And dog spit.

I glance at Bradley in the rear-view mirror. His eyes are downcast, often squeezed closed. He looks in pain, probably from the broken nose and dog bite. Maybe the freezing used when they stitched up the bite on his butt is wearing off.

Physical pain is one thing, but there's probably a hefty dose of emotional pain there, too. His puffy lips occasionally quiver. Is he trying to hold back words? Or tears? There is no evidence of the confident entrepreneur we interviewed at Sophia's on Seventeenth.

I pull the car into the secure holding bay at the back of the station. When we slam the doors, the sound echoes off institutional-grey, polished concrete walls. The fish-eye peephole on the door and the overhead cameras should remind Corbin that from now on, his every move could be watched.

* * *

I take Corbin to an interview room. When I remove the handcuffs, he gives me an icy stare. "Dey weren't necessary." He rolls his shoulders, grimacing the whole time.

I could agree with him. In his shape, he could hardly escape a toddler. "It's policy, Mr. Corbin. Nothing personal."

He winces when he sits down. The crushed flesh in his butt must be excruciating.

He attempts to shuffle the chair closer to the table, and glares when he finds it's affixed to the floor.

Corbin called his lawyer from the hospital, and I expected him to be waiting for us. Fortunately, he's not here yet, and I'm glad we'll have a few minutes alone with Bradley before his lawyer tells him to shut up.

I place a plain paper bag in the middle of the table in front of us. It has a single, crisp fold at the top. He focuses on it for a moment, then drops his eyes to his lap.

It's a long shot, but maybe if I'm nice...

"Would you like something to drink? Coffee or water?"

"No." He slumps, breathing through his mouth. At the tip of his nose, the bandages are starting to tinge with pink. He squirms, trying to get comfortable on the hard metal chair. "Whend's by lawyer going to be here?"

"I don't know, Bradley. Is there anything you want to tell me before he gets here?"

He tosses his head, trying to get a hank of mud-caked hair out of his eyes. "I hab notting to say to you."

"All right then. No problem. Are you sure you don't want something to drink?" I stay calm. If he doesn't talk before his lawyer gets here, I doubt I'll get anything from him, so I try again.

"That is a pretty nice Beechcraft King Air you've got out at the airport. Do you own it outright, or is it leased?"

It's like talking to a brick wall, but I'm persistent.

"Bradley, I'd like to clarify some things about your relationship with Sophia."

He shows no sign of talking, but I carry on, keeping it conversational.

"You told us your relationship was platonic. That you were business partners."

He's mute.

"But if that's the case, it makes me wonder about her pregnancy? Wouldn't that complicate things?"

He winces. Was that because I refer to the pregnancy, or because he's hurting. Hard to say.

He intently rubs his mud-caked cuticles. Flakes of dirt litter the table in front of him. He isn't meeting my eyes, and I take my time studying him. He is disheveled, there are even some twigs entwined in his hair. I suppose it is difficult to look composed or confident when you have mud in your boxers.

He sneaks a quick look at the paper bag between us.

I push. "I can understand you having a physical relationship with her. I mean, no one would blame you. She was a beautiful woman."

I poke at what I hope to be one of his soft spots. "I should say, almost no one would blame you. I wonder what Barbara's reaction would have been if she found you were having sex with Sophia?"

I take an audible deep breath. "And, wow, I can't imagine what she would have done if she thought you fathered her baby. Was that why you had to get rid of Sophia?"

Corbin presses his lips together tightly, or as tightly as the stitches and swelling allow.

I bring up his alibi. "Bradley, on the night Sophia was murdered, you claimed you went to the restaurant and left there after midnight with the night manager. Are you sure you didn't pop out sometime? Maybe go for a snack? Anything like that?"

Hearing footsteps outside the room, he glances quickly at the door and tries to sit straighter, wincing as he does so. When the footsteps recede, he slumps, and his eyes drop back to the mess on the table.

"Well, Bradley, what if I told you we talked to someone who saw you at Sophia's condo that night?"

He shifts in the chair, glancing at the door again.

The flesh around his eyes is so swollen, it's hard to see them darting and shifting from the door to the one-way mirror, and back to the table.

"That this person saw you there at about ten o'clock. Can you think of a reason someone might say that?"

Now he's looking at me. If his eyes could narrow any further without closing completely, they would.

"And that same person saw you leave the building a short time later. And that this corresponds with the time that Sophia died?" I have to give it to him. He's stubborn and keeps his mouth shut. "I don't think this person would mistake you for someone else. They know you well."

He tries to act nonchalant, but his body gives him away. His jugular pulses wildly next to his Adam's apple that bobs when he swallows.

I give him a chance to change his story. A branch to grasp.

"Do you want to tell me why you lied about being at the restaurant all night? Maybe you're having an affair with someone else in that building and didn't want anyone to know?"

I change subjects to keep him off balance, hoping that one of these questions will elicit a response. My goal is to get him to answer just one question. If he starts talking, it will be easier to keep him talking.

"While we were waiting for the folks at the hospital to take care of you, we took a look through your car, Bradley. We found something interesting. There's a package of disinfectant wipes in your glovebox. The same kind that we found in Sophia's trash."

He glares at me and graces me with a sneer, "So what? Doesn't everyone use them since COVID?"

I nod. "Yah, you'd think so. It's just these aren't the normal everyday run-of-the-mill wipes. These are used in the restaurant industry, and your restaurant purchases them by the case." I wait. "Sure, you can claim that others could have those wipes, but it's just one more thing we can use to put you at the scene. And anyway, that's not the most exciting thing we found."

I take the paper bag and slowly unfold the top. Corbin's aloof manner evaporates, and his eyes track my hands like a dog watches when you're cutting him a piece of cheese. I reach into the bag and pull out a baggie, sealed with a bright orange evidence tag. I hold it in front of him. His swollen eyes widen.

"We found something interesting in your pockets, Bradley. Sophia was wearing a pendant just like this the night she was murdered."

His lips tighten.

"Bradley." I pause to make sure he's giving me his full attention. "Do you want to tell me your side of the story?"

He's succinct in his reply.

"Puck you."

* * *

Scott is standing behind the one-way glass. I've reached a standstill with Corbin, so it's his turn. I don't think it's likely, but maybe he will be able to get Corbin to talk. At least we'll keep trying until his lawyer gets here.

Scott opens the door. Corbin looks up, desperately hoping to be rescued. When he sees it's only Scott, the broken man slumps again, finding the pile of dried mud on the table in front of him fascinating.

Scott sets a water-filled cup in front of Corbin. "I thought you might be thirsty."

Corbin doesn't lift his head but looks at Scott from under lowered brows. With a voice muffled by a broken and gauze-packed nose, he manages, "Tanks."

Corbin uses two shaking hands to lift the cup to his mouth. He manages to drink without spilling.

Scott pulls out a chair and places a file on the table in front of him. Corbin lifts his eyes just enough to look at it but doesn't react otherwise.

When Scott opens the file, though, and runs a finger down a column of numbers on what appears to be a financial statement, Corbin can't resist trying to read it. He furrows his brows and blinks a few times as if to clear his vision, but with the shock of dog bite, broken nose, painkillers, arrest, and whatever else is new to him, he gives up and waits for Scott to speak.

"You know, you and Sophia had a great business relationship. A profitable restaurant, great public profile. But I mean, it's even better when it comes with benefits. Right?"

A muscle in Corbin's jaw tenses. He glances up at the door, no doubt willing his lawyer to show up.

"I don't understand why you'd kill her, though. I mean, you had it all. At least from my vantage point. Why would you rock the boat?" Scott shakes his head. "Brad, things were going so well for you. You seem like such a smart guy. What happened? She got pregnant and wanted you to step forward as the baby-daddy?"

Corbin licks his lips and looks up at Scott. I hold my breath...sure he's going to say something... then the door bursts open. Damn it!

Bradley heaves a sigh of relief. "Tank God, Malcob, you're here."

I've seen Malcolm Gentry around. He's a high-profile defence lawyer who likes to have his face on television, and to have his name quoted by journalists. Unfortunately, he's not just a media hound. He's also a freakin' good lawyer. If I murdered someone, Gentry's the lawyer I'd call to defend me. If I could afford him.

"Detectives, what have you done to my client?" In addition to, or maybe because he's a successful criminal lawyer, Gentry is a great actor, but he's genuinely taken aback at the battered man in front of him. He stops dead in his tracks, just inside the door, before rushing to Corbin's side. He leans over and looks more closely at Bradley's face. "What the hell happened? Did they do this?" He turns to glare at Scott and me. Mostly Scott.

His concern is not surprising, although if we had roughed Corbin up, it would only help Gentry's case. Each passing moment, Corbin's complexion acquires different hues of purple as bruises continue to bloom. His normally immaculate white shirt is filthy, his glasses are bent, and I notice one of his ears is filled with mud.

Bradley manages to mumble. "They let a dog loose on me."

The lawyer tightens his lips and plunks his briefcase down on the table. He huffs a sigh. I'm guessing he's communicating his disgust at us and makes a show of retrieving a legal-sized pad of paper. "I'm Malcolm Gentry, and I will represent Mr. Corbin."

There's no point antagonizing him or being a bitch, so I stand and reach out to shake his hand. "Detective Janice Maidstone."

Scott looks up but doesn't offer his hand. "Detective Scott Amble."

Pleasantries, such as they are, are out of the way. And I am right. Once Gentry is there, all hope of getting a statement out of Bradley vanishes. Gentry tells us to leave them alone, and we comply. The last thing I see is Gentry taking pictures of Corbin's face with his cell phone. I wonder if he's going to have Corbin drop his drawers to get photos of the dog bite on his butt.

Chapter Seventeen

Since Corbin is locked up and waiting for trial, Scott and I have moved on to other cases. I'm cleaning up the last bit of paperwork before leaving the office. Tomorrow morning, I'm heading out for holidays at the ranch. Although the break from work hasn't come soon enough, I'm afraid some of the conversations at home are going to be more stressful than working murder cases.

I've been procrastinating about breaking up with Terry and feel obligated to ask if he wants to come along and catch up on old times with high school friends and such.

I breathe a sigh of relief when he shakes his head. "Nah. I'm kinda done with Maple Creek, you know? My parents aren't there anymore, and I sure as hell don't want to run into the ex-wife or her family. You go, have a good time, and next winter we can go someplace warm."

To be honest, I only asked because I thought I should. Our relationship has run its course and it's time to move on. Besides, I'm looking forward to the solitude of the drive with Treacle riding shotgun. I can listen to podcasts, sing to old music, and think about the situation at the ranch. I can't do this with Terry in the passenger seat. He's fidgety and talks too much.

* * *

Mom and Dad are thrilled when I pull into the yard. I'm shocked to see how Dad has sunken into himself since I last saw him. He insists on carrying my suitcase into the house, and I note he has more trouble carrying it than he used to, his long legs shuffling when they used to take the steps two-at-a-time.

Over supper, he tries to keep up with the catch-up chatter, but in the end, leaves Mom and I to carry on the conversation.

"It's just the three of us tonight." Mom tells me, "We wanted to have you all to ourselves. Tomorrow, Richard, and Emily and Harry will be over for dinner."

I keep the conversation light but gently feel them out for thoughts about friends who've moved into town.

Mom admits, "I know the time is coming when we have to leave this house, but I can't quite see it yet. We still manage just fine."

I know Mom's anxious to know about my love life, and sure enough, when she brings out my favourite dessert, saskatoon pie, she asks, "Are you seeing anyone special?"

"Didn't I tell you that I've been seeing Terry Ellars for a few months now?"

She rolls her eyes. "Oh dear, yes, you did. I completely forgot about it."

She looks over at Dad. "I'm getting almost as forgetful as your dad."

"Don't worry about it, Mom," I assure her.

She waits for me to continue, but I dig into the pie, hoping to avoid the third degree.

It doesn't work. She raises her eyebrows, an action she's perfected over the years of raising four kids. It means, in no uncertain terms, tell me more.

"Well, yah, I've been seeing him since, oh, about the beginning of the year."

"Is it serious?"

"No, Mom, not at all. In fact, I'll probably break it off when I get back from holidays."

Her shoulders slump, "Oh, that's a shame."

"No, not really. I mean, it would have been great if it worked out, but I don't think we're after the same things."

"Well, you know best, I'm sure, but it would be nice if you found someone to settle down with."

"I know, Mom. But it's hard finding someone who makes as good a partner as Dad does."

I reach out and touch his hand on the table while telling her, "They don't make them like him anymore."

"Oh, I know they don't," she agrees.

Dad's followed enough of the conversation to interject, "And they don't make them like your mother anymore, either."

He can still make her blush. "Oh, go on now, you old coot. Eat your pie."

* * *

Waking up in my childhood bedroom takes me back to growing up: the creaking of the house, the birds in the trees just outside my window, and the familiar squeak of the windmill bringing up water from the well for the corral tank. This is still home. I forget how much I love this place when I'm absorbed with my life in the city.

Treacle senses I'm awake, and she comes over to put her nose on my pillow. I thread my hand out from under the sheets and stroke the silky-smooth fur.

She waits patiently for me to get dressed and tiptoe down the stairs, just in case Mom and Dad are still asleep.

I should have known better. They are both in the kitchen with their coffee. Mom's reading the online news from the Southwest Booster, and Dad's watching the robins build a nest in the lilac bush just outside the kitchen window.

"Good morning. I'm going to take Treacle out. You want to come with me, Dad?"

He scoffs. "Since when does she need to have her hand held? Why don't you just let her out to do her own thing?"

"I will, as soon as I know she's not going to make trouble with the other dogs. I don't want her to think she's still boss-dog. She's too old to get into a scrap."

He flaps a hand at me, shooing me out of the kitchen. "Go on then, tend to your sissy dog. Then come back and have your coffee."

This is the nicest time of day, early with the smell of green in the air when trees are budding. The wind hasn't come up yet, but it probably will, around eight. It almost always does. I stride to a big old boulder in the corner of the pasture. It looks west over to the prominent ridge that's mostly rock and scrub. Later on, but not right now, I'll ride up there. From the top, I can see as far as Medicine Hat. There's no way storms can creep up on us unseen. We have clear views in every direction for miles and miles.

Knowing that the coffee isn't getting any fresher, I decide it's time to head back to the house. Before going in, I scruff the dogs' ears. "Now, all of you. Play nice."

* * *

Mom looks up from her iPad as soon as I walk in. "Give your sister a call."

"At home or at work?"

"At home, I think."

As soon as I hang my jacket on the pegs in the mudroom, I pick up the phone and dial.

Emily answers on the first ring. I hold the phone away from my ear as a precaution.

"Janice," she squeals, "You're home! Come over for lunch. You know Richard. If we try to gossip at supper

262

tonight, he'll give us the evil eye and we'll have to behave ourselves."

I laugh. "He's always been that way, but it's probably worse since he had to endure so much of it being about him and his divorce."

Emily sighs. "Poor guy. But if you come over, I can fill you in what I know about his plans. Granted, it's not much, but at least you won't into tonight blind."

* * *

Emily and I are sitting around her kitchen table when I ask her about Terry.

"What's the deal him? I still don't have a handle on what happened before he left town."

"He's a strange one," she starts. "He was in your class, not mine, so I didn't get to know him until he came back here after university. Mostly we crossed paths in the co-op, or the bar, and I saw him at the hospital in the ER a few times. He came in for stitches from accidents at the ranch, but nothing serious."

She takes a breath. "I know Sheila, his ex-wife, better." Emily gets up and pours more coffee. "We were in the same high school class. She went to Regina to beauty school, then came back and worked in a shop in town. She married Terry and kept working until they started having kids. I'd only see her getting groceries, supplies with the trucks, that sort of thing. I was shocked one time, though, Janice. Sheila had the two kids in tow, looking like shit. She always used to keep herself nice, but her hair was a mess, she was walking a little hunched over, and even though it was an overcast day, she was wearing sunglasses."

Emily sees me nodding. "Yep, you got it. It looked like she'd been beat up. It wasn't my business to ask questions, but I kept my eye out for her."

"You think it was Terry?" I ask.

263

Emily shrugs. "Who else would it be? It happens more than you think." She corrects herself. "Well, in your line of business, you probably have an idea. Anyway, off and on over the next few years, I'd see her wearing sunglasses when she shouldn't.

"But then, right around Easter a few years ago. I remember the time of year because we just had a blizzard. And I was working nights. Russ, Sheila's dad, pulled up outside Emerge in his pickup. Remember him?"

I nod. "Yah. Big guy."

"Yep. He dropped Terry off. Now, I saw her dad's knuckles, and they were bleeding, and I could see why. He laid a beating on Terry. Terry spent a couple of days in the hospital. Got no visitors. I asked him if he wanted me to call the cops. He said no."

She smiles. "Anyway, Terry got out of the hospital, and the next thing we know, he's packed up and left town. Then I hear he's in Calgary."

She gives me a pointed look. "And you're dating."

"Why the hell didn't you tell me all this before?" I'm angry with her. "If he beat his wife, he's not going to change. He'll do it to the next woman he has a relationship with."

Emily has the decency to look sheepish. "I know. I should have told you right away. At first, I figured you'd only go out a couple of times and then, you know, you don't usually date a guy more than once or twice. But when you kept seeing him, I thought maybe the lickin' his father-in-law laid on him changed him. I know you used to really like him, and I hoped that you two would hit it off."

"Hit it off, Emily? Poor choice of words."

"Sorry Jan. I just..."

"I know what you meant. Maybe this explains a few things. He's never given any indication, at all, that he's going to get violent, but he did get heated about some guy he had a beef with. And Treacle's never warmed up to him. I have to admit, she's always been a pretty good judge of character."

Emily continues her story. "So anyway, Sheila moved to Regina, and her mom sold the farm and moved there too, after her dad died."

"Ouch, so Terry got kicked out and lost what he thought was going to be his ranch once his daddy-in-law died, eh?"

Emily nods. "He sure did, and he never made any bones about how he was going to take over. I bet he was pissed when he lost it."

Emily shrugs and gets up from the table, "Anyway, that's history. Now, what do you want for lunch?"

While she's fiddling with something on the stove, I wonder if it's worth confronting Terry with what I've learned.

Chapter Eighteen

Bradley Corbin's spending Christmas in the 'abandon hope all ye who enter here' Remand Centre. The Ministry of the Justice Solicitor General of Alberta operates this correctional facility that holds inmates awaiting trial or sentencing. It is depressing, crowded, and a terrible place to spend the holidays. Correction — it's a terrible place to be — ever. He will be there until his sentencing hearing in January.

We charged Corbin with second degree murder in the death of Sophia Turnbull, but in return for offering a full confession, the Crown Prosecutor has offered him a deal that will take years off the original, possible twenty-five year sentence.

* * *

It's my last day before heading to the ranch for Christmas. I'll be back to work in time for the spike of crime that usually coincides with New Year's Eve.

Tonight, I am meeting Scott and Monica for our traditional Yule drink. It's a special night, so we've decided to get together at the historic and elegant Pallisades Hotel.

Our department's Christmas party isn't exciting. I'd even go so far as to say it's agonizing. The grungy police-bar hangout has drinks, platters of deep-fried cheese sticks and chicken wings, and a tray of flaccid vegetable sticks. There's even a tired, plastic sprig of mistletoe hung up over the entrance to the hallway leading to the washrooms. Some guys bring their wives or girlfriends, but mostly, it's just cops. It's not much fun, unless you're drunk. I usually try to be working so I'm not expected to go.

I broke things off with Terry last April after I came back from the ranch. I pressed him about what happened with his marriage. I wanted to see if he'd come clean about his assaults on Sheila. He didn't.

I haven't missed him. Neither has Treacle.

Tonight, the evening with Scott and Monica is my only Christmas party. I use it as an excuse to dress up. The heels, which I dug out from the back of my closet, haven't been worn for a couple of years and have a layer of dust on them. At the end of the rod, I pull out and unzip a garment bag. I admire a dress I bought more than a year ago. The dark, almost black, green lace wasn't something I picked out. Emily did. She came for a visit, and as we were out shopping one afternoon, she pulled it off the rack and showed it to me.

"Janice, you have to try this on."

I argued. It was too expensive.

"It's on sale," she told me.

"It's not my style."

"Oh, for heaven's sake, Janice. Your style is pants and a golf shirt. Live a little."

She shoved it into my hands and pushed me toward the change rooms.

Less than half an hour later, I walked out with the dress cradled in my arms, shocked that my little sister has such good taste in clothes.

Even though I'm used to wearing form fitting gear at the gym, I never pictured myself in such a sleek dress. It hugs every curve. Apparently, it's supposed to.

I walk into the hotel lobby, glad I've worn it tonight when I see everyone around me in something festive.

Before I meet my friends in the lounge, I take a detour through the lobby, festooned with sways of aromatic cedar, and real, bushy fir trees. Carols softly play over the in-house speaker system. In the beginning, Scott and I thought a squabble over a venue in this luxury hotel was the motive for Turnbull's murder. I stop for a moment at the ballroom entrance and watch Erin Armstrong experience her fairy tale wedding, before going to meet my friends.

* * *

The oak panelled room with high ceilings and a massive fireplace is buzzing with murmured conversations. I spot Scott first, of course, when he stands to draw my attention as soon as I reach the lounge area. In his dark suit, he could be stepping from the pages of a fashion magazine, and from the covetous glances from more than a few in the general vicinity of his table, I don't think I'm the only one with that opinion.

Decades ago, this room featured an enormous stone fireplace. The sleek glass, chrome and granite, gas-fired replacement doesn't exude the feeling of grace and comfort the old one did. I miss the faint smell of wood smoke and the sound of logs crackling.

I thread my way through tables to my friends on the far side of the room. One chair between Scott and Monica sits empty. On either side of them are their dates. I don't mind being solo.

Monica has other holiday functions where she dresses up, but she knows this is my one and only party, so she promised she'd put forth the effort tonight. Both she and her girlfriend, Shira, wear sparkles, heels, and make-up.

Before I sit down, Scott gives me a hug and peck. Up close, I see his red tie has tiny dancing Rudolf's. "Good God, Janice, you look great. I hardly recognized you."

I stand back and feign a frown. "I'm not sure how to take that comment, Scott. Do I look so terrible at work?"

He backpedals. "You look …fine… you know. But in the office, you're just one of the guys. Tonight, you are definitely *not*." He looks around the table. "Help me out here, ladies!"

They shake their heads, leaving him to climb out of the hole he's dug. I let him off the hook and squeeze his arm. "Don't worry. I'm not offended."

He turns to introduce me to his date. "Janice, meet Stephanie."

I think for a moment before placing her. "Well hello, Stephanie, it's nice to meet you again."

She stands. Her handshake is firm. "It's nice to see you again, too." There's a twinkle in her dark brown eyes that I hadn't noticed when we interviewed her last spring.

Despite how busy it is, a server quickly takes my drink order. While waiting for my wine, I tell them. "I was late because I wanted to swing by and look in on Erin Armstrong's wedding."

Scott and Monica nod, knowing to whom I'm referring.

"The decorations in the ballroom make it look like something out of a fairy tale. Like a winter wonderland. And she is stunning."

More to Scott than the others, I say, "I can't help but wonder what Sophia and Maxwell's reception would have been like."

I realize my last statement is a bit of a downer, especially since Stephanie actually knew Sophia. I hurry to apologize. "Sorry folks, I didn't mean to throw water on our get together."

Stephanie shakes her head. "Don't worry Janice. I didn't know her well."

I'm wondering how to re-inject holiday cheer into the conversation when Scott suddenly stands and reaches out to shake hands with a tall fellow who's come up to our table. He's about our age, early 40s, and dressed to impress in a dark suit. I've noticed his wide smile, square jaw and short, clipper-cut hair before.

I'm not one to blush, but I feel my cheeks blossom. "Hi Dave. Good to see you off the ball diamond."

He lightly places a hand on my shoulder. "Good to see you too, Janice."

Scott turns to the rest of the table. "Hey everyone, meet Dave Scottish, one of the guys on my ball team."

Dave nods and murmurs a greeting to us. "I don't want to interrupt but thought I should come over and say Merry Christmas."

Scott teases him. "Glad you did. You look fine in your suit. You actually look like you could be a banker."

"Very funny, Scott. You clean up pretty well, too."

He doesn't wait for Scott to reply but puts his arm over the shoulders of the woman at his side. "And this is my sister, Dexter. She came into town last night all the way from Miami to be my plus-one at my Christmas party tonight."

Scott gestures at an empty chair. "Do you want to sit down and have a drink with us?"

We're starting to scootch around to make room for a couple more chairs when Dave puts up a hand and shakes his head. "No, thanks. The shindig upstairs in the penthouse has already started and we need to get up there while we're still fashionably late. Much longer and we'll just be late!"

"Sure, no worries." Scott tells him. "Let me introduce everyone, though."

When it comes to me, Dave laughs and tells his sister, "Janice is Scott's partner, and is notorious for stealing his fries."

I laugh with them but wonder if my frequent raids on Scott's plates bother him more than he lets on. "I don't take that many, no matter what he tells you!"

After a few minutes of visiting, Dave and Dexter cast off.

Scott gives me a look.

"What?"

"Nice guy, huh?"

"Yah. I suppose so."

I wait for him to say more, but he's already turned back to Stephanie.

Would I be too suspicious to think that Scott and Dave pre-arranged this chance meeting?

* * *

Early the next morning, Treacle and I head east down the TransCanada highway. It will be Richard's last Christmas living on the ranch. The plan we made last April has fallen into place. Sometimes Dad agrees with it, and sometimes, most times, he forgets that a local rancher has signed a two-year rental agreement for the entire operation.

He and Mom are going to move into a little house in town, so they won't have to worry as much about bad roads and taking care of the yard. It will be closer to Emily, and she can look in on them on her way home from the shifts at the hospital.

I'll go back at the end of February to help them pack and move. They've been in that house since they were married, so it's going to be a monumental job. I'm sure Mom will be in tears part of the time, and Dad will be confused. Even though I know they have to move, I'm sad about it, too. At my heart, home has always meant the ranch and the farmhouse, not a bungalow in town.

The agreement to rent the ranch doesn't include the house. It will stay empty, for now, but we'll keep the heat turned on so the pipes don't freeze. Harry promises he'll check it regularly to make sure the mice don't take over and kids haven't broken in. Mom's not been subtle in her hints that maybe I will move into it. I don't think that day will come, but you never know.

I can't see leaving the police service. I love it, and I'm good at it. Sometimes, in the murky middle of an investigation when we're spinning our wheels, I get frustrated and think doing something else would be a good idea. But then, the satisfaction of putting bad guys behind bars makes it all worthwhile.

I've made a life I enjoy in the city with good friends and a future. If I go back to the ranch, I will have to start all over to build relationships. I think it would be hard to find things in common with most of the folks in the community. Heck, it's hard enough anywhere to fit in as a single woman in her 40s.

Until a decision has to be made, I like the idea of renting out the land. It gives Richard time to get his feet back under him. Maybe his move to the Coast will be permanent, but it's just as likely he'll find being on an island too isolating, and the thick forest of trees claustrophobic. Will he miss the wide-open prairies where there's nothing to block the view to the horizon? I want to leave him plenty of space to come back to the ranch, if that's what he decides he wants.

In the meantime, I have my sidekick, Treacle. And from what Mom tells me, there's a new litter of puppies about ready for new homes. Maybe Treacle and I will bring one of them home.

The End

Born in windy southern Alberta, Bonny grew up in a farming community surrounded by waving fields of wheat and barley. Her best friends were her horses (Beauty, Shorty, Whisper, Lady, and Dancer) and a variety of mongrel dogs.

A university education opened doors to different jobs across many industries. The most impactful of those was as a police officer with the Royal Canadian Mounted Police. She has fond memories of both her fellow officers, and the experiences from the Force.

Bonny finds inspiration in the natural world: the wind in the trees, waving fields of grain, fat and healthy cattle in the field, and bumble bees clamoring about in flower blossoms.

Writing in a variety of genres, she experiments with different characters and voices.

Her childhood fascination with books has never diminished. She hopes her readers find as much pleasure in reading her books, as she does in writing them.